INTRODUCTION

Making Memories by Janet Lee Barton
Amanda Forrester takes her good friend, Josh Randall, home with her for Christmas. . .hoping to keep her match-making family from setting her up with anyone. As the couple makes plans for Christmas, their friendship turns to love—but it's only after making their way through a near miss with death that they finally admit they'd like a chance to start making memories of their own.

A Christmas Wish by Jeanie Smith Cash
Relief at catching a flight fades as Abigail Forrester recognizes her seatmate as Nicholas Creighton, her ex-fiancé. When a storm grounds the plane, and she must depend on Nick to get her home in time for the Christmas Eve gathering at Granny Forrester's. Will bad weather, snow covered roads, and a car accident melt Abby's frozen heart enough to see that her true Christmas wish is sitting right beside her?

Home for the Holidays by Christine Lynxwiler
What's a girl to do when she falls in love with her lifelong best friend? Librarian Lauren Forrester moves to St. Louis so that handsome contractor Jeffrey Warren can find a mate without having to deal with her moods. But when Jeffrey shows up on her doorstep to convince her to come home for a country Christmas, will the hardheaded pair lose their friendship or find something even more precious?

Dreaming of a White Christmas by Kathleen Miller
When EMT Ben Callahan, estranged son of the owner of Callahan & Callahan department store, is called out on an emergency to revive a woman in the store's window display, he quickly loses his patience—and his heart—to Casey Forrester, the exhausted window dresser. Can Casey return to her home town of Pierce City, Missouri, in time for Granny's Christmas Eve celebration, even if it means losing her job and Ben?

Ozark
Family Christmas

*Four Romances Take an
Adventurous Track Home for Christmas*

Janet Lee Barton ✳ Jeanie Smith Cash
Christine Lynxwiler ✳ Kathleen Miller

BARBOUR
PUBLISHING

Making Memories

by Janet Lee Barton

Dedication

To my Lord and Savior for showing me the way
and to my family—I thank the Lord for you daily.
I love you all!

Chapter 1

When Amanda Forrester left the Rosewood Realty office for the day, it was with a huge grin on her face. Not only had she been to closings on the first two houses she'd sold, she'd also received her first listing for the company she worked for. Maybe her move to Oklahoma City hadn't been a mistake after all.

As she got in her car and started for home, she decided to stop at the grocery and buy a steak to celebrate. Maybe she'd buy two and ask Josh Randall, her next-door neighbor, to join her. Actually, she hoped he'd offer to cook them. She hadn't quite gotten the hang of her gas grill yet, and he could grill anything blindfolded.

Amanda rushed into the store and picked out two thick ribeyes. Normally she loved to go up and down the aisles to see everything the grocery offered. It was so much larger than what she was used to back home.

But then, everything here in the city was larger than she was used to. She'd been raised on a farm outside of Pierce City, Missouri, and had been a little apprehensive about moving to a city, but she liked to think she was beginning to adjust to it all.

She paid for the steaks and hurried back to her car. As she drove out of the large parking lot and headed home, Amanda realized she should have called Josh to make sure he didn't have plans for the evening. She sure hoped he was free. A celebration meant more if it was shared with someone else. She turned down her street and grinned—Josh was pulling into his drive just ahead of her. She couldn't have timed things better if she'd planned them.

"Hey, lady, need any help?" he asked as he jogged across the small side yard that separated their driveways and their condos.

"Sure." Amanda began to pull bags out of her car. "And, if you'll do the grilling tonight, I'll provide the steaks."

"Steaks?" Josh looked into the bag she handed him. "Whoa. What are we celebrating?"

"Oh, just my first listing for Rosewood Realty *and* two closings today."

"Wow! That is something to celebrate. I'll be glad to cook for you," he said with a grin.

His lopsided smile never failed to make her feel a little breathless, but as usual, she tried to ignore it. "Sure you don't want to cook inside? It's kind of chilly out."

"Are you kidding? When you have that wonderful

stainless steel grill outside?"

"Yeah, and you know the only reason I have that state-of-the-art grill is because some lucky salesman knew I didn't have a clue what I was looking for."

"Well, you made an excellent decision, to my way of thinking," Josh said, taking another bag from her.

"You are going to have to teach me how to use my own grill one of these days, Josh. It thinks you own it."

Josh laughed as he followed her inside to her kitchen and put the two bags he held down on the counter. "I like it better than my own."

"You've used it *more* than you have your own," Amanda teased him.

"That I have. It's a great grill. What time do you want me to start cooking?"

"Let's get them started in about an hour and a half. I'll put some potatoes in the oven to bake and make a salad."

"Okay. I'll go get changed and check my e-mail. I'll be back in a little while."

" 'Kay. Oh, and would you bring back some sour cream when you come over, if you have any? I seem to have forgotten that."

"See? That's what you get for going grocery shopping without me. I'll bring some." Josh chuckled on his way out the door.

He was right. When they went together, he always prompted her to remember things she might be out of. They'd become good friends when he'd offered to come show her how to light her grill right after she moved in. He'd been in his small backyard next door and had heard her talking to herself—or more accurately, to her grill, trying to convince it to light for her.

She'd offered to share her steak with him that night, and since then they seemed to eat together several nights a week. Josh wasn't shy about asking himself to supper. On the other hand, he was very generous with his help. In the few months she'd lived next door, he'd fixed two leaky faucets—one in the kitchen and one outside. He changed the oil in her car to save her money and he always carried in her groceries if he was around and saw her unloading her car. He'd also told her the best places to shop, the best place to get her car filled up, and he'd even given her the names of his doctor and dentist.

All in all, he'd made the move away from her family a little easier. Much as she hated to admit it even to herself, she did get lonesome at times. She missed her relatives—but not their constant matchmaking.

After each of the cousins she'd been so close to moved away during the past few years—for various reasons of their own—she'd found it impossible to stay in her hometown of Pierce City, Missouri, any longer. With her three cousins gone, her big family suddenly seemed to decide it was their mission to find Amanda a mate. From her parents to her aunts and uncles, they all were determined to find a husband for Amanda.

It didn't matter that she'd told them she wasn't interested. She'd witnessed enough of her cousins' broken romances to know that she'd rather stay single than go through all the heartache they'd endured. She didn't want to hurt her family—she knew their intentions were good—but she just couldn't stay there and go along with their matchmaking plans to set her up with every available man they knew.

So, Amanda opted for moving from Pierce City to Oklahoma City. She felt she really needed to be on her own for a while before she even thought about getting married. Thankfully, she'd been fairly successful at selling real estate at home, in spite of the devastation caused by the tornado that had destroyed most of the historical downtown in 2003. A good part of the town had already been rebuilt and she was happy about that. But when she decided to make the move, she was glad to be able to use her hometown broker's connections to help her find an agency to work for in Oklahoma. After taking the required tests and paying her fees, she'd gone to work for Rosewood Realty as soon as she moved here.

Her parents hadn't been thrilled about the move, but they'd supported her anyway and helped her get settled into her condo in northwest Oklahoma City. But, after they left for home and she was truly on her own, she'd found getting started in a strange city wasn't all that easy. It'd taken a while before she sold her first house and even longer to get a listing of her own. Today truly was a day to rejoice in. She was glad Josh would be there to celebrate with her. Amanda put the foil-wrapped potatoes in the oven and went to change clothes.

She liked her condo and she liked the neighborhood it was in. It was quiet and peaceful. There was a community pool she'd used a couple of times before it got too cold, and there was a walking trail she enjoyed almost daily.

Most of all, she liked her next-door neighbor—probably a little too much for her own good. Josh was the kind of man she could fall in love with if she wasn't careful. He was fun to be with, very nice looking, and, best of all, he was a Christian. She'd been delighted, after meeting him the week after she moved in, to find that he was also in her Sunday school class at church. They seemed to find more and more in common with each passing day. They both liked old movies and the cooking channel on TV. Josh was one of the few men she knew who also liked to shop. Every day she seemed to learn more about him and she liked all of it.

But, she had to remind herself that he was just a very good neighbor—at most a really great friend. He'd shown no sign of wanting their relationship to be anything else and Amanda told herself she wanted things to stay just like they were. She certainly didn't want to lose the friendship they shared.

She changed into a soft yellow velour jogging suit and went back to the kitchen to make the salad and dry rub the steaks with a spicy mixture of seasonings. She set the round table in her dining area and turned the gas log on low. Her fireplace was a two-sided one that could be seen from the living and dining rooms at the same time and she really enjoyed it.

The doorbell rang and she hurried to answer it, knowing it would be Josh. She could feel that the temperature outside had dropped as soon as she opened the door to him. "Come on in. It's getting colder. Maybe we'd better cook on my little electric grill tonight."

"Nah, it'll be fine. I'm dressed for it," Josh said. He had on a heavier jacket than she'd seen him in before. Still, it didn't look *that* warm to her. "Are you sure?"

"I'm sure. I've gone to all kinds of tailgating parties this time of year." He handed her a small white tub. "Here's the sour cream you asked for. Now," he said as he squared his shoulders and grinned at her, "lead me to those steaks."

Amanda chuckled and led the way back to the kitchen, shaking her head. Men. They were so funny sometimes.

꩜

Josh followed Amanda to the kitchen wondering how long it was going to take her to realize that he wanted to be more than just a good neighbor to her. He'd been attracted to her from the first moment he'd met her. He smiled just remembering the day he'd heard her trying very hard to persuade her new grill to light. Finally, he'd peeked over the fence to find her with an instruction book in one hand and a long-handled lighter in the other. He'd watched for a moment as she flicked the gas switch and put the lighter to it. Then she quickly turned the switch back off. She did the same thing several times before he decided she needed help.

"Hi." He'd called her attention away from her frustration, but he could tell from the way she caught her breath and held her hand over her heart that he'd also frightened her. "I'm sorry. I didn't mean to scare you. I'm Josh Randall, your next-door neighbor. Can I help you there?"

"Oh." She'd let out a huge breath. "Yes, if you don't mind. I can't seem to get the thing started and that salesman promised me it was very easy to light."

Josh was already on his way over through their respective gates. "I'll see what I can do."

She'd given him the lighter and opened the instruction booklet. "Here are the instructions—"

"I think I've got it," he'd said as he bent down and twisted the propane tank on, turned the igniter to the burner, and it lit. The flame was visible.

"Ohh." She began to laugh. "I forgot to turn the tank on, didn't I?"

He really liked that she could laugh at herself. "That's all it was."

"Well, thank you, Josh Randall. I'm Amanda Forrester." She'd smiled, held out her hand, and he'd taken it in his. It was small and soft, and he hadn't wanted to let go of it. But she'd gently pulled it out of his grasp and smiled at him. "Would you like to share my steak with me? It's really more than I can eat."

He wasn't about to turn down a dinner invitation from his lovely new neighbor. "I'd like that a lot. Can I bring anything over? Or cook the steak for you?"

She'd chuckled as she looked at her new grill. "Maybe you'd better."

"I'd be glad to." That evening had been the beginning of a friendship that he secretly hoped would grow into something much closer. He could fall very hard for Amanda Forrester, but she'd shown no sign of being any more attracted to him than she was to any of the other men in their Sunday school class, and he certainly didn't want to harm the friendship they shared now. His life had become much more meaningful with her in it.

"Here," Amanda said, shoving the steaks at him and bringing him out of his thoughts. "If you are determined to get a chill, go right ahead. I, on the other hand, am going to stay inside and stay warm."

He loved that spunky side of her. She looked so cute standing there with her arms crossed, he wanted to pull her into his arms and kiss her. Instead, he just grinned and saluted before heading outside, determined to grill the best steak she'd ever tasted.

∞

Amanda sighed and shook her head as she watched Josh shut the door against the cold. She put on a pot of coffee. He was liable to want a cup after standing outside for over ten minutes. She tossed the salad and put it back in the fridge, then went to the back door and looked out through the blinds. She couldn't help but smile. He looked so endearing out there leaning against one of the brick columns that held up her patio cover. She watched as he lifted the grill lid and turned the steaks over. Then he seemed to shiver and warm his hands over the heat. She shook her head and grabbed her jacket from the back of one of the bar stools where she'd left it earlier and went to pour him a cup of coffee. The least she could do for a man braving the cold to cook a good meal for her was take his coffee to him.

His eyes lit up at the sight of her, and he eagerly grabbed the mug she handed him and took a sip. "Thank you. This hits the spot."

"Not too cold for you?"

"Nah. Good grilling weather."

She raised an eyebrow at him as he pulled the collar of his jacket up a little higher on his neck, but he only laughed and raised the grill lid again. She sniffed appreciatively. Those steaks did smell wonderful.

"They are almost done. Another five minutes."

"Okay. I'll go get everything on the table." Amanda headed back inside, trying to ignore the thought that she wished they ate together every night.

Chapter 2

The steak was cooked to perfection. She should probably give him her grill. It just didn't work for her the way it worked for him.

"Mmm, this is wonderful, Josh."

"Thank you, ma'am. I aim to please." He grinned at her before taking another bite.

"Tell me about the Thanksgiving dinner we're helping with at church. What is it we are supposed to do?"

"Just serve, I believe. Our congregation is large enough that we can feed a lot of people in the fellowship hall. The ladies have things so organized that all we have to do is show up and serve those who are less fortunate. The church bus drivers established pick up places years ago and once word gets out about the day and time, they bring full busloads of people right to us each year."

"I just think that is so wonderful." Thanksgiving was the next week and Amanda had been fighting a wave of homesickness for the past few days. She was glad to have something to keep her busy that day. Her family had tried to talk her into coming home for the holiday, but she felt too vulnerable to go. Her mother would be able to tell that she was homesick and she'd have to tell her dad, and he'd insist that Amanda just come on back home. Besides, they'd already started pushing for her to be there for Christmas. She didn't even want to think about that until after Thanksgiving.

"We'll eat there, of course," Josh continued. "It's a good feeling to know you are helping others, but I've always come home knowing I was helped every bit as much as anyone I'd served."

Amanda's respect for Josh raised another notch higher than it had when she found out he was a high school teacher, and she found herself looking forward to serving Thanksgiving dinner right alongside him. Then she wondered if maybe her heart would be safer if she went home for Thanksgiving instead of sharing the day with Josh. She really had to have a talk with herself. For years, she'd been telling her family that she wasn't interested in finding a mate, and now here she was, right next door to a man who seemed the answer to her secret dreams—when she allowed herself to contemplate those things.

"Well, I always make it a habit to count my blessings, but this Thanksgiving I'll have even more to count—a wonderful new home, a great place to work, and a new best friend who knows how to cook the best steak in town."

"Thank you. I have to give some credit to your grill,

though," Josh said, smiling at her.

Amanda shook her head and grinned. "You and that grill."

The telephone rang just as they were finishing their dinner and Amanda sighed when she saw the number on her caller ID. It was Granny Forrester. Her parents had called in the big gun. For a moment she was tempted not to answer the phone but then she'd have to explain to Josh. She quickly picked up the receiver. "Hello?"

"Hello, Amanda dear. How are you?" her grandmother asked.

"Hi, Granny! I'm fine. How are you?"

"Well, I'd be doing a lot better if you'd just come on home for Thanksgiving."

"Oh, Granny. I'd sure like to see you all, too, but—"

"Now, Amanda, you know your mama and daddy are going to be really lonesome if you aren't here."

"I've explained it all to them, Granny. They understand that—"

"That's what they say. But I know they are very disappointed that you won't be here."

"Granny," Amanda said as gently as she could, frustrated as she was, "I really need to stay here this year. It's not like I'm never coming home again."

"Then you'll be here for Christmas?"

"I don't know, Granny. I'm just beginning to get settled here and—"

"Now, Amanda Jean, it's one thing for you not to be here for Thanksgiving, but we're all expecting you to be here for Christmas."

Uh-oh. She'd used her middle name. Still, Amanda tried once more. "Granny, I just don't know—"

"Well, you'd better be making up your mind to be here. That's all I have to say. I love you, darlin'. Talk to you later." With that, her grandmother hung up on her.

Amanda didn't know whether to be upset or relieved. She replaced the receiver on its base and let out a huge sigh. Turning back to Josh, she found that he nearly had the kitchen cleaned up. Oh yes. He was going to make some woman a terrific husband.

"You didn't have to do that, Josh," she said.

"Not a problem." He finished wiping off the table. "You bought the steaks."

"And you cooked."

He shrugged. "I felt funny listening in on your conversation. I figured I'd do better to find something to do."

"It was my grandmother. The family is disappointed that I'm not coming home for Thanksgiving and I think they put her up to calling to convince me to come—or at least that's what I thought at first. Now I think maybe they are just starting the campaign to get me to come home for Christmas."

"Oh. It must be nice to have a big family."

Amanda felt bad. When she'd asked Josh if he was going home for Thanksgiving, he'd told her that he'd lost both of his parents in an automobile accident several years before and he was an only child. His aunts and uncles lived on the West Coast and he rarely talked to them. How ironic it was that here he was wishing *for* family and she was trying to avoid hers.

"It is, most of the time. Mine just seems to be a little too. . ."

"Controlling? Meddlesome? Nosy?" Josh chuckled as he teased.

"All of the above. And, sometimes, all at the same time."

"Oh. I see."

Amanda laughed. Somehow she didn't think he did but that was okay. "But, they are wonderful and I love them. I do miss them, too. I just think I need to be on my own a while before I go back home."

Josh nodded as he leaned against her kitchen counter. "It's not easy to be alone for the first time, is it?"

"No, it's not." *But you've made it a lot easier than I expected it to be.* Amanda caught her breath, thinking for a minute that she'd spoken her thought out loud.

"It will get easier, with time," Josh said in answer to her words, not her thinking.

She sighed with relief that her thought was still only that. "I hope so. Want some more coffee? I have some cookies to go with it."

"Sure. I'd love some."

⚬⚬⚬

Josh would have liked to hear more about Amanda's family, but she didn't seem to want to talk about them anymore so he didn't press it. From what she'd told him, he knew she came from a large, loving family; and he could tell she missed them. Maybe talking about them made it worse and he certainly didn't want to make things harder on her. The last thing he wanted was for Amanda to get so homesick that she decided to move back to Missouri. So, when she changed the subject, he went right along with her.

"How was your day?"

"The kids are all ready for the Thanksgiving break, and they are always a little high-spirited this time of year." He chuckled. "Actually, that's putting it mildly. But it was a good day."

"Much as I like teens, I don't think I could teach a whole room of them. You must have a special calling to be able to."

He shrugged. "I like it—most of the time. Every once in a while I wonder what I was thinking when I decided I wanted to be a teacher. But I don't believe I'd be as happy doing anything else. I love teaching."

"Well, if my opinion counts for anything, your students are very lucky to have you."

Josh laughed heartily at that. If she only knew how very much her opinion counted. "I wish they all thought the same thing, but I have a couple of students who certainly would not agree with you."

"No."

"Yes." He began to tell her stories that had her laughing and then shaking her head at some of his students' antics.

When he left an hour later, Josh pulled up his collar and sprinted across the lawn to his own home. It had turned colder while he was at Amanda's. He lit the gas log in his fireplace before hanging his jacket in the coat closet. Dropping down into his favorite chair, he picked up the TV remote control but only stared at the blank TV screen. He would have liked to stay at her place a little longer but he certainly didn't want to wear out his welcome. He loved spending time with Amanda. She had a way of putting sunshine in any day for him.

And she didn't have a clue how he felt; he was sure of that. Or at least, if she did, she didn't want to deal with it. She'd called him a best friend tonight and while he was glad she thought of him in that way, he was afraid that's all he'd ever be to her.

But he wasn't going to just give up without taking it to the One who was in control. He bowed his head and prayed. "Dear Lord, You know how I feel about Amanda. I can't help but believe You brought her here so that we could meet. Maybe I've got it all wrong, and if so, please let me know, Lord. If I'm right, please let her have an idea of what Your plans for us are. And please help me to be patient until that time. In Jesus' name I pray, amen."

He felt better about it all as he reminded himself that the Lord would guide him in this. In the meantime, he had a pile of papers to grade. Josh got up and went to his computer. They certainly weren't going to grade themselves.

Chapter 3

The next week passed fairly fast for Amanda. She'd been surprised that there were several people from out of town who were relocating after the first of the year and wanted to look at homes that week. Since she was working the desk when they called about a listing, she was busy showing them properties up until Thanksgiving Day and was hopeful of a sale before the end of the week.

She'd also been busy trying *not* to feel guilty about not going home for Thanksgiving, as well as fighting a wave of homesickness just thinking about all the family favorites she'd be missing. Josh had called the night before and made arrangements to take her to church with him and that had helped some—at least until her family called that morning.

She could hear the unhappiness in her parents' voices as they'd wished her a happy Thanksgiving and told her how much they would miss having her with the whole family.

They were all gathering at one of her uncles' homes this year. Thanksgiving was always at a different family member's home while Christmas Eve was always at Granny Forrester's.

In an effort to try to inject a little humor into the conversation, Amanda asked if her aunt Sally was going to make the dressing. It was an inner-family joke ever since the time Aunt Sally had accidentally put too much sage in the dressing. It was almost Christmas green and about as inedible as a tree, too.

She was rewarded by a chuckle from her dad. "No, thankfully. Your mother is making it this year." Amanda heard his leather chair shift as he leaned back, and she pictured him at his desk in the den.

"And it won't be nearly as good with you not here to taste test it for me," Amanda's mother said from the telephone in her kitchen.

"Oh, Mom. You don't need me to taste it for you. You make the best dressing in the family." And she did. Amanda was certain she wouldn't have dressing anywhere near as good as her mother's.

"Well, I count on you to tell me when I've put enough seasoning in."

"Dad can do the same thing."

"I'll help you, dear." Her dad's reassurance to her mom made Amanda miss them even more.

"Thank you, dear. Amanda, you are going to be with others today, aren't you?"

Her mother seemed to need extra convincing that she wouldn't be alone. "Yes, Mom. Remember, I told you that our church is serving dinner today—"

"Oh yes, I do remember it. And you are going with a neighbor?"

"Yes." She looked at her watch. "In fact, we should be leaving in just a little while."

"Well, you have a great day, dear. We'll be thinking about you."

Amanda was near tearing up, knowing her family would miss her as much as she missed them. But she didn't want them to know how close to crying she was. "You two have a happy Thanksgiving, too. I'd better go finish getting ready. I'll talk to you later, okay?"

"All right, dear. We love you," her mother said.

"Yes we do. And, Amanda?"

"Yes, Dad?"

"You really need to think about coming home for Christmas. I know you are trying to be all independent and grown-up, but—"

The doorbell rang just then, and Amanda literally felt saved by the bell as she honestly told her parents that she had to answer the door.

"I love you both and I'll call later, okay?" She quickly hung up the telephone and breathed a sigh of relief. She just was not ready to even think about Christmas right now. She almost ran to open the door and didn't think she'd ever been quite so happy to see Josh. He looked wonderful, dressed in black pants and wearing a rust-colored sweater over a black shirt.

"Hey, lady, you ready to go?"

She loved the way Josh called her "lady." It always

made her feel special. "I am."

"You sure look pretty today," he said, his glance taking in her outfit. "Very. . .Thanksgiving-ish. I don't think that's a real word, but it fits."

Amanda felt herself blush at his compliment. She'd dressed with extra care, choosing a pumpkin-colored dress with brown accessories, telling herself that she wanted to look good for the people they were serving. But deep down she knew she wanted to look good for Josh. "Thank you. You don't look bad, yourself. We almost match, don't we?"

"That we do. Shall we go?"

"Just let me get my purse and coat."

"It's cold out," Josh said, taking her coat from her and helping her on with it. He settled the collar around her neck and his touch sent a sudden charge of electricity down her neck.

Thankfully, he opened the door and she could excuse her shiver as due to the cold air that swept inside. "You are right. It is cold."

"We'll warm up once they put us to work at church," Josh said, helping her into his car. "It'll be nonstop for a couple of hours at least."

That's what she needed, Amanda thought—to stay too busy to think about missing her family and too busy to think about how glad she was to be spending the day with her handsome neighbor.

⤬

This Thanksgiving was turning out to be the best he'd

had in a very long time and Josh was certain it was due to the woman beside him. Her sweet gentleness with the people they were serving settled her even deeper into his heart.

"There you go," she said to one of the ladies in line as she heaped a large spoonful of dressing onto her plate. "Happy Thanksgiving to you."

"And God bless you," the lady replied before moving down the line. As he'd anticipated, they'd been serving nonstop for the past hour and a half, and from the look of the line, the next pair of servers might be there just as long.

"We're here to relieve you," Melinda Benson said, stepping up behind Amanda.

"Oh, is it that time, already?" Amanda asked, looking at her watch.

Andrew, Melinda's husband, held out his hand for Josh's mashed-potato serving spoon. "Has it been like this long?"

"Since the start," Josh answered him with a grin.

"Well, go get something to eat. The ladies outdid themselves this year," Andrew said.

Josh relinquished his spoon and waited for Amanda to do the same before they headed to the kitchen where they could help themselves to the same dinner they'd been serving, without having to get in line. Tables were set up for the volunteers to eat at and after they filled their plates, they joined the rest of the first shift.

The deacon heading up the volunteers said a prayer of thanksgiving, thanking the Lord for all their many blessings and for the volunteers who were willing to give up their family dinners to help those less fortunate. Then it was time to enjoy the meal that had been whetting their appetites while they served.

"Mmm. This is wonderful," Amanda said. "The dressing tastes almost like my mom's and is every bit as good as hers."

"I'm sure she's a wonderful cook, then. I like the sweet potatoes, too. But then I like everything," Josh said.

"It's all just wonderful. I don't know how I'm going to tell my mother that I didn't miss out on any of my favorite dishes," Amanda said. "As unhappy as they were that I didn't make it home for Thanksgiving, I'm not sure she'll be thrilled to hear how good the meal is."

Trisha Lane chuckled from across the table. "I know what you mean. It's kind of like they want you to have a great meal, just not as good as the one you'd have had at home."

Amanda nodded. "Exactly. And truthfully, I'd love to be with them, too. But I haven't been on my own that long and I feel I need to—"

"Get used to that before you got back home," Trisha stated.

"Yes. How did you know?"

"I've gone through the very same thing. And I was so homesick at times, I cried myself to sleep, but I felt I had to stick it out. Now I can go home and come back, and I'm happy in both places. I can't wait to get there and can't wait to come home."

"Oh, that makes me feel so much better, Trisha."

Josh just listened to the conversation between the two women. He was finding out more about Amanda's feelings about being away from family than she'd ever told him.

"I guess I feel even worse because I'm not the only one in the family who isn't there this Thanksgiving," she continued. "Three of my cousins have moved away, also. I'm sure our family feels as if we've all deserted them."

"Four of you left home at the same time?" Josh asked, his brow furrowing. Why would they all have moved away?

Amanda shook her head. "Not at the same time. Casey and Abigail both moved to California—Casey to Cade's Point and Abigail to San Francisco. Then Lauren moved to St. Louis and I came here."

"Well, I guess you can't blame your family for feeling a little forlorn with all of you gone, huh?" Josh couldn't help but feel a little sorry for her relatives.

Amanda shook her head. "I guess not."

"Josh, somehow I don't think you are making Amanda feel any better," Trisha said.

One look at Amanda's face told him Trisha was right. "Oh, I'm sorry, Amanda. I—"

"It's okay, Josh."

"No it's not. I didn't mean to make you feel bad. I just—I guess I'm coming from a totally different mindset. With no family to go home to, a big family seems a dream to me."

"I understand. And I do have a very big one. I don't mean to sound ungrateful for them. I love my family."

"I know you do." And he did. He could tell by the way she talked about them that she loved them. And he certainly wasn't upset that she'd decided to stay in Oklahoma. If she'd gone home to be with them, she wouldn't be here with him. "Personally, I'm glad you didn't go home."

He was rewarded with a small smile and a "Thank you."

But Josh had a feeling that he'd put a damper on her joy of the day and for that he was extremely sorry. Somehow, he'd have to find a way to make it up to her.

Chapter 4

By the time they left the church that evening, Amanda understood what Josh had been talking about earlier in the week. She felt she'd benefited more than those who'd come for the meal. Seeing their humble thankfulness had been a vivid reminder of how blessed she was and she was glad she'd been a part of the serving team.

"What are you doing tomorrow?" Josh asked as he pulled out of the parking lot. "Are you one of those early-bird shoppers?"

Amanda shook her head. "Not me. I'll get my shopping done later. I know I miss some great sales, but I just don't like the frenzied crush."

"Neither do I. I do like the lights going up and seeing all of that, though. How about I take you to the Oklahoma Christmas Tree Lighting tomorrow evening? Then we can grab a bite to eat at one of the restaurants and take in some of the other events downtown."

"I'd like that. I wasn't sure how the city celebrated the Christmas season."

"Well, this will be only our fifth year for downtown OKC, but it gets nicer each year. Last year was the first year for snow tubing. The youth group from church went one night and had a ball. The kids loved it. And we took them to Braum's Ice Rink in Civic Center Park. I had as much fun as they did."

"I've always wanted to ice-skate, but I've never been quite brave enough to try."

"Oh, we'll have to go one night during the season. I'll teach you."

Amanda loved the thought of Josh teaching her to skate, but the thought of her pulling them both down on the ice gave her doubts. "I'm not sure—"

"You'll love it. Just wait and see."

She had no doubt that she would love skating—or trying to skate—beside Josh. In fact, she was so sure she would enjoy it, Amanda wondered if she would be wise to accept his invitation to teach her how to ice-skate. She wasn't sure she should even be going to the Christmas tree lighting. The more time she spent with Josh, the more time she wanted to spend with him—but not necessarily just as the friend he thought she was.

Still, it was the Christmas season and she was looking forward to finding out how the city celebrated. She tried to tell herself that being with Josh had nothing to do with the excitement she felt just thinking about the next evening. But by the time he pulled into his drive and walked her across to her door, she couldn't deny that she was looking forward to going—mostly because she'd be with him.

"The tree lighting is at six," he said as she unlocked her front door. "How about we leave about five so we can find a good place to view it?"

"That will work for me. I have to meet a couple who want to make an offer on a house I showed them yesterday, but that shouldn't take long. I ought to be home on time."

"Good. But if you see you're running late, just give me a call and I'll pick you up at your office."

"All right."

She really wanted to ask him in for some hot chocolate but her telephone started ringing before she could get the words out of her mouth, and Josh just said a quick, "Good night. I'll see you tomorrow," before he sprinted across the lawn.

Amanda shut the door and hurried to answer the phone.

"Amanda, dear!" her mother said with a lilt in her voice. "I thought you were still gone and I was just about to hang up."

"I just walked in the door, Mom. How was your day?"

Her mother's voice changed slightly, taking on a more somber tone. "Well, it would have been much better with you here, but we managed to be thankful for all of our other blessings."

Amanda stifled the chuckle that wanted to escape.

Her mother could be very dramatic on occasion. "I'm glad, Mom. And your dressing turned out great, I bet, didn't it?"

"It was pretty good. At least everyone said it was even better than last year's."

"I knew it would be."

"Did you have dressing, dear?"

"I did. It was different from yours, but it was pretty good." Then she quickly added, "Of course we were starving when we got to eat, so everything tasted real good. But oh, Mom, it was such a blessing to be there today! Since I wasn't with you all, I'm glad I was able to help at church."

"You could have been with us, dear."

Amanda sighed. "I know, Mom. I—"

"Your uncle Jim has a new young man working for him," her mother interrupted. "We think he is just your type and that the two of you would make a wonderful couple."

Of course they did. They thought any available man they met would be perfect for her. "Mom—"

"Really, dear, he's very nice looking and so sweet."

"I'm sure he is, Mom." Amanda could have bit her tongue as soon as the words were out of her mouth. And at her mother's next words, she knew she should have.

"Maybe you can meet him at Christmas."

"I'm still not sure about coming for Christmas."

"Now, Amanda, surely you'll be here for Christmas. We miss you so."

"I. . ." She couldn't deal with this tonight. So Amanda simply opted to put off telling her mother that she had no intention of coming home to meet this new man. "Miss you all, too."

That seemed to satisfy her mother for the moment. "I am glad you enjoyed helping at church, too. It there a nice group of young people there?"

"Oh, yes, there is a really great young adult group."

"Good. I'm glad. What are you doing tomorrow? I'm going shopping with your aunt Lily. She wants to leave at five in the morning."

"Oh, Mom, I don't know how you get up that early to do that. I'm not going shopping. I have to meet with a client. But, I am going to a tree lighting tomorrow evening."

The conversation turned to trees and how her mother was decorating this year and Amanda was very relieved that her mother didn't get back to whether or not she was coming home for Christmas. Missing them so, she'd been thinking maybe she would go home—until her mother brought up the new man they wanted her to meet. And there was a whole month until Christmas. No telling how many men they'd have lined up by then. Amanda had to find a good reason for not going home again. And she had to find it fast.

❦

Josh had been to the city's tree lightings many times in the past, but he'd never had as good a time as he was having tonight. It was all due to Amanda's company.

She was in high spirits when he'd knocked on her door, having made her third sale that day, and her mood had gotten better as the night went on.

She seemed to love the Christmas lights as much as he did as she watched the Oklahoma Christmas Tree Lighting. The sudden burst of twinkling lights when the switch was turned on had the crowd cheering in delight.

"Oh, Josh, isn't it beautiful?" She craned her neck to look up. "It's so big!"

"It's supposed to be the state's tallest cut tree."

"I can believe that. And it's just gorgeous."

And so was Amanda, her blue eyes shining with joy at the profusion of lights.

"Ready to see more of what downtown OKC has to offer?"

"Oh yes!"

Before the evening was over they'd taken a cruise on Bricktown's Water Taxi to see the lights there, then they'd headed over to Braum's Ice Rink in Civic Center Park and watched the skaters. He got Amanda to promise she'd try to skate another night when it wasn't so busy and was just glad she'd agreed to another night out with him. The hot dogs smelled so good they'd decided to have one for supper and go to one of the downtown restaurants another night. Then they took in the Oklahoma Gas and Electric Garden Lights before heading home.

Josh hated to see the evening come to an end, so when he'd walked Amanda to the door and she asked him if he wanted to come in for a cup of hot chocolate, he didn't hesitate to say yes.

He lit the log in her fireplace while she heated the milk and mixed the cocoa and sugar. Then he took a seat at her snack bar and watched as she mixed all the ingredients together and simmered them all until he could inhale their delicious smell. She'd just poured the aromatic liquid into two cups when the telephone rang. He sipped from the cup Amanda handed him and tried not to listen in on the one-sided conversation. But it was impossible not to.

∽

Amanda recognized the telephone number on her caller ID and picked up the receiver quickly. "Hi, Dad!"

"Hi, baby. Your mom said you had a good Thanksgiving but I wanted to check on you myself."

"I had a great day," Amanda said, pretty sure that wasn't the answer her dad was looking for, so she added, "I missed you all, of course."

"We missed you, too. You aren't going to put us through that again at Christmas are you?"

Amanda sighed and shook her head. She should have ignored the call. "Dad, I'm just not sure—"

"Amanda, it will break your mother's heart—not to mention your granny's. Now you just plan on coming home, you hear?"

"Daddy, I'll think about it, okay?"

"Well, you think about it all you want. But we're setting a place for you for Christmas." Then before

Amanda even had a chance to reply, he added, "And we expect you to be here. Night, baby. Love you."

"Da—" The click and buzz on the line told her that her dad had said all he'd planned to say. Forgetting for a moment that she wasn't alone, she moaned and put her receiver down a little too hard.

"Whoa. You okay, Amanda?" Josh asked, reminding her that she had company.

More than a little embarrassed at her reaction to the phone call, she forced herself to smile at him. "I'm all right. Just a little. . ."

"Frustrated?" He grinned and raised an eyebrow at her, as if he could read her mind.

"You could say that. I know you wish you had a big family, Josh. And I do truly love mine, and I would love to spend Christmas with them—but I just don't think I can handle any more of their unending matchmaking!"

"Matchmaking?"

"Yes. That's the main reason I left home. They've been trying to marry me off since I graduated. And I do want to get married—one day. But I think I need to be on my own for a while between living with my parents and getting married."

"That makes sense."

"Well, they don't see the need in it. And since my cousin Lauren left home," Amanda continued, "if it wasn't my parents trying to set me up, it was my aunts and uncles. And even Granny got in the picture, introducing me to the man who does her yard work for her. And it's not like I haven't asked them not to—over and over again." She let out a big sigh.

"Oh. I had no idea, Amanda."

"I know. It's just that none of the men they seem to think would be perfect for me have interested me at all. We have nothing in common. So, my family tells me that I'm too picky or too hard to please—even just too stubborn to see that someone they pick could be right for me. I guess maybe I am, but I'd at least like to feel a little spark of attraction for someone." She shook her head. "And besides, it doesn't do much for my ego, with my family thinking that they have to find me a mate. Don't they trust me to find my own, when the time is right?"

"I, ah—"

"I don't think there is anything wrong with refusing to 'date, just for the sake of dating,' do you?"

Chapter 5

No, of course not! You don't see me dating just for the sake of it, do you?" He didn't add that the only person he wanted to date was her—and dating just to date certainly wasn't something that Josh wanted Amanda to be doing. He wanted to be the one to take her out when she decided she was ready to start seeing someone. And if they did start to date—when they did—he didn't want her to be dating him just to be going out with someone. He wanted it to be because she cared about him.

She'd told him once right after they met that she wasn't interested in blind dates or any other kind of date, and he'd thought maybe she'd suffered from a breakup. Instead, her family had evidently set her up with so many wrong men that she was a little sick of the whole dating scene entirely. He was glad he'd gone slow, fearing that he would scare her off if he let her know how much he cared about her. And yet—perfect timing was one thing, but what if his was off and because of his dawdling, she went home and met someone she could really be interested in?

"That's what I keep telling them," Amanda said, continuing their conversation. "But if I'm stubborn, then I got it from my family because they just don't give up. They probably already have two or three lined up for me to meet if I go home for Christmas. And they've started the campaign to get me there."

He had no doubt that she was right. She hadn't gone home for Thanksgiving and if they'd missed her half as much as he would if she went home, he was certain that her family was going to try to get her to come home for Christmas—to set her up once more. The thought that she would be seeing other men if she went home, and perhaps meet one who did have something in common with her, had Josh's mind whirling with ways to keep that from happening.

Amanda stirred her cooling hot chocolate and sighed. "I dread going so much, but I know they won't let up until I agree."

Josh hesitated for a minute or two before deciding to pitch the idea that came to mind. After all, he was desperate and the stakes were high. If she didn't agree to his idea, he could well lose her. "Why don't I go home with you?"

"They'd think I'd brought you home to meet them, because, well, because, they'd think we're dating here. I can't lie to them, Josh."

"No, and I wouldn't want you to. Why don't you just tell them the truth? Tell them I'm the guy next door and have no place to go for Christmas."

"You don't know what you'd be letting yourself in for, Josh. Before you could even say hello to them, my family will jump on the very fact that I brought you home and have us paired up as a couple."

Like having them think Amanda and I are serious about each other would bother me. "Don't worry about that, Amanda. I can handle it if you can."

"Josh, you don't know my family. They'll be planning a wedding before we—" The phone rang again, cutting her off. She looked at the caller ID and moaned. "They've called in the big gun *again*. It's Granny."

She gave a big sigh before answering on the third ring. "Hello, Granny. You're calling awfully late—nothing is wrong is there?"

There was a long pause as Amanda listened to her grandmother. Josh had to stifle a guffaw when she closed her eyes and shook her head. Evidently her grandmother stopped to catch her breath as Amanda said, "Now, Granny, you know I haven't promised to come home—"

Cut off again, Josh thought as Amanda's side of the conversation halted. It appeared she was losing ground to the older woman when after several moments of watching Amanda rub her temple, she tried to get another word in, "Oh, Granny—"

Interrupted again, it was a few more minutes before Amanda said, "Really? Do you think they will?"

Then, finally, a chuckle from Amanda. "Oh, all right, Granny. I'll be there to hang my ornament. But

I'm bringing a friend with me—my next-door neighbor has no place to go for Christmas."

Another pause and then Amanda grinned. "No, it's not a girl. Josh Randall is my neighbor and I'm bringing him home with me."

Something must have come up at her granny's because the next words out of Amanda's mouth were, "I love you, too. Night."

"No questions about me?" Josh said as she hung up the receiver.

Amanda laughed. "Oh, there will be plenty of questions about you. But right now I'm sure she's calling my parents and then everyone else in the family to let them know I have a man in my life." She quirked a delicate eyebrow at him. "Are you sure you're ready for this?"

Not only was he ready, he couldn't wait to meet Amanda's family. "I think so. I know I will be by the time we leave. What made you change your mind and tell her you'd come?"

"Well, your offer to go with me helped. But if you could have heard her. . ." Amanda shook her head. "I didn't have a chance. She pulled out all the stops: She and the whole family miss me terribly; she may not be here next year. . . . I thought that was hitting below the belt, but that's Granny for you."

"Oh, I can see how that would get your attention."

"Well, as if that wasn't enough—"

"There's more?" Josh asked, chuckling.

"There is always more. But she's trying to talk all three of my cousins into coming home, too, and it will be so great to see them, if they do. And, hopefully there will be safety in numbers for us all."

Maybe she really didn't need him to go if the cousins were going to be there, but Josh wasn't about to mention that thought. He was quite happy that she'd told her grandmother that he was coming with her. Surely she wouldn't change her mind.

❦

By the next evening, Amanda had a few misgivings about taking Josh home with her for Christmas. She'd had calls from her parents and her grandmother again. They were thrilled that she'd decided to come home but, most of all, they were delighted that she was bringing a man with her.

"What is he like, dear?" her mother asked.

"He's a very good neighbor, Mom. But we're just friends. He has no family to go home to."

"Oh, the poor dear. Well, we will try to make up for that. What does he look like?"

"Oh, he's tall and broad shouldered. He has dark hair and blue eyes. He's nice looking."

"Hmm. And what does he do for a living?"

"He's a schoolteacher, Mom."

"A teacher?"

"Yes. He teaches high school."

"How nice! And you met how?"

"Mom, we live next door to each other and I was having trouble with my gas grill. He came over and helped me light it."

"I see. He came to your rescue. I can't wait to meet him."

"Mother, we are only friends. That's all."

"I understand, dear."

She might understand the words, but Amanda knew her mother well and her mother's next words didn't surprise her at all.

"You know your dad and I started out being best friends, too."

"I'd forgotten, I guess," Amanda said. How could she have forgotten that? It was going to be harder than ever to convince her mother that she and Josh were only friends, now. Still, she had to try. "But not everyone is like you and Dad, Mom. You two were meant to be together."

"Yes we were. And you never know where friendship will take you, dear. We're all looking forward to meeting your young man."

"Mother!"

"I'm sorry, dear. I meant to say your *friend*. I'll give the spare room a good cleaning. Are there any dishes he particularly likes, dear?"

"Mom, Josh will like anything you make. He's not picky and he's very easygoing." As Amanda spoke the words, she realized how true they were.

Her call-waiting beeped and she looked at the caller ID. It was her grandmother. "Mom, that's Granny on the other line. I'll call you back, okay?"

"No need to call me back tonight. I'll talk to you later in the week, dear. Love you."

"Love you."

Amanda clicked over to her grandmother's call. "Hi, Granny!"

"Hello, Amanda dear. I won't keep you but a minute. I just wanted to know if you thought I should make your friend an ornament to put on the tree."

"Granny, that's up to you. But keep in mind that we are just friends and you'd need to let him bring it home with him."

"Oh, of course I would, dear. I just thought it would make him feel more a part of things."

"Whatever you want to do is fine, Granny." They all had their own special collection of wooden ornaments to hang on her grandmother's tree and each new member of the family was provided with one. It would be nice for Josh to have something to hang on the tree, but she knew her grandmother was trying to find out if they were more than just good friends.

"His name is Josh, isn't that what you said?"

"Yes, it is."

"Well, I'm looking forward to meeting him. I just wish all of you girls would settle down and have some great-grandchildren for me before I leave this land."

"Oh, Granny. Now, don't you be counting on me for that. Josh and I are just good neighbors."

"And he had no place else to go?"

"No, ma'am. His parents have passed away and he was an only child."

"Oh, dear, we'll have to make this Christmas special for him."

"He wouldn't want anyone to go to any extra trouble, Granny. I'm sure he's just glad not to have to spend Christmas alone."

They talked for a few more minutes, but Amanda ended the call as soon as she could. The more she talked, the more her grandmother was going to think there was more to her and Josh's relationship than there really was.

Dear that Josh was, he truly didn't know what he was letting himself in for. Her family could be loud and boisterous and loving, and she wasn't sure Josh was ready for them. She should probably let him out of his offer. By the time they arrived at her parents', her family would probably already have the wedding planned—and that would present more problems down the road.

Maybe she could cancel at the last minute. If she did it now, she'd have no peace. But she did want to be part of the family Christmas, to hang her special ornament at Granny's, and to see her cousins.

And with Josh along it would be such a blessing to go home and not dread being "fixed up." Nonetheless, she was sure that even though she would say Josh was just a friend, her family would assume that he was more, because of the very fact that she was bringing him home with her. To them that would mean she must care about him, and they certainly wouldn't hinder what they thought might become a serious relationship.

By the time her family actually figured out that there was no romance, it would be time to come home. Or, better yet, maybe they would continue to think that she and Josh might be serious about each other—at least enough so that they would quit matchmaking for a while.

Oh, what a blessing that would be!

She found herself looking forward to introducing her family to Josh. She knew they would like him. She just hoped they wouldn't be too much for him. She knew her cousins would take a liking to him and, for a moment, she couldn't help wishing she'd been able to introduce him as the man she was dating instead of just her next-door neighbor.

Josh found he was looking forward to Christmas more than he had in years. He'd spent more of them alone than he cared to think about and he wondered what being with a huge family like Amanda's would be like. Aside from the matchmaking—which he didn't like the idea of any more than Amanda did—he was sure they were a warm and loving family. It would be enlightening to see them together.

He wondered if he should buy gifts for everyone or just for her parents and started to pick up the telephone to call Amanda and ask but then decided to run next door and talk to her. She opened the door almost immediately, and he could tell she was on her way out or just getting home.

"Hi! Did I catch you at a bad time? Are you coming in or going somewhere?"

"I was just about to go out to the store. I wanted to take

some cookies in to work tomorrow and I'm out of nuts."

"Well, come on. I'll run you to the store—if you'll let me taste test those cookies."

"That's a deal."

It wasn't until they were on their way that Amanda asked, "What were you coming over for? Did you need to borrow something?"

"No. I wanted some gift ideas for your family." Just as he figured, she shook her head.

"Josh, you don't need to take presents."

"I know I don't have to, but I really would like to. I haven't spent a Christmas with a large group in so long. I'm really looking forward to it."

Amanda chuckled. "I'm glad. But I'm not sure you'll feel the same way after you've heard my dad's hunting stories for the fiftieth time."

"He likes to hunt? What kind of hunting does he like to do?"

"Just about any kind. He likes to fish best but not in the wintertime."

Hunting and fishing. Her dad shouldn't be too hard to buy for. "Does your mother have any hobbies?"

"She loves to cook, just like we do. And she likes to read."

A cookbook for Mom. "What about Granny?"

"Granny likes everything. She loves to cook. She loved to sew, but her eyes aren't quite as good as they used to be, so she does all kinds of other crafts. Crocheting is a favorite. And she loves to fish, too."

Well, Granny shouldn't be too hard to buy for, either.

"But really, Josh. They don't expect you to get them anything. They are just thrilled you are bringing me home for Christmas."

Josh smiled as he turned into the parking lot of the grocery store. They couldn't be any more pleased than he was. Christmas with Amanda and her family—the prospect had him almost as excited as a kid.

Chapter 6

"Want to help me put up my tree tonight?" Josh asked as she got out of her car the next evening. "I'll order pizza."

"That sounds like fun. I'd love to. I'll bring cookies."

"I was hoping you would."

The walnut chocolate chip cookies she'd made the night before were delicious. It was a good thing she'd made a double batch. "What time do you want me to come over?"

"As soon as you get changed and grab the cookies." He grinned. "The tree came with pre-strung lights and I have it up. I just need some help spreading out the branches so it looks real and then we can put on all the ornaments."

"I'll be right over." She hurried into her house and quickly changed into jeans and a sweatshirt decorated with Christmas trees of varying sizes. She'd been planning on putting her own tree up that evening, but it would be much more fun to help Josh. Maybe he'd return the favor and help her decorate hers another time.

She filled a ziplock plastic bag with cookies, slipped on her jacket, and hurried over to Josh's condo. She was always a little surprised when she went inside his home. It had a definite masculine feel, yet felt very warm and homey at the same time. The rich brown-leather sectional faced the corner fireplace. His tree stood beside the fireplace and it was huge. It had to be at least eight feet tall and once all the branches were arranged it would be very full.

The lights were lit and Josh had already added the topper. He'd started pulling out the branches to give it more shape and make it look fuller. "Just step right up and start wherever you want. I have some gloves, if you'd like to put them on. The needles are a little sharp. They make these trees seem real these days, don't they?"

Amanda pulled on the gloves he handed her. "They certainly have improved them. I love real trees, and my parents insist on one, but they are expensive and so I decided to buy an artificial one. Want to help me decorate mine tomorrow night? I'll make a pot of soup and maybe more cookies."

"Sure. I'd be glad to help you."

They sung carols with the Christmas CD Josh had put on as they shaped the tree and put on the ornaments he'd brought out earlier in plastic boxes. He had quite a collection started.

Just as he placed the last brightly painted ornament on the tree the doorbell rang and Josh went to answer it. The pizza deliveryman's timing was perfect. Josh pulled some bills out of his pocket and thanked the man before closing the door and turning to Amanda.

"Let's eat in here so we can enjoy the tree." Josh set the wonderful-smelling box on the oversized ottoman in front of his sofa. "I'll get paper plates and some soft drinks and be right back."

He was back in a flash and set the ottoman with a flourish before flipping open the pizza box. "Mmm, smells delicious, doesn't it?"

"It certainly does. I never realize I'm so hungry for pizza until I get the first whiff of a freshly baked one."

They each helped themselves to a slice and settled against the sofa to look at the tree while they ate.

"I know a lot of people wouldn't put up a tree if they weren't going to be here for Christmas Day," Amanda said, "but I just love looking at the lights at night."

"So do I."

"I'm not sure mine will compete with your tree, though. It's lovely, Josh."

"That's because you helped with the ornaments. I usually manage to have them all on one side or the other, and it nearly always looks a little lopsided."

Amanda chuckled just picturing it. "Well, it's not lopsided tonight. I bought one of those stands that rotate the tree all around. I hope it works right."

"We'll get it to work," Josh said.

Amanda found herself looking forward to the next night and putting up her own tree. Having Josh there to help would make it an even more special event.

"Does your family have any special traditions at Christmas?"

"Well, my cousins and I have always spent Christmas morning at Granny's, where we have hot chocolate and rolls with her and then hang our special ornaments on her tree. Then that night the whole family gathers there again to open presents and celebrate Christmas with her. The next day will be at my parents' house, where we'll open more presents and have Christmas dinner."

"No." Josh shook his head. "I'm sure I'll love it all. I'm just glad to have somewhere to go."

Amanda was still having second thoughts about this—thinking her family might overwhelm him or that he might be wishing he hadn't volunteered to go—but thinking about him spending the day alone made her glad that he was going.

"I love turning out the lights and just leaving the tree lights on," Josh said as they finished the pizza. He flipped off the lamp on the end table and the lights on the tree seemed to glow brighter. "Isn't that beautiful?"

"Yes, it is," Amanda said. With the Christmas music in the background and the twinkling lights, sitting side by side on the sofa took on a different feel. There was something warm and cozy and. . .kind of romantic about the moment. But they were just friends. Amanda jumped up and began gathering their plates and glasses. "I guess I'd better be going. Surprisingly, I'm showing houses again tomorrow morning."

Her appointment with her clients wasn't until eleven the next morning, but suddenly she felt a need to go home. She and Josh were just good friends and she didn't want to ruin their great relationship by weaving dreams that were unlikely to come true.

∽

Josh walked Amanda to her house, wondering why she'd suddenly decided to hurry home. It was only nine o'clock. Maybe she was just tired of his company—but it didn't seem that way as she told him not to forget about the next night.

"Oh, I'm not likely to forget. Soup and cookies, right?"

"Right."

"You didn't stay long enough to have any of the ones you brought over tonight."

"Those are yours; you enjoy them."

"Thank you—for the cookies and for helping me tonight."

"It was fun. I enjoyed it."

"So did I." It was getting cooler out and he didn't want her catching cold. Since she didn't ask him in, he turned to go. "See you tomorrow."

"At six, okay?"

"Six it is." He turned and waved before jogging over to his place. It had been a wonderful evening to his way of thinking. Trimming a tree with Amanda made all the difference in the fun of it all. But he couldn't help wondering if he'd done the right thing by pushing her to take him home for Christmas. Maybe she was having second thoughts. He certainly hoped not. As he entered the living room and looked at the tree glowing brightly in the otherwise dark room, it dawned on him that he might have scared her off by turning off the lamp. It had felt just right to him to be sitting beside her, admiring their work. But he had to admit he would have liked to have put his arm around her as they sat there—would have liked to thank her for helping him. . .with a kiss.

He shook his head. There was no denying that he cared about Amanda a great deal. In fact, he was sure he was falling in love with her, but he didn't want to ruin the relationship they enjoyed now. He wasn't sure what to do. Should he let her know that his feelings for her were growing or just pretend that they were best friends? Maybe during this trip the Lord would make things clearer to him and he would know what to do.

∞

Amanda found herself looking forward to decorating her tree with Josh so much that she decided it would be best to invite most of their Sunday school class over, too—with others around it wouldn't seem nearly as romantic as the night before. When she called Josh to let him know, he seemed pleased and she didn't know whether to be glad or disappointed that he didn't appear to mind that they wouldn't be spending the evening alone.

She baked all afternoon—three different kinds of cookies, plus corn-bread sticks to go with the soup she had simmering when the first guests arrived. Trisha Lane came with Mark Edwards. They'd only been dating for a few weeks. Josh came over next, and then Andrew and Melinda Benson showed up. John and Carey Reynolds were also there, as were most of the rest of their class.

But even in a room full of people, Amanda was aware of Josh's every move. And he never seemed very far away from her. He took charge of putting the tree into the revolving stand and he was there to help her put the topper on the tree. She liked the way he just pitched in and helped her serve dinner, standing by her side and handing out the bowls after she ladled soup into them. And it felt natural and right to have him by her side. For a minute, she let herself think of how it would feel if they were a couple like Trisha and Mark, but she quickly shook that thought out of her mind. The fact that he was going home with her for Christmas—to keep her family from setting her up with any of the men they'd chosen for her—only meant he was a very good friend coming to her rescue and she needed to keep that in mind.

But that was hard to do, especially when Trisha was helping her make hot chocolate for everyone and bluntly asked, "Are you and Josh seeing each other?"

"We see each other every day just about, Trisha. We live next door to each other."

Trisha threw her a look that said Amanda knew

that wasn't what she meant. "You know what I mean. Are you dating?"

Amanda shook her head and tried not to give away how much she wished she could say yes to that question. "No. We aren't dating. We're just really good friends." And that's probably all they'd ever be, much as she was realizing she'd like there to be more—but she wasn't going to tell Trisha that. And even though her mother had said she and Amanda's dad had started out as best friends, Amanda just wasn't sure how you could get around the friendship phase into the romantic phase—and she didn't know if Josh would even want to try to get there.

"Well, I'm glad you asked him to go home with you for Christmas. He sounds really excited about it. I can't imagine what it would be like to have no family to share the season with."

Amanda was a little surprised that Josh had mentioned it to the others and relieved that he hadn't told them exactly why he had offered to go. She didn't want everyone to know that her family seemed to think she needed help in the romance department. "No, neither can I," she agreed with Trisha. "Not with the huge family I come from. Grab that plate of cookies, will you?" Amanda picked up the tray of hot-chocolate mugs, and they rejoined the party.

Josh was at her side to take the heavy tray from her. "Mmm, this smells delicious," he said before placing it on the coffee table so her guests could help themselves. "What is a tree-trimming party without hot chocolate?"

Her tree did look pretty. It wasn't decorated with the homemade wooden ornaments like her grandmother's was, nor the sequined balls that her mother liked, but it suited her just fine. She liked the painted glass ornaments that Josh used so much that she had gone out and bought some for her own tree. She loved the way the lights picked up the different-colored Santa Clauses and snowmen. And the revolving tree stand worked beautifully.

"I'm going to have to get us one of those stands next year," Melinda said. "I love the way the lights seem to twinkle as it goes around."

"I do, too," Amanda said.

"It makes it easier to decorate, too," Mark said. "You only have to stand in one spot and let the tree turn to you."

All in all, the evening was a huge success, and in some ways it was even more romantic than the night before—with Josh staying behind to help her straighten up after everyone else left. He brought empty cups to her and helped her load the dishwasher.

"It was a nice night. Everyone seemed to enjoy themselves, don't you think?"

"I'm sure they did. I know I enjoyed it," Josh assured her as he placed the last cup in the rack.

"So did I," Amanda said, thinking that this is what it would be like if they were married, talking over their evening with friends, and—Amanda clamped down on that unexpected thought. Where had it come from?

Chapter 7

Amanda didn't want Josh to go home. She wanted to sit beside him and look at her tree lights in a dimly lit room. She wanted him to pull her into his arms and kiss her. But Josh seemed to have other ideas. He put on his jacket as soon as they went back to the living room, and she tried to hide her disappointment.

He stood looking at the tree as he buttoned up. "Your tree looks really great, Amanda."

"Thanks to all of you. I couldn't have done it by myself. Thank you for getting it into the stand. I don't think I'd have been able to do it without help."

"You're welcome. I was glad to help. We have the same taste in ornaments; do you know that?"

Amanda chuckled. "I do. In fact, I liked yours so well I decided to start my own collection of the same kind. I hope you don't mind."

"Not at all." Josh shook his head as he walked to the door. "How about helping me shop for Christmas?

We could go to Quail Springs Mall and maybe take in a movie one night this week."

Her heart expanded with happiness at his invitation. "Sure. I have some shopping to do, too. And at least it won't be quite the crush of the day-after-Thanksgiving shopping."

"Okay, how about Monday evening?"

"Sounds good to me."

He opened the door and turned back to her. "Want to ride to church with me tomorrow?"

"Sure."

"I'll warm the car up before I come and get you."

"You don't have to—"

"It's cold outside." Josh cut off her protest. "You don't need to see me out. I'll see you in the morning." He gave a wave and closed the door behind him.

Amanda locked the door and leaned against it. It wasn't the perfect end to the evening but at least they'd be spending time together the next few days. And it was really better that he hadn't stayed. It was getting harder to pretend all she felt for him was friendship. Here she was, picturing them as a married couple!

Her family was going to fall in love with him. Of that she had no doubt. He'd be helping her mother and grandmother with anything they requested of him and he'd be talking to her dad and uncles about the football games, hunting, fishing—anything they wanted to talk about. And that presented another problem. They'd like him so much they'd be really disappointed when they realized that she and Josh really were only good friends.

She pushed away from the door and told herself she should probably just let Josh out of his offer to go to Granny's with her for Christmas. But she didn't want to. She wanted him to go—and not only to keep the matchmakers at bay. She loved being with him and she wanted him to have a good Christmas, too. He must be looking forward to it or he wouldn't have mentioned it to their Sunday school class. Much as she wished his reason was because he wanted to be with her as much as she wanted to be with him, Amanda was pretty sure that he simply wanted to experience what Christmas was like with her big family. Well, it appeared he was going to find out.

❧

As Josh sat looking at his Christmas tree, he wished Amanda were there with him. He hadn't wanted to leave her place tonight. He was looking forward to spending Christmas with her and her family more each day. But he was having a hard time pretending that the reason he wanted to go was to help her out. It was more that he felt he was protecting his own interests. But how was he ever going to be able to let her know that? He had a feeling he wouldn't be accompanying her home for Christmas if he did. And if he did, would he ruin what they shared now? He sighed deeply. He didn't know what to do except leave it all in the Lord's hands. Surely, He'd let him know if the time was ever right to let Amanda know he was falling in love with her.

He chuckled to himself, thinking about her asking

if he minded that she'd decorated her tree similar to his. How could he mind? It was just one more thing they had in common. He wondered if Amanda realized how many of the same things they liked. Each day he seemed to find more that they had in common. They would make a great couple; he was sure of it. Maybe one day Amanda would see it, too. In the meantime, Josh was going to enjoy each and every minute with her.

On Monday they went to Quail Springs Mall and began their shopping. For Amanda's mom, he found a cookbook they both wanted by one of their favorite food-network cooks. Amanda bought her mother computer software so that she could adjust her recipes to any amount depending on how many she was cooking for. She also mentioned that she would like to have it herself so her mom had better like it, and Josh made a mental note to go back and get one for her.

They browsed for presents for the aunts and uncles and cousins, but as they were both starving, they decided to do the shopping for them on the coming weekend.

They went to a nearby Italian restaurant for supper and Josh was glad when they were shown to a table for two in a secluded corner. After they'd given their orders to the waiter, he quizzed Amanda about what Christmas was like with all of her family.

"It's fun most of the time. But it's loud. Everyone seems to talk at once."

Amanda chuckled, making him think that she really didn't mind it. Her next words told him he was right.

"We pride ourselves on being able to keep up with

several conversations at one time. Are you sure you're ready for all this? How many conversations can you keep up with at a time?"

Josh leaned back in the booth and grinned at her. "You forget—I teach high school."

"Oh, that's right. Well, you'll fit right in, then. My dad and uncles tease us all about it, but they love it. They pretend not to hear, but they listen in often. We know, because they'll say, 'Huh? What did you say?' if they miss anything."

Josh had to chuckle. "They sound fun."

"They are for the most part. And I do love them all very much, in spite of the meddling, the matchmaking, and the never-ending advice."

"I'm sure they love you very much and only want what they think is best for you," he said. From what he'd heard about her family, Josh found himself eager to meet them. He could only hope that he would measure up in their eyes.

"I know they do. I just wish they would trust that I can figure out what's best for me on my own—with the help of the Lord."

Josh also hoped that she would come to realize—with the help of the Lord—that *he* was best for her.

Once their appetites were sated, they continued their shopping. For Amanda's dad, they went to a sporting goods store and Josh found a book on how to make the flies he loved to fish with. Josh added some special supplies to make them, hoping that they weren't any her dad already had.

After that, they went to a huge craft-supply shop in the area and found some specialty thread that Amanda assured him Granny would love. They stopped for hot chocolate on the way home and Josh couldn't remember when he'd enjoyed shopping for Christmas so much. Of course he'd never had much shopping to do—and then it was mostly for a few friends and coworkers. This was different and much more special. He wasn't sure what to get Amanda, but he wanted it to be something she would keep always. He'd kept her so busy helping him decide what to get her dad and grandmother, he hadn't been able to get a clue on what to get her other than the recipe software. He'd get that, too, but it wasn't quite special enough. He resolved to watch her closely on their next shopping expedition to try to get an idea or two.

❦

Amanda got ready for bed that night thinking that she had never had such a good time Christmas shopping. It was so different going with a man. Josh wanted so much to get something special for each person and he hadn't settled for anything less. She knew her parents and grandmother were going to love the presents he had picked out for them. She was more convinced than ever that her mother and Granny were going to fall in love with Josh right off the bat. How could they not? She was having a hard time resisting that very thing.

Amanda was afraid she was dangerously close to

losing her heart to him. Why had she let herself think that bringing Josh home for Christmas would make things easier for her? Oh, it would put a stop to the matchmaking for the time being, but only until her family realized that she and Josh were truly only friends. No, in the long run, it was going to make things much harder because she didn't know how she was ever going to be able to hide her growing feelings for him. And what if she couldn't? What would that do to their friendship?

"Dear Lord, please help me *not* to fall completely in love with Josh. I don't want to ruin the relationship we have now and I'm not sure it could survive if he knew I was thinking of him romantically. Please help me to stop thinking of him that way and especially help me not to let him or my family know that I have been. In Jesus' name, amen."

She should never have accepted his offer, but now he seemed so happy and excited about spending Christmas with her family that there was no way she could change her mind—especially now that he'd bought them gifts. She'd just have to make the best of it and pray that she and Josh came back to Oklahoma City with their friendship intact.

Chapter 8

The next weekend the Bensons threw a Christmas party for their Sunday school class and Josh seemed to just naturally assume Amanda would ride with him. She knew she probably should have taken her own automobile, but she couldn't bring herself to turn down a warmed-up car and his company. Besides, it was fun showing up at the party together as if they were a couple, and most of the class had begun to treat them as if they were one.

" 'Bout time you two showed up," Melissa said. "We've been waiting on you to get started."

"Started on what?" Amanda asked, looking around the living room. She couldn't see that anything needed to be done. The tree was decorated beautifully, as were the mantel and the rest of the house as they passed through the dining room to the family room.

"We're going to have a gingerbread-house contest. Come on out to the kitchen, everyone, and I'll hand out the makings," Melissa said.

"What fun! I haven't made a gingerbread house in years," Amanda said.

"I've never made one in my life," Josh said, "but it sounds like fun."

"We don't actually have to make the gingerbread, do we?" Trisha asked.

"No. I bought these kits from a local bakery," Melissa answered as she and Andrew began handing them out, one box to each couple, or in the case of singles, pairing them with another as a team to work together. "The directions are on the box and I have extra icing, gumdrops, and other candies, so you have no excuse not to make a dazzling house."

Amanda was more than pleased when she and Josh were paired together and sent off to one of the small folding tables that had been set up for each team.

"Do we get to eat these when we are finished?" Mark asked.

"No," Andrew said. "We'll be giving them to the children of some of the members who are receiving Christmas baskets from the church. A lot of folks are having a hard time making ends meet this year."

"Oh, well that is a good cause. Guess I'll resist the temptation to nibble as I work."

"Don't worry, Mark. The pizza man will be showing up at any time, and I made desserts this afternoon," Melissa assured him.

"I'm glad she told us she was feeding us," Josh whispered to Amanda. "I probably would have done a little taste testing myself."

Amanda only chuckled as they got to work on their house. Josh turned out to be very adept at cementing the walls together with icing. The roof was another matter, though. It took several minutes to get it to line up just right. Then the fun part began as they decorated the small cottage.

"I just love gingerbread houses. I saw a beautiful glass gingerbread-house decoration the other day, but it was a bit more than I wanted to spend for a tree ornament. It was lovely, though. It was so detailed and colorful. Maybe next year I'll feel like I can get one like it since I won't have so much to buy."

"It sounds great. Do you remember where you saw it?" Josh asked as he lined the walk with red and green gumdrops.

"No." Amanda shook her head. "I think it was at one of the stores in the mall, but I just can't remember. You would like it. It would go great with your collection."

Josh nodded and looked thoughtful for a moment. "Maybe on our next shopping expedition we'll find out where you saw it."

"I do need to pick out a few more things, but you don't need to feel you have to go with me." Then, thinking that sounded rude—as if she didn't want him with her—she added, "Unless you have shopping to do for others. But I don't want you thinking that you need to do any more shopping for my family."

"I have a few more things to get. How about we go on Monday evening to finish up? We're leaving next weekend, right?"

Amanda nodded, trying to ignore the little shiver of anticipation that ran down her spine. She put icing on two small candy canes and put them on either side of the front door. "I thought we could leave on Friday afternoon, if that's all right with you. That way I'd be there in time to go to Granny's the next morning like always."

"That's fine. We can leave earlier if you decide you'd like to. School is out until after the New Year, so I'm free as a bird until then. I can't begin to tell you how much I'm looking forward to meeting your family."

And that was the reason she could not—and would not—back out of accepting his offer to go with her. His excitement about sharing Christmas with her family was almost contagious, or at least that's what she kept telling herself that her growing excitement about the trip was all about.

The doorbell rang and Melissa and Andrew hurried to answer it.

"Pizza man!" Melissa called back to them. "It's time to take a break and gather round the kitchen island."

"She's not going to have to call me twice," Mark said.

"Nor me," Josh added.

"We ought to have a gingerbread-house judge to see who's made the prettiest one. I think Mark and I would win," Trisha said.

Amanda craned her neck around to look at their project and shook her head. "No way. Mine and Josh's would win."

They were in the middle of teasing rivalry when

Andrew and Melissa came back with the pizzas.

"Look at that," Andrew said. "Leave them without food too long and they revert to their childhood. We'd better feed them quick or they're liable to get quite cranky." Once he said the blessing for the food, it didn't take long to empty the last box of pizza.

Eating did seem to settle them all down before they went back to their house making. By the end of the evening, Amanda figured it was a good thing their projects weren't judged—they were all adorable and she prayed that the children who received them would be delighted.

Amanda and Josh stayed after everyone else left so that they could help Melissa and Andrew straighten up the family room and kitchen, and pack up the houses they'd all made. As the women packed the gingerbread houses in deep pastry boxes to be taken to church and given out, Josh and Andrew took them out to the Bensons' vehicle. They came back in from one trip to the garage laughing and disappeared into the front of the house before coming back for another box.

"What are you two up to?" Melissa asked her husband.

"You'll see later." Andrew winked at her and gave her a kiss on the cheek before they took another box back out to the garage.

"Men." Melissa shook her head and grinned. "No telling what they are plotting."

"You're right about that." Amanda chuckled and nodded. She'd seen her dad and uncles pull one prank after another often enough to recognize the signs. "We'd better be on our guard."

Melissa insisted that they have a cup of hot chocolate before heading out into the cold night air and Amanda thoroughly enjoyed the next half hour of small talk. She was feeling more and more at home in Oklahoma City and knew that a lot of her ease was due to the three people at the table. She sent up a silent prayer thanking the Lord for sending them into her life.

"I guess we'd better be on our way," Josh said. "We wouldn't want to be late for Sunday school."

"No, that wouldn't be good," Andrew said. "Especially for me as I'm teaching the class this quarter."

Melissa retrieved their coats from the closet in the entryway and Josh helped Amanda with hers before putting on his own.

"Thank you so much for your hospitality," Amanda said to the Bensons as they all stood in the entryway.

"Thank you for coming." Melissa gave her a hug.

Andrew cleared his throat and pointed up to the small chandelier hanging above the women.

There, hanging right above their heads, was a large clump of mistletoe tied to one of the crystals with a red ribbon. Andrew pulled his wife into his arms and planted a quick kiss on her lips as Amanda watched, slightly bemused. Then, before she realized she was still standing in the same spot, Josh had turned her face toward his and touched his lips to hers in a kiss so light and sweet Amanda almost thought she'd imagined it.

"Merry Christmas," he whispered.

"Merry Christmas," Amanda found her voice and whispered back.

"So that's what you two were up to," Melissa said with a chuckle. "I should have guessed."

Amanda felt her face flushing with embarrassment—and what she hoped no one knew was pure happiness.

Chapter 9

Amanda was so quiet on the way home that Josh was afraid he might have overstepped the boundaries of their friendship by kissing her. But that clump of mistletoe was too good of an opportunity to pass up. He hadn't been able to resist the chance to kiss her.

Now he could only pray that he hadn't ruined things. He hadn't been able to tell how she felt about his kiss. Oh, color had flushed her face, but he didn't know if it was because she was surprised by his kiss— or angry. And yet, for a second he thought he'd felt her lips cling to his. But maybe that was because it's what he wanted to believe. At any rate, he was doing way too much thinking when he should be trying to break the silence in the car.

"Amanda?"

"Yes?"

"I think our gingerbread house was the best one."

She gave a soft chuckle and the tightness in his chest

eased a bit. "I think so, too. I'd forgotten how much fun it was to decorate one."

"It was a first for me, but I really enjoyed it." *Just not nearly as much as I enjoyed kissing you.* He pulled into his drive and shut off the engine. "Want to ride to Sunday school with me tomorrow?"

Amanda hesitated for only a minute before answering. "Sure. It does seem a little silly for us to take two cars when we're going to the same place, doesn't it?"

"It does." Josh met her coming around the back of his car and they walked briskly over to her front door. It felt as if the temperature was falling by the minute. "I'll have the car warmed up, too."

Amanda grinned at him in the glow of her porch light. "That's one of the perks of riding with you—a toasty car."

"I aim to please," he said as she unlocked her door and turned back to him. She looked so pretty looking up at him; Josh wanted to kiss her again. But there was no mistletoe hanging over her head and he wasn't sure what her reaction would be. So, he just gave her a wave as he turned to go. "See you in the morning."

"See you then."

⌘

Amanda shut the door, her heartbeat still fluttering, as it had been ever since Josh's kiss. She told herself not to read too much into it. Kissing under the mistletoe was only a Christmas tradition. It meant nothing.

Well, that wasn't entirely true. It meant a lot to her.

It meant she could no longer deny her feelings for Josh—certainly not to herself and most probably not to her family. And in about a week she was going to have to pretend that they were *only* friends when she knew she wanted more. And how did *that* happen, anyway? She hadn't wanted to fall in love with anyone—didn't want her family finding her a mate. She'd wanted to be on her own a while before she even thought about marriage. She'd lived in her parents' house all her life and felt like she should at least be able to support herself and know what it was to make a living before she settled into a relationship. Or so she thought.

Now all she could think of was the man next door and what it would be like to be able to introduce him to her family as the man she was going to marry. Yet, until the kiss tonight, Josh hadn't shown that he felt anything more toward her than friendship. And she really didn't think that tonight was an exception. He most probably was just carrying out a simple tradition. She wanted to think the kiss meant something to him, but how could she find out without putting their friendship on the line? They lived next door to each other, went to the same church, and enjoyed each other's company now. If he felt uncomfortable about her growing feelings for him, how long would that last?

And if he felt uncomfortable, how much more so would she feel? She might have to change churches just when she was feeling at home—might have to move to keep from seeing him each day.

Amanda moaned and sent up a silent prayer. *Dear*

Lord, what have I done by letting myself fall in love with my best friend here? I don't want to lose the friendship we have. But if it's possible that he could care for me, too, please help me to know. And if it's not, please help me to be able to hide how I feel from him and from my family. In Jesus' name, I pray, amen.

༄

Their Monday night shopping trip had to be canceled because Amanda had a surprisingly busy day with new clients who were moving to the area right after the New Year and wanted to find a house. She was hoping to end the week with a sale, and Josh was hopeful that she would, but he missed her company.

With their trip to her hometown nearly upon them, Amanda insisted that he go on with his shopping trip. It was nowhere near as much fun as shopping with her had been. Since she wasn't with him to show him the decoration she'd liked so much, Josh visited every store he thought might have it but left without that special present for her.

He spent the next few days trying to find the perfect gift for Amanda and had about given up when he decided to visit a Christmas store in a mall on the other side of the city. When he finally spotted the colorful glass gingerbread-house ornament that looked like the one Amanda had described to him, he couldn't resist. If for no other reason, he wanted to get it for her to remind her of the night they'd made the houses and kissed under the mistletoe. It even looked a little like the gingerbread house they'd made together. He browsed the aisles to see what else he could find and then he spotted the perfect ornament for the two of them—if their relationship ever got to the point he'd prayed for. To the point where he could tell Amanda how much he loved her.

The delicate glass ornaments were small but detailed clumps of mistletoe that looked real. They would be sure to make them both remember the first time he kissed her. Josh didn't know when he would give Amanda one—a lot depended on this Christmas with her. But he bought two. He knew he wanted one for his tree and hoped with all his heart that one day they would be able to put both ornaments on the same tree. In case that didn't happen, he wanted to make sure that each time Amanda put the ornament on her tree through the years, she would think of him.

They'd planned on getting together that afternoon and evening to finish Amanda's shopping, and then they planned to wrap the presents for her family at her place. Josh carefully wrapped the gifts he'd bought Amanda that morning and slipped them into a bag. He felt as if he'd finally found presents that would let Amanda know how special she was to him. He could only pray that he was special to her in the same way.

Chapter 10

Amanda and Josh ended their final Christmas shopping trip with a meal at one of their favorite Mexican restaurants before going back to Amanda's to wrap presents. When they got home, Josh ran into his place to pick up the presents he'd already bought and brought them back over to Amanda's so they could get all their wrapping done together.

When Josh rang the doorbell, Amanda opened it to find his hands full of bags of the gifts they'd picked for her family and her heart melted. He was so sweet to want to choose gifts that were just right for them. "Come on into the kitchen. I have paper, tape, ribbon, and bows all laid out on the table."

She had the makings for hot chocolate ready and a plate of the cookies she knew Josh loved nearby. They'd barely gotten started with their wrapping before the telephone rang. She could tell from her caller ID just who it was. "Hi, Granny!"

"Have you been watching the weather, Amanda dear?"

"Well, no, should I be?" Granny loved to watch the weather channel on TV just as much as Amanda and Josh liked to watch the cooking channel.

"They are calling for a major snowstorm to move in. You might want to leave a little earlier than you'd planned. You don't want to get caught in it."

"No, we wouldn't want to do that," she assured her grandmother. "We'll watch the weather forecast and make a decision, okay?"

"All right, dear. And you be sure to tell your young man to drive carefully."

"He's not—" Amanda clamped her mouth shut on the denial. Josh might not know it, but she wished with all her heart that he *was* her young man. "He'll be careful, Granny. I'll see you Christmas Eve morning, okay?"

When she hung up, she went to get the TV remote so they could get the weather forecast. "Granny says bad weather may be moving in and she thinks we should leave earlier."

"Oh?" Josh stopped his wrapping and watched the news with her. There was, indeed, a chance for bad weather moving in before Saturday. "Maybe your grandmother is right. It might be best if we leave tomorrow. What do you think?"

She was all packed for their trip, except for the presents that would be put in the back of his car. "Well, I can be ready. But will it be an imposition for you if we leave earlier? It will mean one more day with my family and they—"

"Amanda, I am looking forward to Christmas with your family. It can't get started early enough for me."

She'd tried to warn him on more than one occasion that her family could be overwhelming. But she had a feeling that if anyone could handle her family, it would be Josh Randall. "Well, then I'll leave the decision on when to leave up to you."

"Okay. We'll finish our gift wrapping and keep listening to the weather, but if things don't change, I think we need to leave no later than tomorrow morning."

"Okay." Amanda had been looking forward to the three-and-a-half- to four-hour trip home in Josh's car. She certainly wasn't going to complain about leaving early. She'd just have to be on her toes and not give away how much she cared about him.

❧

They'd decided to leave Friday morning, and as Josh put his and Amanda's luggage in the trunk of his car and the colorfully wrapped presents in the backseat, he couldn't believe how excited he was about this trip. He'd made up his mind that at some point during this visit with her family, he was going to have to let Amanda know how he felt about her. He prayed she felt the same way about him, but if not, he'd have to depend on the Lord to help him through the hurt. He just couldn't keep spending time with her without falling more and more deeply in love with her, and it was time to find out if she could ever feel the same way about him.

Amanda looked so pretty today. She was dressed in jeans and a bright red sweater; her blond hair was pulled back from her face and her blue eyes were bright and shining. She could protest all she wanted, but he had a feeling she couldn't wait to see her family again.

"Buckle up," he said as she got in the car.

"Yes, sir!" She saluted as she pulled her seat belt around and secured it. "It is looking like snow, isn't it?"

Josh backed out of the drive and headed toward the turnpike. He looked out the window and nodded. "I think it may be a fast-moving storm. I hope we're leaving in time to dodge it."

He turned the radio to a station that was playing Christmas music and before long they were both singing along with the familiar songs. They were on the other side of Tulsa when it started to snow. Beautiful as the big flakes flying at them were, Josh hoped it got no worse. He could see where they were going now, but the snow was sticking and he feared the roads could become dangerous if they didn't drive out of it soon.

"Oh, isn't it pretty, Josh?" Amanda asked. "I hope we have enough at home to make a snowman. I love playing in the snow."

"It's beautiful," he agreed. He looked forward to helping her make that snowman. It'd been a very long time since he'd felt so happy this time of year, and he knew his happiness was because of the woman sitting beside him. He'd been looking forward to sharing Christmas with her and her family for weeks now, and he prayed that they liked him and that before this visit was over, their matchmaking days for Amanda would end.

But until then, he needed to know how she wanted him to act when he met her family for the first time.

"Amanda, when we meet your parents—how are you going to introduce me?" The snow was falling fast and steady now. He couldn't take his eyes off the road but he listened closely for her answer.

"Why, as my next-door neighbor who had nowhere to go, like we planned. Josh, it's getting worse out there. Can you see the road?"

"For now I can. Will that keep them from trying to set you up with someone while we are there?"

"Well, I figure that no matter what I tell them, they are going to assume we are—" Wind hit the car and whipped it to the side. "Josh—"

"I'm going to have to pull to the side of the road, Amanda. It's getting too bad to see and if I don't do it now, I won't know where the edge of the highway is." Josh couldn't see behind them, either, but he didn't want to tell her that. He eased over to what he hoped was the shoulder of the road and safely out of harm's way.

But Josh had no more than applied the flashers on the car when the sound of screeching brakes came from behind them and made his heartbeat thud in his chest. He quickly grabbed Amanda and pulled her into his arms. Bracing for the crash he was sure was coming, he sent up a silent prayer. *Dear Lord, please let us get out of this alive.*

The expected crash never came. Only a whooshing kind of sound was heard as a vehicle flew past them and then there was a sudden silence.

"Josh?" Amanda eased out of his arms.

"We're all right, but I don't know—" They looked around to find the automobile that had come off the road behind them, stopped down the embankment just shy of a tree.

Josh and Amanda left his car almost at the same time. They rushed over to the car and Josh thought he heard a sob as the driver opened the door. "We're all right. We're all right."

Josh peeked inside and saw a badly shaken woman trying to calm two young children. But they were, indeed, all right. *Thank You, Lord.*

"Do you need any help getting out of here?" Josh asked the man.

"No, I don't think so. I just hit a really slick spot back there. I think the car is all right. I'll turn it around and pull in behind you."

"I have some cookies in our car, if you think the children would like them," Amanda said to the woman. Tears were streaming down the woman's face, in what must have been relief, as she nodded.

Amanda took off toward his car, and Josh followed. By the time the man had the car back on the shoulder, Amanda had a bag of cookies ready.

"I'll take them over," Josh said. "You just stay here and get warm."

❦

"What's this?" Josh asked as he entered the car and shut his door against the cold. Tears were flowing down Amanda's cheeks. "Honey, it's all right. We're okay. That family is all right, too."

Amanda only nodded and sniffed. Josh pulled her back into his arms and she began to sob. "Amanda, we're all right."

"But—but we could have been killed and—I'm so sorry I've pulled you into trying to deceive my family, Josh. I'll understand if you want to turn around and go back to Oklahoma City."

Josh was still shaking on the inside from their close call. Had that car taken a slightly different path, they both could have been killed and he would have died without ever letting Amanda know how he felt. He sent a silent prayer upward, thanking the Lord again for watching over them and for giving him another chance to tell Amanda that he loved her.

"Amanda, you didn't pull me in. I offered to come with you. The last thing I want to do is turn around and go back home. Besides, you can't take the blame for the weather. I was the one who should have realized we needed to leave earlier. If anything had happened to you, I would never have been able to forgive myself."

Still sniffling, Amanda looked up at him with those big, tear-filled eyes. "I promise you, I'll make sure my family knows that you aren't in love with me as soon as we get there so you won't feel any pressure to act as if you are."

Josh pulled her into his arms. He had to tell her now. "Oh, Amanda, I can assure you that letting your family think I'm in love with you won't be an act."

He heard her quick intake of breath but he didn't give her a chance to say anything. His lips claimed hers in a kiss he hoped left no doubt in her mind just how he felt. His heart sang with joy when she kissed him back. Knowing Amanda as he'd come to over the past few months, Josh was sure she wouldn't have responded the way she did if she didn't feel the same way.

When she ended the kiss and pulled back, Josh reached into the backseat and pulled a small package out of one of the sacks. "Here; open this."

Amanda ripped open the paper and opened the box the mistletoe ornament came in. She pulled it out and held it to her heart. "Mistletoe."

"I wanted you to always remember our first kiss when you hang that ornament. And I've been hoping that it would be hung on *our* tree one day." He hurried to say the words that he'd wanted to say for weeks. "I love you, Amanda—with all my heart. And if you are willing, we can tell your parents a simple truth—that we are engaged. Will you marry me?"

Amanda answered him with another kiss that told him all he needed to know, before she even said anything. When it ended, she whispered, "Oh, Josh, I love you, too. I've loved you for weeks—and yes, oh yes! I will marry you."

❦

Amanda had never been happier in her life than when she and Josh pulled into her parents' drive and hurried up the porch steps. The front door was opened before they got there and her parents welcomed them with open arms.

"I'm so glad you got here safely. We heard there've been several accidents due to the storm," her mother said, giving her a hug and trying to pull Josh into it, as well.

"We had a close call, but it turned out to be a blessing," Amanda said. "Mom, Dad, I'd like to introduce you to my fiancé, Josh Randall."

As her dad shook Josh's hand and her mother gave him a bear hug, Amanda thanked the Lord above for seeing them home safely and for giving her the best Christmas ever. Tomorrow she and Josh would join her family at Granny's to carry on her family's tradition, but they'd already begun to make special Christmas memories of their very own.

JANET LEE BARTON

Janet has lived all over the southern U.S., but she and her husband plan to now stay put in Oklahoma. With three daughters and six grandchildren between them, they feel blessed to have at least one daughter and her family living in the same town. Janet loves being able to share her faith through her writing. Happily married to her very own hero, she is ever thankful that the Lord brought Dan into her life, and she wants to write stories that show that the love between a man and a woman is at its best when the relationship is built with God at the center. She's very happy that the kind of romances the Lord has called her to write can be read by and shared with women of all ages, from teenagers to grandmothers alike.

A Christmas Wish

by Jeanie Smith Cash

Dedication

To Jesus, my Lord and Savior, who made this all possible. To my son, Donny; my mother, Wanda; and my brother-in-law, Marvin. You went to be with the Lord before you had a chance to read this book. Thank you for your love, support, and confidence in me as a writer. I miss you but know that I will see you again. To my own special hero, Andy. You are always there for me, and I love you. To my daughter, Robyn; son-in-law, Dave; grandchildren, Daniel, Chelsea, and Justin; my father, Don; and sister, Chere, for your love and support. To my critique partner and special friend, Barbara Warren, for your help, love, and support. A special thank-you to Kathleen Y'Barbo, Christine Lynxwiler, Janet Lee Barton, and Rebecca Germany for giving me a chance.

As for God, his way is perfect;
the word of the LORD is flawless.
He is a shield for all who take refuge in him.
PSALM 18:30 NIV

Chapter 1

Abigail Forrester ran through the airport, pulling her luggage behind her. Thankfully, she had decided to fly out of San Francisco. The way she dodged in and out of passengers on the way to her gate, people would surely think she was crazy. But she had no choice. If anything held her up, she'd miss her flight. Out of breath, with her heart pounding and a pain in her side, she rushed into the security checkpoint and dumped everything onto the conveyor belt. She said a prayer of thanks when she slid through the doorway and didn't set off the alarm. After her bags were checked, she made a mad dash for the gate and arrived just as the agent was about to close the door.

"Please wait. That's my flight!" Abby handed him her ticket, hoping that because she'd been upgraded to first class, he'd still allow her to board.

He frowned momentarily but reached to accept the coupon. "Follow me, please. I'd suggest you give yourself a little more time in the future. Another second and you would have missed this flight."

"I know, and I'm sorry. I really appreciate this; I was unavoidably detained." Heat filled Abby's cheeks as she remembered the reason she had been delayed. As manager of a travel agency in Tracy, California, a small town about fifty miles from the airport, she took pride in being organized. How could she have left her wallet locked in the drawer of her desk at work? She'd had to call Bonnie Cranston, owner of the agency, who had offered to bring the wallet to her. The hour-and-a-half wait for Bonnie to arrive had almost caused her to miss her flight.

"I'll take those for you." The flight attendant lifted her bag and placed it in the compartment above her head as Abby took her seat and sighed in relief.

"You almost didn't make it." The man's deep voice echoed from the seat next to her.

Abby froze. She'd recognize that voice anywhere. *Oh, Lord*, she prayed silently, *let me be mistaken. Please don't let it be him.* She slowly turned to look at the man beside her. She wondered which of them appeared more shocked.

"Nick?" She swallowed against a suddenly dry throat and forced her gaze to meet his. "What are you doing here?"

"I've been at a medical convention for the last two days." The dimples she remembered so well creased his lean cheeks as he smiled at her. "Do you live in San Francisco?"

"N–no," she stammered and could have kicked herself for allowing him to still affect her this way. She fastened her safety belt before answering, hoping to get a grip on her emotions. "I live about fifty miles inland."

"Jared said you'd moved away, but he didn't say where." Nick placed the magazine he'd been reading back into the seat in front of him and adjusted his medical bag to give her more room.

Oh, Lord, I know You have a reason for everything. But of all the people to find in the seat next to me, why did it have to be Nicholas Creighton?

He hadn't changed at all. His muscular six-four frame didn't sport an ounce of fat. Eyes a brilliant shade of green, dark brown hair that barely brushed his collar, and a warm, welcoming smile that still had the power to turn her bones to liquid. How could she be so attracted to him when he'd crushed her the way he had? Even now, hurt nearly overwhelmed her at just seeing him again. The chance that she might run into him once she arrived at Granny's house had crossed her mind. But she hadn't been prepared to see him this soon.

Nick and her oldest brother, Jared, had been best friends when they were growing up, and they had gone to medical school together. Nick specialized in surgery, and Jared was a pediatrician.

"How's Janine doing?" She nearly choked just saying that name. She had spent hours on her knees the night Nick had told her he was going to marry Janine, asking the Lord to please make the other woman go away and praying that Nick would change his mind and come back to her. But that had been fourteen months ago. She hoped she'd gained some perspective since then, but considering her reaction to his unexpected presence, it didn't look hopeful.

A flash of pain appeared in Nick's eyes before he answered, making her wonder if they might be having problems. "I'm sorry; maybe I shouldn't have asked."

"No, it's all right," he said softly and patted her hand. "You don't know do you?"

"Know what?" she asked, frowning slightly.

Nick took a deep breath before answering her. "Janine died eight months ago."

Abby gasped at his words. "I'm so sorry. I had no idea. My family didn't say a word." *Oh, Lord, when I asked You to make her go away, I didn't mean for her to die! I just meant for her to move somewhere away from Nick; I didn't want her to have him. I was jealous, but I never meant for anything to happen to her.*

Nick interrupted her prayer. "It's okay, Abby. I'm sure they were trying to protect you. I didn't exactly make points with your family after hurting you the way I did." He glanced over at her, and she could see regret reflected in his eyes.

"Jared wouldn't tell me where you were when I asked—not that I blame him." His gaze slowly scanned her face. "If you were my sister, I'd probably react the same way. He said he loved me like a brother, but you had made a new life for yourself, and he felt it was best if I stayed away from you."

An odd mixture of emotions gripped Abby. Sadness filled her heart at his loss, but she wasn't ready to forgive the hurt he'd inflicted. Still, her conscience rebelled at the way she had prayed; it wasn't okay. Ashamed, she realized she hadn't acted with a very Christian attitude. *Please forgive me, Lord.* Suddenly it dawned on her what Nick had just said. She sat up in her seat and looked at him. "You asked about me?"

"Yes." He smiled sadly, adjusting his medical bag under the seat in front of him to make more room for his feet. "After Janine died, I wanted to try to reach you to explain. I know I hurt you terribly, but there is an explanation that I couldn't give you until now."

His hopeful look almost swayed her as she looked into his too-familiar eyes and felt a stab of long lost love. But at the last second, she came to her senses, pulling her gaze from his as she reached up to turn off her air vent. "You don't owe me an explanation, Nick. What we had was in the past. We've both made separate lives for ourselves now."

The captain's voice came over the intercom, interrupting their conversation. "Please fasten your seat belts and prepare for takeoff."

The plane taxied to the end of the runway. As they began their ascent, fear swelled in Abby's chest, stealing her breath away and leaving her light-headed. She gripped the side of the seat until her knuckles turned white.

"Still don't like to fly, I see." Nick patted her hand gently. "It'll be all right."

Once the plane ascended into the air and leveled out, Abby released her death grip on the chair arm, and her heartbeat slowed down to almost normal. She knew it was crazy to be in the travel profession and be afraid to fly, but she hadn't been able to get past the fear that always welled up inside of her. Just the thought of being so high off the ground caused her to break out in a cold sweat.

"Going home to Granny Forrester's for the traditional Christmas Eve gathering, I presume." Nick relaxed in his seat and offered her a gentle smile.

"Yes, I look forward to it every year. Besides, Granny would be heartbroken if any of us were missing." She glanced away, trying to fill her thoughts with Granny and home rather than the hurtful memories the man sitting beside her brought to mind.

"Yes, she would. Jared and Amy invited Scotty and me to come for Christmas Eve. I hope it won't make you uncomfortable; they didn't want us to be alone."

Panic gripped her at the thought of spending more time in Nick's presence. How would she manage this? She had been with him for only a few minutes and already the painful memories flooded her mind. It wouldn't be easy, but she couldn't deprive him of being with his sister for the holidays. She adjusted her seat belt to give her a moment to compose herself before answering him. "I can understand Amy wanting you to be there. You should be with your sister on Christmas Eve. Who's Scotty?"

"My son."

Shock rendered her speechless for a moment. *Nick and Janine had a son together?* Her chest tightened as she fought to control emotions she'd thought she had put behind her. *Please, Lord, help me. I need to get over this, or it's going to be a very long week.*

"I—I didn't know you had a son," she stammered, avoiding eye contact. "How old is he?"

"Eight months and he's quite a little guy."

"Eight months?" Abby looked up at him. "Did Janine die in childbirth?" Abby couldn't believe she'd just asked that. She'd been so shocked, she'd just blurted out the first words that had come to mind. She searched his face, hoping she hadn't inflicted more pain with her thoughtless question.

"Yes," Nick said just as the pilot announced they were descending into the Denver airport. He smiled in her direction as if to let her know that he knew she hadn't meant to be unkind.

"I'm afraid I have some bad news, folks," the pilot announced just as they landed. "It's snowing so hard here in Denver that they've grounded us for an indefinite time. We aren't going to be flying tonight, and they can't promise anything for tomorrow."

"Oh no!" Abby jerked upright in her seat. "I can't stay here for two days. I won't make it to Granny's house in time to decorate the tree."

"I don't think we have much choice." Nick laid a hand on her arm in an effort to calm her. "They can't fly in these conditions."

"I have a choice." Abby pulled her tingling arm out from under his warm hand. She unfastened the seat belt and took her bag from the flight attendant.

"Abby, what are you planning to do?" Nick unfastened his own belt, and it clanked against the airplane wall.

His shoulder brushed hers as he stood up. It was times like this that Abby wished airplanes were larger. "I'm going to rent a car and drive." She slipped the strap over her shoulder, adjusting it to a more comfortable position as Nick reached under the seat for his medical bag.

He leaned over and said softly in her ear, "You can't drive thirteen hours in this snowstorm."

She moved her head as his warm breath tickled her ear, to avoid the intimate feeling it evoked. "Oh yes, I can." Abby said a silent prayer of thanks as the wall of people started moving toward the front of the plane. She followed, trying to put as much distance as she could between herself and Nick. Just as soon as there was an opening, she quickly headed out the door and up the long ramp.

"Abby, wait!" Nick called. "There's no way you're going to drive that far in this weather by yourself."

Chapter 2

A line had already formed at the rental car desk by the time Abby stepped up to wait her turn. She set her bag down and turned to face Nick as he came up behind her.

"Don't try to talk me out of renting a car. Whatever I have to do, I'm going to be at Granny's for Christmas Eve." She raised her chin stubbornly, crossing her arms in front of her.

Nick smiled, shaking his head and reaching into his pocket for his wallet. "I'm not going to try to talk you out of it. I'm going to go with you."

Abby's heart did a little flip at the thought of spending thirteen hours in the car with Nick. Certainly a change from what she'd been feeling a short time ago on the plane. She'd only been with him an hour and a half, and the wall of protection she'd managed to build had already begun to crumble. She couldn't let that happen. The guy broke her heart fourteen months ago.

Abby knew in her mind that she should detest him,

but her heart wasn't listening. She had to get a grip on her feelings. She could not allow herself to get involved with him again.

She thought for a minute before answering, but she couldn't come up with an excuse that would make sense. "All right. We're going to the same place, so I guess it would be foolish to rent two cars. We can split the cost."

"That's fine with me." Nick pulled his credit card out of his wallet.

The tall, dark-headed man behind the counter motioned them forward. "How can I help you?"

"We'd like to rent a four-wheel drive, please." Abby set her purse on the counter.

The man tapped a few keys on the computer. "We have a Chevy Trail Blazer available."

Abby glanced at Nick, and he nodded. "That's fine; we'll take it."

"I need the name, driver's license, and credit card of the person who will be driving." The clerk laid the contract on the counter.

"We'll both be driving," Abby said, digging in her purse for her wallet.

"You'll have to put it in one name and then pay extra for the other driver."

"That's fine." Nick handed him his credit card and driver's license.

"Hey, wait a minute," Abby protested as she continued searching for her wallet. "I planned to put it in my name with you as the extra driver."

"Abby, it's going to be a long trip," Nick said. "What difference does it make whose name it's in?"

She started to argue, but she hesitated when she heard the fatigue in his voice. He had been in a conference for the last two days. He was tired, yet he'd agreed to drive through with her in spite of that fact. "I guess it doesn't make any difference. But I'm paying my half."

"Fine. We can settle up later. Let's just get this done so we can get on the road. It's going to take longer to drive than it would in normal weather, so the sooner we get started the better."

Nick's arm brushed Abby's as he reached for the pen, sending chills of awareness up her spine. She stepped back away from him and waited while he signed the contract.

"Okay." Nick slid his credit card back into his wallet and grabbed his bags. "We're all set. Let's go get your luggage before we pick up the Blazer."

"This is it; I didn't check anything." She slid the bag back on her shoulder and picked up her purse.

His eyes widened. "Where's your guitar? You never go anywhere without it."

"I don't play anymore." Nick's penetrating glance made her uncomfortable. She didn't want to discuss this.

"Why not?" He didn't budge, waiting for an answer.

"I just don't. Look, it's not a big deal. As you said, we need to get the car so we can get going. We have a long trip ahead of us, and right now I need to find a restroom before we go."

"The restrooms are right over there." Nick indicated the two doors down and across from them.

"I may be a little while. I need to call my parents, and it should be a little quieter in there."

Nick nodded as he sat on a bench and laid his bags on the floor next to him. "No problem," he said, removing his cell phone from his pocket. "I'm going to call Maggie to let her know I've been delayed and see how Scotty is doing."

Abby left him there and walked to the door that said WOMEN. Tactfully ignoring a tearful young girl sitting alone on a bench, she walked to the other side of the expansive room and pulled out her cell phone. After a couple of rings, her father answered.

"Hi, Daddy."

She heard the concern in her father's voice as he answered. "Hi, sweetheart. Are you all right? Where are you? Your mother and I have been worried."

"I'm fine, but we're grounded in Denver, and they don't know for how long. So we've rented an SUV, and we're going to drive." She freshened her makeup at the sink while she talked to her father.

"Abby, I don't think that's a good idea. You're going to be driving in snow and nasty weather all the way through. It's snowing here, too."

"We'll be all right, Daddy. We have to get there so I can help hang the ornaments on Granny's tree, and I'm not missing the Christmas Eve gathering. This is the only way, but we'll be careful. I promise."

"You've said 'we' several times now. Surely you

aren't traveling with someone you just met. I've taught you better than that."

The sternness in her father's voice brought a smile to her lips. "No, Daddy. I know him very well. Amazingly enough, Nick Creighton happened to be in San Francisco for a medical convention, and we wound up on the same plane. He's driving through with me."

Her father's silence spoke volumes.

"Daddy, I know how you feel about the way Nick treated me, but that was a long time ago. We're just two people who need to get to the same place," Abby said as she placed her makeup back into her purse.

"You be careful. Remember how devastated you were the last time."

"I know, Daddy, but I'm not going to allow that to happen, so you don't need to worry."

"Well, I do worry. I like Nick. I always have. But after the way he hurt you, I don't want you involved with him." He paused. "I have to admit, though, being with Nick is preferable to you driving through alone."

Abby hung up the phone with a promise to call again soon and headed past the young girl who still sat in the same place on the bench. Something about her tugged on Abby's heartstrings, and she hesitated.

Lord, if You want me to talk to this girl, please give me the words to say. Abby sat down on the bench beside the young woman.

"Hi. My name is Abby. Is there anything I can do to help?" The young girl glanced up, and the desolation Abby saw in her expression wrenched her own heart.

The girl studied Abby for a moment and shook her head. "No one can help."

Abby laid her hand on the young girl's arm in a comforting manner. "Sometimes it helps to talk to someone. Why don't you start by telling me your name?"

The girl sobbed. "My name is Sandy, and I don't know what to do. I brought my boyfriend to the airport. I thought he just planned to go home to visit his parents. But before he boarded the plane, he told me he wouldn't be coming back." More tears rolled down her face.

"Well, no wonder you're upset." Abby went to the sink and wet a paper towel. She returned and handed it to Sandy.

"I just found out a week ago that I'm six weeks pregnant." Her slender shoulders shook as she cried. "Can you believe he said he'd send me the money for an abortion, but he wouldn't marry me because he doesn't love me?" She wiped her face with the towel Abby had given her.

How did this little girl get hooked up with the wrong guy at such a young age? She looked like she should still be home playing with paper dolls, not sitting in an airport bathroom pregnant and alone. *Lord, please comfort her.*

Sandy folded the paper towel in her hand. "I could never destroy my baby. I already love it. I want to be a good mother but I'm scared." She looked up, and her tear-filled eyes begged Abby to understand.

"You love your child, Sandy, so that's a step in the right direction." Abby patted her arm gently. "Do you have family that could help you?"

"I can't tell my family." Her eyes widened. "My father will be so angry he'll kick me out. He won't love me anymore if he knows what I've done."

Abby was appalled; she couldn't imagine a father who would kick out his child when she was in trouble. Her father would never abandon her, no matter what the circumstances.

"Sandy, I know someone who loves you unconditionally. His name is Jesus, and He loves you so much that He died on an old rugged cross to save you. He is the Son of God." Abby squeezed Sandy's hand, a smile on her face.

"You're a Christian?" She shifted on the bench until she faced Abby. "So is my grandmother. She asked me to go to church with her."

"Are you close to your grandmother?"

"Yes. I love Nana, and I know she loves me, but my father wouldn't let me see her after my mother died four years ago. He doesn't believe in God." She fidgeted on the bench. "I hadn't seen Nana until I turned eighteen last month."

"That must have been hard on both of you."

"Yes, it was. I try to spend as much time as I can with her now. She told me that Jesus loves me, too. But I've done things I shouldn't have, and now I'm pregnant and I'm not married. Jesus probably won't love me now." She hung her head.

"Jesus still loves you, and He is willing to forgive you no matter what you've done. That's what I meant when I said His love is unconditional."

Her eyes brightened as she looked up at Abby. "Do you think He might forgive me then?"

"I know He will." Abby smiled. "He loves us so much He is willing to forgive us no matter what we've done."

"I'll have to really think about what you've said." Sandy picked up her purse from the bench beside her. "Maybe I'll go talk with my grandmother and tell her about the baby."

"She loves you, Sandy. I'm sure she'll help you." Abby reached for a small tablet she always kept in her purse. "Here are a few scriptures I'd like you to read." Abby wrote down First John 1:9; Romans 3:23; Romans 10:9; John 3:16; and Romans 10:10, then added her cell phone number and handed the paper to Sandy. "I'll be happy to talk to you some more, or if you feel more comfortable, talk to your grandmother. But you need Jesus in your life. He will help you through this."

"Thank you." Sandy stood and slipped on her coat.

"Will you be all right?" Abby asked as she slipped into her own jacket.

"Yes, I feel better now. I think I'll stay at Nana's tonight."

"That's a good idea. I'll be praying for you." Abby smiled. "Be very careful driving home."

"I will. I have four-wheel drive." She slipped the strap of her purse over her shoulder and started toward the door.

Abby followed her out. Before Sandy left, she turned to Abby with a smile.

"I'm so thankful you came into the restroom today. I'll think about what you've said."

She left, and Abby whispered a prayer. "Please, Father, watch over her and her baby. Bring her to the saving knowledge of Your Son, Jesus Christ. I pray her grandmother will welcome her and give her the help she needs. In Jesus' name I pray, amen."

Nick got up from the bench across from the restroom and walked toward her carrying his bags. From the look on his face, she knew he wondered what had taken her so long.

"Why don't you let me carry that bag for you?" he asked and glanced toward Sandy as she walked away.

Abby watched the young woman disappear into the crowd and smiled. "That's okay. I can get it; you have enough to carry."

"Is that someone you know?"

"No, but she's upset and needed someone to talk to." Abby told him what had happened in the restroom as they walked across the airport.

"Nice guy." He shook his head. "I hope her grandmother will help her; it's not easy raising a child alone."

Abby glanced over at him, realizing that was something he knew in a personal way.

Chapter 3

Nick glanced up at the sky as they stood waiting for the shuttle. If the weather didn't let up, they were in for a miserable trip. He had to be crazy to let himself get caught in this situation, but he couldn't let Abby drive alone. He knew how stubborn she could be. She would go whether he went along or not. Besides, he owed her something for the way he had treated her fourteen months ago.

He breathed in the fragrance of her perfume, thinking how good it felt to have her sitting next to him again. She hadn't changed much in fourteen months. Five-four and slender built—her reddish-gold hair still hung in curls nearly to her waist. He remembered how her bright blue eyes sparkled when she laughed.

He hoped someday she would let him explain why he broke their engagement to marry Janine and understand that, under the circumstances, he felt it had been his only option.

The driver pulled up next to the SUV and called Nick's name.

"Be careful; it's really slick," Nick said as they stepped out of the van. Ice and snow covered the parking lot, and damp air hit them in the face, chilling them to the bone. Fortunately, he had ignored Abby's protest when they left the airport and held on to her arm, even though she insisted she could make it to the van on her own. She had slipped twice and would have fallen without his support.

"I'll walk you to the car before I get the bags." Nick smiled to himself when she didn't object. By the time Abby was seated, the driver had their luggage unloaded and Nick stowed them in the back of the SUV. She had just fastened her seat belt when he climbed in and started the engine.

∝∾

Abby wanted to protest and insist that she'd drive. After thinking about it, however, she decided being independent had its merits, but she knew her limitations and Nick had a lot more experience driving in this kind of weather.

"It'll only take a few minutes for the engine to warm up, and I'll turn on the heater," Nick said, rubbing his hands together to try to get warm.

"That would be good. I'm freezing." Abby's teeth were chattering.

Nick slipped off his coat and laid it over her legs. "That should help."

The jacket, still warm from his body heat, felt good. "But you'll be cold without it." She started to hand it back to him, but he laid his hand over hers. She jerked away as sparks of awareness shot up her arm at his touch. If he noticed her reaction, he didn't respond to it.

"I'll be fine; this sweater is heavy." He turned on the defroster and cranked it up to the highest setting for her. "I'll change it to heat and defrost as soon as it gets warm," he said and pulled out of the parking lot.

Abby smoothed the coat over her knees. He was just as warm and devastating as she remembered, but what they'd had together must remain in the past. She'd made a new life for herself. A happy life. She had been happy, hadn't she? Of course she had.

They had been on the road for about two hours, and Abby realized she'd been dozing when Nick yelled, "Hang on!" jolting her awake as the car jerked to the right, the tires sliding over the ice-coated road. Nick fought the steering wheel, trying to avoid a head-on collision as another car spun into their lane. Abby screamed as the Blazer bumped over the side of the embankment and slammed into the ditch. She jerked forward as her air bag went off. Her seat belt tightened, cutting into her waist and across her shoulder. Dazed and disoriented, for a moment her mind didn't register that Nick was calling her name.

"Abby—Abby! Are you all right?" She felt his hand against her face as he brushed her hair back.

"My cheek hurts." She touched her face and noticed

a smear of blood on her hand.

Nick examined her cheek and reached into the back for his medical bag. He deftly opened a package of gauze, folded it into a square, placed it against the open wound, and taped it just below her temple.

"You have a cut here, but I don't think it's deep enough to need sutures. That will hold it until we get someplace where we can do a better job." She squinted as he shone a pin light across the side of her face. The bright light against the darkness hurt her eyes.

"The air bag scratched your face and neck." Nick continued to check her for injuries. "Do you feel dizzy, nauseous, or hurt anywhere else?"

"I don't think so." She sat up suddenly and looked at him. "Are you all right?"

"I'm fine—just a little scratched up, too, from the air bag. But I'm thankful they went off." He set his medical bag back on the seat behind him. "We missed the other car. It spun out of control on the slick pavement. I need to go see about them. Stay here, and I'll be right back."

Nick returned in a few minutes and slid back into the car. "They must have been okay; they're gone."

"Your quick reaction saved our lives." Abby thanked the Lord she hadn't been driving.

Shaken and still a little disoriented, she peered through the windshield. "It's really nasty out there."

"Yes, and it's getting worse by the minute." He placed his hand under her chin and gently turned her head toward him, checking the bandage on her cheek.

Evidently satisfied with the results, he turned the key in the ignition and started the engine. "We need to find a couple of rooms at a hotel and continue on in the morning. It isn't safe to drive anymore tonight. We were fortunate this time. I'm not going to take any more chances with you in the car."

Abby only hesitated for a minute; she knew Nick had a point. As much as she wanted to be home in time to hang the ornaments on Granny's tree, she wanted them to get there safely. It had been a tradition, for as long as she could remember, for the boys to set up the tree the day after Thanksgiving. They hung the lights and glass bulbs. Then on Christmas Eve morning, the girls had hot chocolate with Granny and hung the wooden ornaments. Abby looked forward to it every year.

"You're right." She drew in a shaky breath and picked up the contents of her purse from the floorboard where they had been dumped when the SUV hit the ditch. "We don't want to have another accident."

"I'll do my best to get you there in time." She held the flashlight for Nick while he rolled the airbag up and taped it against the steering wheel, out of the way. "I know how important it is to you."

"I appreciate that." She moved the flashlight over so he could see to roll and tape her air bag to the dash. "But as much as I want to be there, it's more important that we get there in one piece. Granny would have a fit if she knew we were driving in this weather."

"Yes, she would." He took the flashlight and laid it on the seat between them. She figured he wanted it to be handy in case they needed it again. "We need to get going, but we have a problem. Even if we can get out of this ditch, the snow is accumulating so fast on the windshield the wipers are having a difficult time keeping up. I doubt that we can see far enough ahead to find an off-ramp. But we can't stay out in this for long or we'll freeze."

Nick made several attempts to get out of the ditch, and Abby could sense his concern. Even with four-wheel drive, the tires couldn't seem to get traction. "Slide over here and guide the car. I'm going to try to push it as you give it gas and hope that will be enough." Nick slipped his coat on and went around to the back of the Blazer.

Abby rolled the window down, but she could barely hear Nick with the noise from the wind and snow blowing into her face. He had to be freezing out there.

"Okay, hit the gas real easy," Nick yelled.

She pressed carefully on the gas pedal, and the car eased forward. It hit the pavement slipping and sliding on the ice, heading back toward the ditch. She couldn't see Nick. Panicked, she prayed he'd had time to move out of the way. Her nerves tightened and her palms began to sweat as she fought frantically to keep the car on the road. It bumped the edge of the ditch and spun in a circle before she could get it under control. Abby sat, shaking, with her head resting on the steering wheel, her heart in her throat.

Nick opened the door and laid his hand on her shoulder. "Are you all right?"

Her heart thundered in her chest as she breathed a sigh of relief and thanked the Lord that Nick was okay. "Other than being scared half out of my wits, I'm fine." She glanced up at him. "You're soaked." She slid over so he could get in.

"Just my coat. I'm dry underneath." He slipped his jacket off once he was in the car and tossed it into the backseat.

Abby fastened her seat belt, and Nick pulled back onto the road. "We'd better start praying," he said. "We aren't going to be able to see to drive for very long in this."

"You drive and I'll pray." Abby bowed her head. "Lord, You know our situation here. Please send us some help. We need to find an exit and a hotel so we can get out of this weather. In Jesus' name we ask, amen."

"Amen," Nick repeated.

A half hour later conditions had not improved. "Nick, this is really scary. I know you can't see any better than I can. A lot of good it does to have a cell phone if it won't work when you need to call for help."

"I know. We must be in a dead zone." Nick cast a sideways glance at Abby and offered a reassuring smile. "There is no other option but to keep driving. Maybe a highway patrol car will come by before too long, to help us."

Fighting the urge to panic, Abby instead returned the smile. "I hope so, because if we run out of gas, we won't be able to keep the heater going, and without heat we'll freeze before morning."

"It'll be okay." He gave her arm a squeeze. "The

Lord will take care of us."

Two hours had gone by. Abby glanced again at the fuel gauge. Every time she looked, it had dropped a little lower. If they didn't find help soon, they would run out of gas.

"There's a truck coming up behind us," Nick said. "When he passes us, I'm going to try to stay behind him. That way I can follow his lights. He sits up high enough he can see better than we can."

Nick stayed behind the trucker for the next several miles. The snow accumulated so thick on the windshield that the trucker's lights were all they could see. The gas gauge, nearing empty, made her more nervous by the minute.

"Look at that!" She could see his bright smile in the reflection from the map light he'd left on. "There must be an exit ahead. He's giving a signal."

"That's great." Her body tensed for a moment. She sure hoped he knew where he was going and wouldn't lead them all into a ditch. They'd just have to trust the Lord in this one. "We can follow him off and find a hotel."

At the bottom of the ramp, a sign indicated Goodland, Kansas, to the left. The truck driver went straight across. "Nick, he is our answer to prayer. Look, he led us off the exit and then went back onto the freeway."

"You're right, Abby." This time Nick's smile was broad, warm, and genuine. "The Lord is faithful. It's amazing how much He loves us and that He always provides our needs."

Nick pulled into a parking space at the Howard Johnson Hotel. Abby scrambled out of the car, determined to pay for the rooms, since Nick had paid for the rental car. As she started toward the lobby, her feet slipped on the icy pavement and she went down hard on her left knee. Before she could get up, Nick stooped down beside her.

"Are you hurt?" He wrapped his arm around her waist.

"I think I'm okay. I just skinned my knee a little." She winced as Nick helped her to her feet.

"Did you bring some snow boots?" She glanced down as he pointed at her feet. "I don't think those tennis shoes are good on ice."

She glanced over at his feet and realized he had on more suitable shoes with waffle-style soles. No wonder he could get around better than she could.

"I think you've done more than skin your knee a little," Nick said as he looked down at her leg.

Abby realized he was right; blood had soaked through her jeans. Her knee throbbed and burned along with the abrasions on her face and neck from the air bag, but she didn't tell Nick that. He held her arm as he led her to the counter.

"We need two rooms," Nick said, handing the clerk his credit card. "Nonsmoking, please."

The clerk returned Nick's card and gave him the two room keys. The clerk glanced at Abby and back at Nick, noticing their injuries.

"Do you need a doctor?" He started to reach for the

phone there on the counter.

"No, I am a doctor," Nick said as he slid his wallet back into his pocket. "But you do need to write up a report, because she fell in your parking lot and injured her knee."

"I'll see to it right away," the clerk said, glancing at the hotel roster, "Dr. Creighton."

Nick helped Abby to the elevator with the bellhop following with their luggage. Abby didn't argue because she didn't want to embarrass Nick in front of the clerk and the bellhop. But she would be taking care of her knee and other injuries herself.

Chapter 4

When Nick and Abby reached their rooms, the bellhop brought their luggage in behind them. He placed her bag next to the closet and took Nick's into the adjoining room. After he pocketed the tip Nick handed him, he left, closing the door.

Nick pulled a folded blanket from the closet shelf and handed it to Abby. "Wrap this around you. You need to slip out of those jeans so I can see what you've done to your knee, and then I'll take care of the places on your cheek and neck. Do you have any others that need attention?"

"Just a few bruises from the seat belt; nothing that won't heal in time. I appreciate the offer, but I can take care of my knee and other injuries myself." The excitement of the day caught up with her suddenly and she slumped, exhausted, into one of the tan chairs across the room from the bed.

"Abby, I can see you're as tired as I am. Let's get this done so we can both get some rest."

"You can go to your room anytime. I'm not stopping you. I can take care of myself," she insisted stubbornly. "I'm sure it's not that bad anyway."

"Let me be the judge of that. I'm the doctor here, and I'm not going anywhere until you let me see your knee." He stood there, clearly determined. "So the longer you resist, the less sleep we'll both get, and tomorrow is going to be another long day."

Abby sighed and closed her eyes for a moment. She knew he meant what he said—if she didn't let him doctor her knee and other injuries, she'd never get to bed. She was just too tired to continue this argument.

"Fine!" She grabbed the blanket and stomped into the bathroom, shutting the door with a loud click. When she pulled her jeans off and got a look at her knee, she sat down on the toilet lid as her stomach lurched. Her head swam, and she wasn't sure if she was going to be sick or faint. She felt like she might do both, so she sat there for a few minutes. When she came out a little later, she had the blanket wrapped securely around her and sat down in the chair. Her stomach felt even queasier, and she was still light-headed. She had wrapped a hand towel around her leg. Her knee was a lot worse than she realized, and she had a huge bruise across her shoulder and her stomach from the seat belt. That bit of information she'd keep to herself—as she'd told Nick earlier, the bruises would heal in time. He didn't need to know exactly what bruises.

When Nick reached over to remove the towel, Abby said, "You'd better lay that under my foot. Otherwise we'll get blood on the carpet."

∞

Nick frowned when he looked at her knee. "You've really done some damage. Are you all right? You look a little pale."

"I'm fine."

Nick studied her for a moment. She didn't look fine. He'd bet she was nauseated and hoped she wouldn't faint on him. She'd never been very good with cuts of any kind and especially her own. "Sit still then while I get my bag. I'll be right back." He went into his room.

A minute later, he came back with his medical bag and knelt down in front of her, opened an antiseptic pad, and gently washed the area around the deep laceration.

"No matter what I do, it's going to hurt. I think the least intrusive would be to set you on the edge of the tub and wash it in warm water."

"Okay."

She started to stand, but he lifted her before she could protest and carried her into the bathroom and set her on the edge of the tub. When he had her settled, he turned the water on and let it run until he had it adjusted to a comfortable temperature.

"I could have walked in here, you know." Abby looked up at him.

"I know, but this way we didn't drip on the carpet." It was also an excuse to hold her. He loved having her in his arms, even for a short time. "This is going to hurt. I'll do it as gently as I can. Are you ready?"

She took a deep breath and let it out slowly, then nodded. Nick gritted his teeth when she cried out as the water hit the open wound.

"I'm sorry, honey. I wish there were another way, but it has to be done to keep it from getting infected." Tears rolled down her cheeks, but she didn't complain as he washed the wound with soap and water. He patted it dry, then covered it with an antibiotic ointment and bandaged it. Next, he took care of her cheek and the abrasions on her neck and hands.

"All done. Are you all right?" Nick asked, gently watching her while he waited for an answer.

"Yes. I appreciate you doing this for me." She smiled and dried her feet so she could step out of the tub.

Someone knocked on the door. "That will be room service. I ordered us sandwiches." Nick opened the door and stepped back so the young man could set the tray on the table. Nick gave him a tip, and he left.

"I wasn't sure I'd be able to eat anything, but my stomach feels a little better now, and I'm starving." Abby sat down across from him. They joined hands, and he blessed the food.

"We should try to get an early start. I'd like to leave around seven in the morning if that's all right with you." He tore the paper from a straw and stuck the straw in his drink.

"That's fine. I'll be ready. I just hope the weather is better tomorrow." Abby sipped her root beer.

"I hope it is, too. But at least if it isn't, I'd much rather drive in the daylight." Nick finished his sandwich and leaned back in the chair.

"Even if we don't make it in time to hang the ornaments, I want you to know how much I appreciate you driving through with me, to try to get me there." Abby brushed the hair away from her face.

"I wanted to come with you, and I'm going to do the best I can to get you to Granny's on time. I know how important it is to you to be there." Nick looked at her and smiled.

They had finished eating, so she helped him pick up the papers from the food and tossed them into the wastebasket.

Nick went to his room and took a shower while he waited for Abby to get settled into bed. When he was through, he knocked on the adjoining door.

"Come in." She pulled the blankets up over her.

"Here's some ibuprofen; it'll help with the pain so you can rest." He handed her a glass of water and two tablets.

"Thank you." Abby took the water and swallowed the tablets.

"Sure; if you need anything, just knock on the door. I'll see you in the morning."

"Okay, good night." She slid down in the bed and closed her eyes just as he went into his room. He glanced back as he shut the door. She looked so beautiful—her image would stay with him the rest of the night.

❧

The next morning Abby had a hard time finding a pair

of pants loose enough not to rub against her sore knee. After going through everything in her suitcase, she finally settled on a pair of black sweatpants. They would be comfortable since they would be riding in the car all day.

Nick knocked on the door adjoining their rooms.

"Come in. I'm almost ready," she said as he opened the door.

"How's the knee?" He sank his large frame into a chair across from her and placed the two cups he had in his hand on the small table beside him.

"Sore. I decided to wear my sweatpants. They won't rub it like my jeans would." She glanced over at him as she placed the last of her clothes in her suitcase and zipped it closed.

"I can imagine it is sore. Sweats are a good choice in this case." He smiled sympathetically. "I'll change the bandage when we stop for the night."

"I thought we'd make it home by tonight." She stopped what she was doing and looked at him.

"I don't think so. From the looks of the weather report, we'll have to take it slow. It's snowing too heavy out there for the plows to keep the roads cleared, and we'll be driving in this all the way. I don't want to take any chances, and as long as we make it in by tomorrow evening, you'll be there in time to hang the ornaments," Nick assured her. "Do you want to eat breakfast here or grab something at a fast-food place on the way?"

"Are you hungry?" Abby asked. "If so, we can eat here."

"I have a cup of coffee, so I'm fine either way. I

brought you a cup of hot chocolate." He handed her one of the cups he'd set on the table. "Be careful; it's really hot."

"Thanks. With this I'll be fine for a while, so we can wait and stop on the way." She reached for the chocolate and slid the lid open, blowing into the top to cool it before taking a sip.

As they got into the Blazer, Abby noticed the dark clouds hovering overhead. The countryside was covered in thick layers of snow. It was still coming down steadily, and it didn't look like it would let up any time soon. Normally she loved the snow and enjoyed the beauty of it, but not when they had to be out driving in it.

She glanced at Nick as he pulled out of the icy parking lot. His strong hands on the steering wheel expertly maneuvered the SUV on the slick road. She thanked the Lord that he had come with her—even though being this close to him rekindled feelings she had hoped were long gone. She knew there was a reason for their being on the same plane. She didn't believe in coincidence; the Lord had a reason for everything that happened.

Abby adjusted the sweatshirt she had draped over her legs and moved her purse from her lap to the floorboard.

"Are you warm enough?" Nick started to reach to turn the heater up.

"Yes, I'm fine. The heat feels good."

Abby realized at that moment the reason she'd avoided dating the last fourteen months. She had declined every dinner invitation she'd received. She didn't have any interest in going out with anyone who had asked her. Now she knew why. She still had feelings for Nick. Sitting so close to him, she could smell the fresh scent of his cologne, a familiar fragrance, her favorite. Memories flooded into her thoughts of the happy times they'd spent together. She shook her head—time to get her mind back where it belonged. She couldn't afford to think about the past. It hurt too much.

"What do you do for a living in the little town fifty miles inland from San Francisco?" Nick asked. "Tell me about your job and where you live."

This subject she felt safe discussing. "I have a small one-bedroom apartment in a town called Tracy. I manage a travel agency in the mall there. My office is about two miles from my home, so I don't have very far to drive each day to get to work. I can park just outside the door, so I don't have to be out in the wind and weather when it's nasty out."

"Manager, huh? Well, that doesn't surprise me, since you had your own agency back home. Do you like your job and living in Tracy?"

She knew what he wanted to know—if she was happy.

"Yes, I do." She took a sip of her hot chocolate. "The owner of the agency only comes in occasionally. She is good to me, and the agents I work with are nice people."

"Have you ever regretted giving up your agency and moving away from Pierce City?" Nick sipped his coffee.

"To be honest, I'd have to say yes. But I'm adjusting."

"I'm sorry, Abby, for everything." His voice grew soft.

"Nick, that was a long time ago." She squirmed in the seat. "A subject better left alone."

∾∾

Lord, I believe Abby is the mate You've chosen for me, and You know how much I love her. Help me to be patient, to be able to win her trust and love once again. Please give me an opportunity to make things right between us, Nick prayed silently.

Just as he ended his prayer, he heard a loud *pop*, and the SUV began to swerve all over the road. He knew immediately they had blown a tire. He took his foot off the gas but didn't hit the brakes, allowing the vehicle to slow down as he guided it to the side of the road.

Abby's blue eyes widened. "What happened?"

"We've blown a tire," Nick said and unfastened his seat belt. "I hope and pray there's a spare in the back."

He climbed out of the car, and his boots sunk to his ankles in the deep snow. He shivered in spite of his heavy jacket. Wind and snow pelted him in the face as he made his way to the back of the Blazer. He opened the hatch to look for a spare and jack to change the tire—not his favorite thing to do in this weather. It didn't look like he had to worry about it; they didn't have a jack. He closed the hatch and climbed back inside. The warmth from the heater felt wonderful as he rubbed his hands together in an attempt to get the feeling back into his frozen fingers.

"We have a bit of a problem." Nick sighed and laid

his arm across the steering wheel. "There's a spare, but we don't have a jack."

"Great!" Abby turned toward him in the seat. "Now what are we going to do?"

"I'll try my cell phone and call AAA. Maybe we're in a place where it will work this time." Nick pulled his phone out of his pocket, flipped it open, dialed, and waited while it rang.

Please, Lord, I pray it will go through. We need some help here.

"It's ringing."

"Hello, AAA road service, how can I help you?" a woman's soft voice asked.

"We're on Highway 70 just a few miles from Russell, Kansas. We've blown a tire."

"Do you have a spare, sir?" she asked.

"Yes, but we don't have a jack and we need some fuel. We're almost out of gas. We're in a light blue Chevy Blazer." He then gave her the license number shown on the rental agreement and estimated the closest highway mile post. Nick wasn't leaving it to chance that another SUV would be mistaken for theirs.

"I'll send a rig out as soon as I can, but it may be a little while. We're swamped with calls. We have been all morning. There are a lot of people stuck in this weather."

"Okay. Thank you. I'm afraid we won't be going anywhere, so we'll be right here when he's free," Nick said and closed his phone before slipping it back into his pocket.

"Well, that didn't sound too promising." Nick frowned. "I have a feeling we may be here awhile. They're very busy. She said she'd send a rig as soon as one becomes available."

Nick locked the doors and turned on the flashers. "I guess we might as well get as comfortable as we can." He slumped down and laid his head against the head-rest of his seat.

"Abby, I'd like to explain to you why I broke our engagement." He closed his eyes and waited, hoping she'd agree to listen.

"Nick." She hesitated as if she were thinking about it, and his hopes rose, but in the next moment, she dashed them completely. "Please, let's not talk about that—not right now."

He sighed, gritting his teeth to hold back his disappointment. "All right, but one of these days we need to talk about it."

"Well, that may be, but please, not now."

He heard the crack in her voice. This was hard for her. He was to blame for that hurt, and his chest tightened with regret. Still he was frustrated at her continued refusal to listen to him. He hoped his explanation would make it a little easier for her. Maybe it would help to know that he had a good reason, as unfair as it was, for what he'd done. That is, if she'd ever allow him to give her his explanation.

Nick closed his eyes, and the memories of that night flooded his mind. Janine had come to him after his brother had been killed in Kuwait. She made him promise he would never reveal what she planned to tell him. After he gave his word, she told him about her pregnancy and that the child she carried belonged to his brother. She wanted to draw up a business arrangement with him. If he would marry her and give the baby his name, she would sign papers giving him sole custody, along with an annulment the day after the child's birth. If he wouldn't agree, she would have an abortion. He cringed even now at the thought of her destroying the baby.

Abby had shown such compassion to the young girl at the airport, and he loved her even more for it. He prayed that she would allow him to explain and would show him some of that compassion—and understand that he'd had no choice in the decision he'd made the night he'd broken their engagement.

Chapter 5

It's been two hours since we called." Abby shivered and wrapped her coat more securely around her. "I wonder how much longer it'll be before they get here."

"I don't know, but surely it won't be too much longer. I'll start the engine and turn the heater back on for a little while so you can get warm."

"I'm okay. I know we're low on gas and you're trying to conserve what we have. If we run out, we won't have any heat. I can wait a little longer."

"It won't take that much to run it for a few minutes. You're freezing, and I don't want you to get sick."

"Nick, I'm really sorry I got you into this. It was a foolish idea to try to drive in this weather. Now you're out here in the middle of nowhere, stuck, freezing in the snow, and it's all my fault. I didn't want to disappoint Granny, but she wouldn't want us to risk our lives to get there."

"I came because I wanted to, Abby. I knew the risks.

Besides, we're going to be fine. AAA will be here before long, and we'll soon be on our way again."

Abby sighed and leaned back against the seat. Nick had always been such a special person, and she could see that hadn't changed. She didn't know if she'd ever be able to trust him again, but during the time they'd been together on this trip, she had regained her respect for him. After all, he didn't have to come with her, yet he hadn't hesitated, even with the severe weather conditions. He'd also done everything he could to help and protect her. She kept thinking about the situation they found themselves in. What if help didn't get here in time and this would be the last chance she had to find out what had caused Nick to break their engagement fourteen months ago and marry Janine? Maybe she should listen to his explanation. Otherwise she might not ever know.

She watched him for a moment. He looked so handsome, relaxed there next to her, his head resting on the seat. Just looking at him took her breath away. She still had feelings for him, but he had hurt her, and she was leery of him. Although, if she were honest with herself, she had to admit she was glad he had come with her. Even though she wasn't ready to accept him back into her life, she didn't want him completely out of it, either. Maybe what he was going to tell her would make a difference. She'd listen to him and then reevaluate the situation.

"Nick," Abby said softly, "I've thought about what you said earlier, and I've decided, if you want to explain what happened fourteen months ago, I'm ready to listen."

He opened his eyes and scooted up in his seat as he turned toward her. She swallowed nervously. Had she made a mistake? Would what he had to say make things worse? Whether it did or not, she had to know.

Abby sat quietly and listened as Nick explained exactly what had happened with Janine.

∽

He flipped the map light on so he could see her face. The anguish he saw there and knowing he had caused it nearly ripped his heart out. Closing his eyes, he paused for a minute longer to regain his composure. He looked at her and said, "I couldn't let her destroy my brother's baby, Abby. Scotty is all I have left of Nathan. I didn't have any other choice. I just couldn't let her have an abortion. I'm sorry. If there had been any other way, believe me, I would have taken it. I never meant to hurt you."

Nick paused for a moment to give Abby time to take in all he'd just shared with her, praying she would understand and forgive him. He loved her so much. She was his life. He hoped they could still have a future together. When she didn't say anything, he continued.

"Abby, I felt terrible, and my heart ached and still does about the way I treated you. I had no choice but to break our engagement without giving you an explanation." At the sight of the tears welling in her eyes, he ran his hand through his hair and swallowed hard before continuing.

"I still have a difficult time understanding how my

brother could have gotten himself into a situation like this. Nathan's Christian principles were as strong as mine are. But he loved Janine to distraction, and I have no doubt this child belongs to him." He paused and swallowed again, having a hard time keeping his own emotions under control while he finished what he had to say.

"I had no choice. I signed the necessary papers, agreeing to keep her secret until after the annulment and she'd left the area."

Abby glanced up at him as tears spilled over and ran down her face. She impatiently wiped them away. Talking about this was hard for her. Nick knew her well enough to know that she would feel compassion for him even though she didn't want to. He'd hurt her that night, and she wasn't sure she could trust him. He couldn't blame her for not ever wanting to suffer like that again.

Nick saw tears well in her eyes again and felt like a heel, hoping as he finished his story she would understand and it would ease some of the pain and disappointment he knew she was feeling.

"There's something else that Janine failed to tell me—one very important factor," Nick continued as Abby reached into her purse for a tissue. "Janine had a severe heart condition, and the doctor advised against her carrying the child, explaining that if she carried the baby to term, she'd never live through the strain of childbirth." He had to stop and clear his throat. His emotions were about to get the better of him in spite of his efforts to keep them under control.

"She left a letter with her lawyer to be given to me after her death. In the letter, Janine explained that she loved Nathan, and she wanted their baby to have a chance."

"If she loved him and the baby so much. . ." Abby paused for a moment and looked at him. "How could she even consider having an abortion?"

"I asked myself that same question. Looking back, I'm sure she wouldn't have had the abortion if I'd refused, but I didn't know her well enough to realize that. She probably felt that threatening to do so was the only way to guarantee that I would agree to her terms. She knew I would love and give her baby the home she wanted for him. In her letter she asked for my forgiveness for placing me in such a position. She just didn't know what else to do; she had to know her baby would be loved and cared for after her death." Nick shifted to a more comfortable position.

"In the letter she also gave me permission to tell you the whole story." He didn't add that Janine's letter said she hoped he and Abby would reconcile and raise the baby together. Nick would keep that part a secret for now and pray for Abby's love and understanding— along with the right time to share that information with her.

"It was just a business arrangement, Abby. We were never intimate. It wasn't a real marriage. I had an obligation to my brother's child, and I couldn't see any other way. I'd made a promise not to reveal Janine's secret before I realized what it would cost us. I never dreamed that what she was about to tell me would change our plans."

She was quiet for so long that Nick had decided she wasn't going to comment at all, but then she turned in the seat and faced him.

"I understand that you were faced with a difficult choice, Nick, but you devastated my world. I loved you so much—you were my whole life. I respect your having the courage to honor a promise, but we were engaged. You had an obligation to honor me, too, and I feel you owed me an honest explanation that night. What you did to me was unfair, and I'm sorry, but I don't trust you not to hurt me again."

"I'm sorry, too, Abby. Not telling you the truth was a terrible mistake. I know that now, and I hope you know I would never hurt you intentionally. I love you. I've never stopped loving you. Can you honestly tell me that you no longer have any feelings for me? If you can truthfully tell me that, then I'll take you home and I won't bother you anymore."

Abby squirmed in the seat next to him. He prayed it was because she couldn't bring herself to sever their relationship completely and she'd admit that to him.

After a moment or two, she sighed. "I can't tell you that. I do still have feelings. But I'm not willing to pursue them right now. I need time to think and time to pray. I can't promise anything."

"I understand how you feel, and I'll give you all the time you need." As hard as it would be to wait, at least that gave him some hope.

Nick glanced up as lights reflected in the rearview mirror. "I think that's our tow truck. Stay inside here where it's warm." He grabbed his jacket from the backseat, opened the door, and stepped out as the large truck pulled up and parked in front of their SUV.

"I'm sure glad to see you." Nick walked up to him.

"Yeah, it's a bit too chilly out here to sit for very long. You have a spare?" the driver asked.

"Yes, but it's a rental, and we don't seem to have a jack." Nick opened the trunk and pulled out the spare tire. The tow truck driver took the tire, rolled it over to the flat, and proceeded to change it. Nick sure was glad this wasn't his line of work, and he felt for the young man having to be out in weather like this changing tires. But he was certainly thankful for his help. When the driver finished changing the tire, he added gas to the fuel tank. Nick gave him his AAA card, signed the necessary papers, and climbed back into the SUV with Abby.

"Man, it's cold out there. Even with my gloves on, my hands are frozen." He blew on his fingers to try to warm them and then started the engine. "We can use the heater again. He gave us enough gas to get us to the next town, which he said would take about a half hour from here."

With the snow coming down so hard, it was difficult to see very far ahead. Nick carefully maneuvered the Blazer onto the icy road. They certainly didn't want to wind up in another ditch.

This was crazy. Anyone with any sense wouldn't be

out driving in this weather at all. But he'd do just about anything to make Abby happy, and he knew how important it was to her to be at Granny's for the hanging of the ornaments and the family Christmas gathering. He'd pray for safety and do his very best to get her there on time and in one piece.

"That heat feels good." Nick kept one hand on the steering wheel and held the other in front of the vent to warm his fingers.

"Yes, it does. I'm freezing, and I haven't been out of the car. I can't even imagine how cold you are."

"I'm beginning to thaw out now. As long as I've known you, you've prayed for a white Christmas. I presume that hasn't changed." Nick grinned. "You sure got your wish this year."

Abby laughed. "No, it hasn't changed. I always pray for snow at Christmas. But I'm afraid I got more than I bargained for this time." As her laughter faded, she said, "I just hope it doesn't keep any of the family from making it this year."

"I wondered, now that all four of you girls have moved away, if you would all make it to Granny's this year." Nick turned the steering wheel slightly when they began to slide a little on the slick, icy road. He felt Abby stiffen next to him and then relax as the car stopped skidding before she answered him.

"It's been touch and go for a while, but at least two of us will be there. Amanda is living in Oklahoma City; she's the closest to home. She's a real estate agent there. She's bringing a friend named Josh Randall. Lauren called Granny and said she couldn't come, but I keep hoping she'll change her mind at the last minute and make it after all. You remember Jeff Warren?"

"Sure, we went to school together." Nick corrected the car again and slowed down just a little. The roads were getting worse. He didn't know how much longer they would be able to continue to drive in this.

"He and Lauren have been best friends for years. When Granny called and told him Lauren wasn't coming home for Christmas, he decided to go to St. Louis where she's living now and see if he could change her mind. I'm praying he'll be successful."

"I'm sure Granny was pleased about that. Where does Lauren work in St. Louis?"

"She's a librarian there, and she loves it. Granny is thrilled that two of us are coming for sure. She's upset over Lauren and Casey, but she's praying and is hopeful they'll make it, even if it's at the last minute. Casey called and said she couldn't come. She's living in Cade's Point, California, which is a town by the beach not too far from Los Angeles. She works for a large clothing company. Part of her job is creating the front window design for the holidays, and she feels she needs to be there for the Christmas party. I keep praying something will change. If the reason she isn't coming has to do with someone special she wants to spend Christmas with, then I hope she'll decide to come and bring him with her." She grinned, her eyes lighting with excitement. "It would be great if the four of us could be there after all."

"Yes, and if that happens, we'll have a full house this year." Nick smiled. "I hope it works out. Everyone loves Granny, and it's hard to think of disappointing her."

"I know, I just can't imagine being anywhere else for Christmas. I've always been home with my family. I guess we're really fortunate." Abby opened a package of gum, offered him a piece, and took one for herself before placing it back into her purse. "So many people don't have a family to be with."

Chapter 6

Nick thought about the Christmases he had spent with his family. Now his brother was gone, and they would never have another Christmas with him. Yes, Abby was fortunate to have her family all together to celebrate with. He had to try to concentrate now on making new traditions with Scotty. He would be the best father he could possibly be and try to make Scotty's world as happy a place as he could for the little guy.

Nathan, I'll do the best I can to make your son a good home. I'll raise him to know the Lord, the way I know you would have if you had been given the chance.

Abby glanced over at Nick. She hadn't thought about how he must feel. This would be a difficult Christmas for him and his family without his brother, and she knew how much Nick had loved him. They had been very close growing up, only eighteen months apart.

He'd miss Nathan terribly.

She remembered how hard it had been for Nick when Nathan told him he had enlisted and that he'd be deployed overseas. Nick had taken every extra shift available at the hospital to keep himself busy. She'd hardly seen him for weeks after Nathan left. Nick came to see her one evening and apologized for neglecting her. He explained that he and Nathan had talked just before his brother shipped out. Nick told her that after spending a lot of time in prayer, he'd finally come to terms with his brother's decision. Even though it would be hard, he'd felt he could accept it. Then Nathan had been killed shortly after his deployment.

"Nick, I'm so sorry. I didn't think. I know it's hard for you this year. I'm glad you're both going to be with us for Christmas instead of being alone. By the way, where are your mother and dad?"

"Mom and Dad are taking a cruise. They just couldn't handle being at home this year for the holidays. They needed something different. Since we lost Nathan in October, we didn't celebrate the holidays last year. And this will be the first Christmas since Janine's death, so it's been hard for them—for all of us—but having Scotty helps."

"I can certainly understand their feelings." She couldn't imagine losing either of her brothers.

"Abby." Nick interrupted her thoughts. "My parents don't know that Scotty isn't mine. No one does but you."

"Why?" Abby asked, confused that Nick would

keep this from his parents.

"I can see by the shocked look on your face you don't understand," Nick said.

"No, I don't understand." Abby looked over at him. "I would think it would be a joy to them to know they had a part of Nathan in his son."

"Janine didn't want anyone to think ill of Nathan, and she was afraid they would if they knew the truth about Scotty. You know how some people are in a small town. We love them all, but you always have a few that gossip every chance they get. Martha Ogalberry would have a field day with this. I can just see it. She'd tell Henrietta Stallings, and it would be all over the church in no time."

"Yes, you're right. I can understand her not wanting you to tell anyone else. But I know your parents would be thrilled to know they still have a part of your brother in his son."

"I'm sure they would, Abby, but I promised Janine I wouldn't tell anyone. The letter she left gave me permission to tell only you."

"Nick, I understand your loyalty to Janine. But I think under these circumstances, you need to think about what your brother would have wanted. You have to make a decision as to what is best here. She was trying to protect your brother's reputation, and I can relate to that, but maybe she didn't stop to think about how much it would mean to your mother and dad. They would really benefit from knowing you have Nathan's son. You don't have to tell anyone else, so that way you can still keep her secret." Abby thought about what she had said and wished she'd kept her mouth shut. She was no longer a part of Nick's life; she probably shouldn't have commented at all.

"Nick, I'm sorry. This isn't any of my business. Please just forget what I said and do what you think is best."

"If I hadn't wanted you involved, I wouldn't have told you any of this. I value your opinion, and you may be right, but I have to think about it and pray before I make a decision."

"I think it's a good idea to let the Lord guide you in this. That way you know you won't make the wrong choice."

A little while later, Abby was getting hungry. With the time lost on the flat tire, they had missed breakfast, and it was now well past time for lunch. Her stomach growled audibly. Heat filled her cheeks in embarrassment, and she hoped Nick hadn't heard. But he chuckled.

"Obviously you're hungry. I think we need to find someplace to get you something to eat. It shouldn't be much farther to the exit. When we get into town, we can get some gas and find a restaurant. I'm getting hungry, too."

They took the next off-ramp and pulled into a service station so Nick could fill the gas tank. Next door to the station, they found a small country restaurant. He parked the Blazer and shut off the engine. The cold wind whipped Abby's hair into her face as she stepped out of the car, causing her to shiver. She sniffed appreciatively upon entering the cheery dining area with its shiny white walls, red checked curtains, and tablecloths to match. Something smelled wonderful, and her stomach growled again.

Nick grinned as she felt the heat creep into her cheeks. "I'm sorry," she apologized.

"You're hungry; you can't help that." Nick pulled a chair out for her to sit down and then sank into the one across from her. On every table sat a candle, a vase with two poinsettias—one white, one red—with a sprig of Christmas greens in each. A red-and-green-checked bow decorated the vase.

Across the room sat a large stuffed Santa and Mrs. Claus in a rocking chair.

"Look at that, Nick. Aren't they cute?"

"Yes they are. You obviously haven't lost your love for Santa." He chuckled.

Abby grinned. "No, I guess in that respect I'll always be a little girl at heart. I love Christmas."

Abby glanced around. In front of a large picture window stood a Christmas tree tall enough to reach the ceiling, decorated with red and green lights, bulbs, and lots of small wooden ornaments. It gave the room a festive glow.

The waitress came to the table, set two glasses of water in front of them, and handed them each a menu. "Hi, welcome to Annie's Kitchen." She smiled brightly. "My name is Ellie. What can I get for you to drink today?"

"Root beer for me, please." Abby smiled and placed her purse on the chair next to her.

"I'll have a Dr Pepper." Nick slipped off his jacket and hung it on the back of his chair.

"I'll be back to take your orders in a few minutes." The waitress left to get their drinks while they looked at the menu.

Abby opened her napkin and spread it across her lap before she sat back to read her copy of the menu. "I think I'll have a cheeseburger and fries."

"Sounds good. I'll have the same." Nick took her menu and set them on the edge of the table. When the waitress returned a few minutes later with their soft drinks, Nick gave her their orders. She took both menus and headed toward the kitchen.

"I told you all about my job and apartment in California." Abby reached for her glass of water and took a drink, more for something to do than because she was thirsty. "So now it's your turn. Are you still working at the hospital?" Nick's cologne wafted toward her. The familiar scent brought back memories of meals they had shared in the past, causing her heart to ache with what should have been as she waited for him to answer.

"No, I decided about six months ago to take my dad up on his offer and go into practice with him and your brother. There are four of us sharing the medical building now. Brad Collins joined our office. He specializes in obstetrics and gynecology. He moved here from Kansas City shortly after you left. He's a good doctor, one of the best in his field, and we were thankful to have him join us."

"That's great. And your joining your dad should have made him happy. I know that's been his desire ever since you started med school. It's convenient for the patients, too, to have a general practitioner, a pediatrician, an orthopedist, and an OB/GYN all in one office."

"Yes, it's working out well, and I'm happy as I can be. But my life will never be completely happy without you." Nick looked directly at her, making her uncomfortable. She squirmed in her chair and quickly changed the subject.

"Do you have an apartment or a house?"

Nick sighed at her response and took a sip of the water to wet his dry throat before he answered. "Janine had a rental, a two-story house. I lived there until just recently. I occupied the upstairs, and she lived downstairs. Five months ago I bought forty acres and had a five-bedroom house built. It's a two-story with a full basement, and I had a barn with ten stalls built back behind the house for the horses." He smiled.

"You have horses?" she cried softly. Riding Granny's horse, Cody, out across her twenty-acre farm was one of the things Abby missed.

"Six of them and two more on the way. It's between Pierce City and Wentworth. You'll have to come out and see it and the horses."

The waitress came back and placed their orders in front of them, along with bottles of ketchup and mustard. "Let me know if there is anything else I can get for you."

"Abby, is there anything else you want?" Nick looked over at her.

"No, thank you. This is fine." She smiled up at the waitress, and the girl nodded her head in response as she walked away.

"I'd love to see your place and the horses while I'm here." Abby smiled at Nick as she unwrapped her straw and put it in her root beer, trying to ignore the information about Janine and that she was ever a part of Nick's life. "Tell me about Scotty. What does he look like, and who keeps him when you're working?"

His gaze softened. "Scotty is the delight of my life. He looks just like Nathan. He hardly ever cries except when he's hungry, and he's been sleeping all night since he was six weeks old. I'm very fortunate. He's a good baby. I have a daytime housekeeper-nanny, Maggie Shepherd; she takes care of Scotty and keeps the house up."

"I know Maggie; she's a nice lady." Abby studied Nick as she ate her cheeseburger and fries. She could see the love in his eyes when he talked about the baby. Nick and Nathan had looked so much alike, people would never question whether Scotty was Nick's.

"Yes, Maggie's a special person. She's warm and loving, and she takes good care of Scotty. I don't have to worry about him when I'm away, like I have been the last few days for the convention and now our travel delay. Maggie loves him as if he were another one of her grandchildren. She's been keeping him since he was born, so he loves her, too. I'm as comfortable leaving him with her for a few days as I am leaving him with my mother."

"Have you thought about what you're going to tell him when he's old enough to understand? Are you going to tell him about your brother, or are you going to raise him as yours?"

"I've thought about it a lot. I'll probably tell him about Nathan, but we'll see when the time comes."

"If you do decide to tell him, have you thought about how your parents are going to feel when they realize you've kept this from them?"

Nick looked at her for a moment before he answered. "I've thought about that, too, but I haven't come to a decision yet." He took the last bite of his cheeseburger and finished his Dr Pepper.

Abby didn't say any more. She just prayed he'd make the right decision. When he saw that she was finished, he reached for the bill. "I'll pay it." Abby grabbed for it, but Nick beat her to it.

"I've got it." Nick pulled out his wallet and headed to the counter.

Not wanting to make a scene, Abby didn't argue with him. She waited until they got into the car.

"Nick, I'm paying that bill," she insisted. "You paid for the food yesterday. It's my turn."

"We can settle up when we get to Granny's, okay?"

Abby hesitated. "All right, but only if you promise you'll let me pay half."

"Fine." Nick started the car and turned on the heater.

"It's still snowing and getting deeper by the minute. I don't know how much longer we can drive in this."

"How far are we from Pierce City?" Abby wrapped the sweatshirt back around her legs.

"It's about six and a half hours. I hope the plows have been out on the highway."

Nick switched over to four-wheel drive and pulled out onto the road. "From the looks of the weather, even if they have, they'll have a hard time keeping up, so I doubt we'll make it that soon."

Abby closed her eyes and laid her head back on the seat to rest for a few minutes. The next thing she knew, she'd been napping for three of the five hours they'd been on the road. She sat up and looked out the window, watching the snowflakes continue to drift over the countryside. The quiet seemed almost eerie. Nick reached over and turned on the radio, searching until he found a station playing soft music.

Abby appreciated the break in the silence until the song came on that had been playing the night Nick had asked her to marry him. The happiest night of her life—so she had thought at the time. He had taken her out to dinner at a nice restaurant in Springfield. When they'd finished their meal, he had flipped open a small, black velvet box, and inside lay the most beautiful engagement ring she had ever seen. A solitaire diamond encircled with emeralds. She hadn't even hesitated when he'd asked her to marry him. She immediately said yes, beaming with excitement because she'd loved him more than anything. Everything had been wonderful in her world. Amazing how things can quickly change.

"Where are we?" she asked, her voice flat.

"Are you okay?" Nick glanced at her.

"Yes, I'm fine." But she wasn't. Tears filled her eyes, and she blinked rapidly to try to keep them from escaping and rolling down her face. She thought she had put this behind her, but obviously not, since just hearing that one song brought all of the hurt hurling back in one swoop.

"This is Vinita, Oklahoma. We're about an hour and a half from home. But in this weather it will probably take us a couple of hours to drive it." Nick leaned forward slightly. The snow had accumulated so thick on the windshield that Abby knew he could hardly see through it. "A sign back there said there's a Holiday Inn Express & Suites at the next exit two miles ahead. I can't see a foot in front of me. I thought maybe we could make it on in tonight since we're close to home, but it isn't safe to drive any farther. We need to book two rooms for tonight and pray the weather will be better in the morning. Then we can drive on in tomorrow. If we get up early, we can still be to Granny's in time for you to hang the ornaments with the girls."

"I hope the other girls are there." Abby worried about them, knowing they were traveling in this weather, too. The snow continued to fall, and there didn't seem to be any hope of it ending any time soon.

"I'll call my parents when we get settled in our rooms to see if they made it yet and let them know where we are. I'll be glad when we get there. It's almost as if we're out here alone with nowhere to go. It's a strange feeling. Are you sure we can make it another two miles in this?" Abby leaned forward and squinted to try to see through the windshield better.

"Nick, stop!" she cried.

Chapter 7

Nick didn't dare slam on the brakes, so he tapped them several times, gradually bringing the SUV to a stop. They passed a car that had slid nose first into the ditch. Since the taillights were still on, the accident must have just happened. He pulled over to the side of the road, out of the way of any traffic that might be coming, and backed up carefully until they were just ahead of the car. "Stay here, Abby." Nick slipped into his jacket. "I'll go see if anyone is injured and if there is anything I can do."

"I should go with you; you might need some help." She started to unfasten her seat belt.

"There's no need for you to get out in this weather unless it's necessary. I'll go check and let you know if I need help, okay?"

"All right, I'll wait here. But please be careful."

Nick nodded and shut the door. Wind and snow hit him square in the face, instantly chilling him to the bone. He slipped and slid all the way down the side of the ditch, sinking almost to his knees in the cold, wet snow making it difficult to move. Finally, he reached the door of the car. Concern filled him when he didn't see any attempt being made to get out of the ditch or any movement at all. He knocked on the window; it seemed several minutes went by before it rolled down just a tiny crack. "Are you all right? I'm a doctor; is anyone hurt?"

"We're okay, but the car is stuck," the man behind the wheel said. "We called AAA. They're sending a truck out, but the dispatcher said it would be about thirty minutes before it could get here. We appreciate your stopping. We have a full tank of fuel, so we can run the heater. We'll be okay."

"I'm glad you're not hurt. Merry Christmas." Nick waved and headed back up the side of the bank to the SUV. He opened the door and climbed in beside Abby.

"Are you all right, and is anyone hurt in the other car?" Abby handed him some tissue to wipe the snow off of his face.

"No, fortunately. They're just stuck. A tow truck is on its way." Nick slipped out of his wet jacket and laid it out in the backseat again to dry. There wasn't much he could do about his wet pants, but they'd be at the hotel soon. He started the engine and eased back onto the road. He'd be glad when they got to Granny's. This was the worst trip he'd ever made, and he wasn't looking forward to battling this storm the rest of the way home. Driving in this weather was just plain foolish. He'd much rather be sitting in front of a fire with Abby than out here on an icy highway. Of course, there was no way for him to know whether she would ever agree to sit by a fire with him again in the future. That thought didn't set well with him at all.

∞

Abby stared out the window at the snow-covered countryside. Snow this time of year made it seem more like Christmas, but she didn't like driving in it. She watched Nick as he expertly maneuvered the SUV on the slick road. She had never met anyone who even held a candle to him, as the saying went. She realized, having spent all of this time in such close quarters with him, that she loved him just as much as she had when he'd broken their engagement. She didn't want to love him, but she'd be lying to herself if she denied her feelings any longer. But was she ready to rekindle their relationship? She didn't know the answer to that question. She'd pray and ask the Lord to guide her and help her to make the right decision.

"There's the exit for the hotel." Nick flipped on the turn signal and took the off-ramp. "I'll be glad to get out of this weather and into dry clothes. I just hope it's better in the morning."

"I hope so, too." Abby unfastened her seat belt as Nick parked in front of the hotel and turned off the engine. He came around and opened her door while she put on her jacket. She took the hand he offered to steady her on the slick pavement. She certainly didn't want another skinned knee.

The clerk signed them in and handed them their

keys, and they went up to their appointed rooms. After the bellhop left, Nick knocked on Abby's door.

"Abby, it's me," Nick said.

Abby went to open the door. "Come on in."

"Are you hungry?" Nick asked and reached for the room service menu.

"Yes, I'm starving. I hope they have something good in there."

"Well, let's take a look and see." He sat down beside her on the blue sofa and opened the menu, holding it where they could both read it.

"I think I'll have a turkey sandwich and chips," Abby said and leaned back against the sofa. "That will be fairly light. I don't want to eat something heavy and then go to bed on a really full stomach."

"Yeah, I agree. I think I'll order a club sandwich." He laid the menu on the dresser and reached for the phone. "Do you want milk or a soda?"

"Milk, please. If I drink a soda I'll be up all night." She sighed.

Nick dialed the room service number listed on a small card sitting next to the phone and ordered their supper. "She said it would be about twenty minutes. I think I'll go take a quick shower."

"I'm going to take one, too, and then call my parents to let them know where we are."

After Nick went to his room, Abby slipped out of her sweatpants. She covered her injured knee with a piece of plastic bag and the tape Nick gave her to keep it dry while she showered. The warm water felt so good. She didn't know when she'd been so tired. She washed her hair, then stepped out onto the small rug. After drying with the large, fluffy towel, she removed the tape and plastic bag from her knee and threw it in the trash. When she was finished, she dressed in a pair of green sweats and went out to call her parents.

Nick knocked on the door just as she hung up the phone. She opened it, and a young man followed Nick in with their orders and placed them on the table. He thanked Nick for the tip and left.

They sat down at the table, and Nick said a blessing. Abby opened the lids, handed Nick his plate, and placed a napkin in her lap.

"I just talked with Maggie, and Scotty is doing great. I sure miss the little guy. Did you get a chance to call your folks?" Nick asked.

"Yes, they were relieved to hear from me and know we're okay." She took a bite of her sandwich, chewed it, and swallowed. "Amanda and her friend Josh arrived safely last night. I'm so thankful to know they're all right. They haven't heard any more from Lauren and Casey."

"I'm sorry. I know you're disappointed. I'm glad Amanda and her friend made it okay, and I'll be glad when we get there, as well. Anything can happen in this kind of weather. It isn't safe to be traveling in it."

They finished their meal, and Nick helped Abby clean up the trash.

"Let's change the bandage on your knee before I go to my room." Nick sat in a chair and opened his medical bag. Abby pulled the leg of her sweats up enough that he could remove the tape and gauze. She closed her eyes and braced herself, expecting the gauze to stick to the wound and pull the top off. When she didn't feel any pain, she opened her eyes, surprised to see the bandages already in the trash. Whatever Nick had used on her knee hadn't stuck to the bandage. Relieved, she leaned back and relaxed while he put on a new one. He smelled so good. Being here with him stirred her senses. His strong hands were gentle as he worked on her knee. The touch of his fingers on her skin sent a tingle of awareness up her spine.

"It looks pretty good—no sign of infection," Nick said, jolting her from her thoughts as he put his supplies back into his bag and closed the top.

She was thankful for the interruption. What was she doing? She couldn't allow herself to think like that.

"I called the desk and requested a wake-up call for five o'clock. That should give us plenty of time to get ready to leave and still make it to Granny's in time for you to hang the ornaments." He cupped her chin in his hand and placed a kiss on her cheek. "Good night. I'll see you in the morning," he said and left, locking her door behind him.

Abby lay awake for a long time, thinking and praying. She knew there was a reason the Lord had brought her and Nick together. Was it in His plan for them to have a future? Could she put what happened with Janine in the past and give Nick another chance? She had been so jealous of Janine, but the thought of her dying so young disturbed Abby. She'd never wanted anything like that to happen. She couldn't help but feel bad. It had to have been hard for Janine to know she was dying and that she would have to leave her baby to be raised by someone else.

Abby's heart ached at the thought of what she must have gone through. Nick would be a good father to Scotty, but a child also needed a mother. She sat up in the bed. Was this the Lord's plan? The reason He had brought them together? Did He want her and Nick to raise Scotty?

∞

The next morning Nick knocked on Abby's door at five thirty. When she opened it, he handed her a cup of hot chocolate and a doughnut. "I thought this would tide us over until we get home."

"Thank you. I appreciate it." She smiled as he sat down across from her.

They quickly finished their breakfast and grabbed their luggage just as someone knocked on the door. Nick went to answer it. When he opened the door, the hotel manager was standing there.

"Dr. Creighton, I'm sorry to bother you, but there has been an accident. One of our guests just fell down the stairs. I called 911, but they said it will be a while before they can get here."

Nick grabbed his bag and followed the man down the hall, with Abby close behind them. At the bottom of the staircase a man sat on the floor beside a young woman whose leg lay at an odd angle. They both appeared to be in their mid twenties. Even to Abby, who'd never had any medical training, it was obvious the woman's leg was broken.

Nick stooped down next to her. "This is Abby, and I'm Dr. Creighton. Looks like you took a pretty good fall."

She looked up at him. "This isn't a very nice way to end our honeymoon." Tears welled in her brown eyes. "I'm sorry, Kevin."

"Honey, it was an accident; you don't have anything to be sorry for. Dr. Creighton, I didn't want to try to move her. She fell from about midway up the stairs. I'm Kevin Standridge and this is my wife, Cindy."

"That was a wise decision. It's nice to meet you both, but I wish it were under different circumstances. Let's take a look at you, Cindy. Do you hurt anywhere besides your leg?"

"I hurt all over." She looked up at him. "But I think I'm just bruised. My leg is the only thing that really hurts. I'm sure it's broken."

"I could pretty well guess it is, but let's take a closer look. I'll try to be as gentle as I can."

When Nick touched her leg, she cried out. "I know that hurts. I'm sorry. It's definitely broken in at least two places. There isn't a lot I can do here. You need to go to the hospital to be X-rayed. Kevin, I don't want to move her." Nick turned to the hotel manager and asked if he could get them a pillow and blanket. He returned with it and Kevin placed the pillow under Cindy's head while Nick covered her with the blanket.

"Hopefully that will make you a little more comfortable until the ambulance gets here." Nick smiled sympathetically.

Abby prayed for Cindy as she gasped in pain when she tried to shift into a more comfortable position on the floor. "Cindy, I know the floor isn't very comfortable, but I'd be best if you try not to move until the ambulance gets here and they can get you to the hospital for X-rays."

From the looks of Cindy's leg, Abby knew she had to be in a lot of pain. In all of her twenty-two years, Abby had been fortunate never to have had a broken bone. Therefore, she didn't know from experience, but she could imagine how badly it had to hurt.

"Oh, I feel sick." Cindy placed her hand over her mouth as if she was going to vomit.

Abby ran to the counter. "Do you have anything she can use?"

The man at the counter handed her a plastic wastebasket. Abby ran back and handed it to Cindy, then went into the restroom and wet a couple of paper towels and took them to her.

"Thank you," she said just as she lost the contents of her stomach.

Kevin took the paper towels from Abby and bathed Cindy's face, all the while crooning lovingly to her.

"There's the ambulance." Nick said as sirens sounded from a distance. He explained Cindy's injury to the paramedics when they came in the door with a gurney.

Kevin shook Nick's hand. "Thank you, Dr. Creighton. We appreciate your help, and it was nice to meet you and

Abby. I don't know how far you have to go, but it's nasty out there. We'll keep you in our prayers for a safe trip."

"I couldn't do much," Nick said. "But you'll be in our prayers, as well. Cindy, I wish you the best."

"Thank you," Cindy said as the paramedics wheeled her out the door with Kevin following.

Chapter 8

W ell, we've had a pretty exciting morning. I sure hope Cindy will be all right." Abby picked up her purse and overnight bag from the floor next to the stairway.

"It will take some time but I think she'll be okay. I hope her leg won't require surgery. I didn't feel any obvious splinters in the bone, but you never know for sure until you see the X-rays."

He was a good doctor. Abby was touched by his kind and caring attitude. "I'll keep them in my prayers. I'm glad she gave me her card with her e-mail address. I gave her mine, and she said she'd send me a note to let us know how she's doing. I feel for them. Cindy said they'd only been married a week. Fortunately, she said their honeymoon was over and they were leaving to go home. It would have been really awful if she had fallen on their first day." Abby glanced down at Cindy's business card. "Wow, it says on her card she's a Christian romance author. They aren't very far from

Pierce City. They live in Springfield. What a story for a new book, huh?" She giggled as they went out the door and headed for the parking lot.

❦

Nick chuckled. "Another author to add to your collection." He knew how she loved to read Christian romance. When they were together, she must have had more than a hundred books in her collection.

"Do you still have all of your books?" he asked as they climbed into the Blazer and closed the doors.

"Yes, I still have them, and I've added a few since I saw you last." She grinned and reached to fasten her seat belt. "I still collect my favorite authors. I went to the Christian section at the bookstore and bought their new ones before I left so I could bring them with me."

"You've read those same authors for a long time. I remember seeing their books on your shelves." Nick glanced over at her.

"Yes, I still have every book they've written in my bookcase at my apartment."

"Books and dolls—you always did love them." Nick smiled at her. "It's nice to have hobbies you enjoy."

❦

Abby smiled to herself. Nick had always been tolerant of her love of books and dolls. Actually, he had always wanted her to have anything that made her happy. She knew that wasn't always true in every relationship. She had friends who weren't so fortunate.

She had spent a long time in prayer last night before she went to sleep, asking the Lord to please help her to make the right decision about Nick, and she believed He'd given her an answer. He helped her to realize that Nick was everything she had ever wanted in a husband. She couldn't ask for a more dedicated Christian man; plus he shared her beliefs. After much soul searching, she decided she'd put her trust in Nick one more time.

"You're awfully quiet this morning. Are you okay?" Nick asked softly.

"Yes, I'm fine. I've just been thinking. I spent some time in prayer last night, and I've made some decisions." She looked at him, and tears filled her eyes. She blinked, and they spilled over, making a path to her chin. She wiped them away with the back of her hand. "I love you, Nick."

He pulled the car over to the side of the road and parked. As he turned, he drew her into his arms. "I love you, too, Abby, with every part of me. You are my life. I haven't been whole since the night we parted. If you can find it in your heart to forgive me and give me another chance, I promise I won't ever hurt you again."

"Through long hours of prayer as I lay awake last night and with the Lord's help, I came to the realization that under the circumstances with Janine, you made the only choice you could have made."

∽

Nick's heart sang with happiness. He'd waited so long

for this day. *Thank You, Lord*, he breathed silently as he kissed Abby, holding her close. He cupped her chin, gently lifting it where he could see her face. "I love you so much, Abby. I want to spend the rest of my life with you, doing everything I possibly can to make you happy. Would you be willing to move back to Pierce City? Will you marry me, be my wife, and be a mother to Scotty?"

His chest tightened as he waited anxiously for her to answer.

"Yes, I'll move back to Pierce City. I haven't truly been happy since I left. Just being with you will make me happy." She ran her fingers through his hair. "And yes, I'll marry you. I look forward to being your wife, and I'll do my best to be a good mother to Scotty."

He breathed a sigh of relief and gently squeezed her hand. "I have your ring in my safe at the house. We can go by and get it on the way to Granny's." He looked directly into her eyes for a moment. "Now I'd like to know why you won't play your guitar anymore."

She looked away. "Because it brought to mind too many hurtful memories. You loved to hear me play, and every time I picked up my guitar, I saw your face. The way you used to close your eyes and listen so intently when I'd play and sing—it broke my heart, so I put the guitar in Granny's bedroom closet and closed the door. It's still there."

"Abby, I'm so sorry." He placed a finger under her chin and turned her head toward him. "Will you play it again for me?"

She looked at him for a moment and then nodded.

"One more thing before we drive into town. You need to prepare yourself for what you're going to see. I know you saw all the coverage on the damage Pierce City suffered from the tornado. But watching it on television and seeing it in person is a totally different thing. The whole downtown was devastated. There wasn't much left standing. They're rebuilding, but it doesn't look anywhere near the same as it did when you left." Nick kissed her once more before he started the car and pulled back onto the highway.

⤶

They drove into Pierce City about an hour later. "Oh, Nick!" Abby cried, placing her hand over her mouth in shock. "I can't believe this. You weren't kidding when you said the tornado didn't leave much. It did so much damage." The devastation was incredible. Sadness washed over her. A few of the original buildings still standing had been repaired, but most of them were gone. She remembered the last Happy Neighbor Days gathering she had been to. She could close her eyes and picture it as it had been.

"It breaks my heart. Almost all of those quaint old buildings are gone now. But we're very fortunate there weren't more killed or injured, and that's the most important thing. The Lord really protected our families. Fortunately, they live three miles out in the country. They're far enough away from town that they weren't affected by the tornado, and for that I'm very thankful."

"I know, sweetheart." Nick sighed. "I am, too, and as you can see, they're rebuilding the downtown area. It won't be long now. They're almost finished. The businesses will soon be back up and functioning again. It will never be quite the same, but as close as they can make it. The love and closeness of the people in this town can never be destroyed, and that's what matters."

Abby smiled sadly as they drove the rest of the way through town on their way to Nick's house. So many memories flashed through her mind. She had grown up in this quaint little town.

"You're right, and I'm thankful to see they're almost done. I love this town and all of the people in it. I always have. It will always be my home."

Nick stopped in front of a set of gates and unlocked the chain holding them closed, then slid the gate open and got back into the Blazer. A few minutes later, he parked in front of a large Victorian-style house. She loved it. It was exactly what she would have built. It stood two stories tall with a wide front porch, and it was surrounded by trees. A large red barn almost as big as the house sat back and to the right side of the property. It was quite an impressive place. Since they were short on time Abby waited in the car while Nick went in to get her ring. But she intended to have a full tour of it when they had more time. Excitement at the thought of living in this beautiful place with Nick made her giddy. She wanted to get out and do a little dance around the yard. She refrained herself but just barely. Wouldn't that be a sight? She laughed.

Nick placed some Christmas packages in the trunk and then slid in beside her a few minutes later and started the car. As they drove back down the long driveway, Abby glanced behind her.

"I love your house. I can't wait to see the inside." She turned back around and refastened her seat belt. "It's so beautiful out here with all of these trees. I'll bet it's gorgeous in the springtime when all of their branches are filled with lush green leaves."

"It's our house, and it is beautiful in the spring. That's one of the reasons I built out here in the country. It was with you in mind. I prayed every night that one day soon you'd share it with me." Nick glanced over at her, a smile creasing his handsome face. He stopped to lock the gate and then headed toward Pierce City so the girls could have their traditional breakfast with Granny and hang the ornaments.

They drove up the long driveway, and just as they pulled up in front of Granny Forrester's house, Abby's cell phone rang.

Abby slid her phone out of the case and answered. "Hello?"

"Hi, Abby, this is Sandy. Remember me? We met in the women's restroom at the Denver airport."

"Sandy, I'm so glad to hear from you. How are you?"

"I'm just fine. I've moved in with my grandmother now, and she is going to help me with the baby. I wanted to call and tell you that I read the scriptures you gave me. Between reading them and talking to my grandmother, I've asked Jesus to come into my heart."

"Sandy that's wonderful. I'm so thrilled."

"I just want to thank you for caring enough to take the time for a lonely, devastated girl you didn't even know. You are a special person, Abby. Because of you, I have found Jesus and He has changed my life. Have a very nice Christmas, and I'll be in touch again soon."

"That's great, Sandy. I'm so happy for you. You have a Merry Christmas, too. I'll keep you in my prayers and look forward to hearing from you again." Abby hung up the phone and shared their conversation with Nick.

"That's fantastic, sweetheart. You just never know where the Lord is going to give you an opportunity to witness for Him. We need to always be ready for any opportunity He lays before us. A few short minutes in that airport bathroom and you helped lead a lost soul to Jesus." He smiled and wrapped his arm around Abby's shoulders as they walked up the steps that led to the wide front porch. Before they went in the door, Nick drew Abby into his arms and kissed her. "Can we sit on the swing for a minute before we go inside?" Nick asked.

"Sure." Abby walked across the porch with him, and they sat on the swing. Nick reached for her hand and slipped the engagement ring onto her left-hand ring finger. "Now it's back where it belongs." He smiled and kissed her forehead.

"I'd like for you to open this gift before you go in. The others I put in the trunk. I'll give them to you tonight when we have the traditional gathering around the tree." Nick handed her a small, brightly wrapped package.

Abby tore the paper and opened the box. "Oh, Nick!" she cried softly. "It's perfect. I love it." She grinned and lifted the Christmas ornament from the bed of cotton. "A wooden guitar. It looks exactly like mine." It had "Branson" with a date painted on the front. She looked up at him, confused. "Why does it have last year's date instead of this year?"

He smiled. "I bought it last year, along with the others. We were separated shortly afterward, and I never had a chance to give them to you. I kept them, praying I'd have another chance. I'm glad you like the ornament. I wanted you to have it to hang on the tree this morning."

"Thank you, Nick. I'll cherish it, and it will always be a special reminder of just how blessed we are to have another chance to be together."

Nick drew her to him again and kissed her. She loved the secure feeling of being held in his strong arms.

As they sat in the quiet, country atmosphere on her grandmother's porch, Abby realized that the Lord had brought her and Nick back together to raise a beautiful little boy and that He had gotten them home safely in time to spend Christmas with her family. He used the situation for her to witness to a devastated young girl, bringing Sandy into the family of God. The Lord certainly worked something good out of their suffering. Romans 8:28 came to mind: *"We know that all things work together for good to them that love God, to them who are the called according to his purpose.*" Sitting there in Nick's arms, Abby prayed silently, thanking and praising the Lord for all of their blessings. She had made a Christmas wish, asking God to provide a way for her to be home for Christmas. Not only had He granted that request, but He had reunited her with Nick, her true love, her soul mate.

JEANIE SMITH CASH

Jeanie lives in the country in Southwest Missouri, in the heart of the Ozarks, with her husband, Andy. They were blessed with two children, a son-in-law, and three grandchildren. When she's not writing, Jeanie loves to spend time with her family, spoil her grandchildren, read, collect dolls, crochet, and travel. Jeanie is a member of American Christian Fiction Writers. She loves to read Christian romance and believes a salvation message inside of a good story could possibly touch someone who wouldn't be reached in any other way.

Home for the Holidays

by Christine Lynxwiler

Dedication

This book is dedicated to my husband Kevin, who was first my best friend, then the love of my life. It's been a wonderful 25 years, honey. Here's hoping for many, many more together. Thank you for being the most supportive, encouraging hero a girl could ever have!

Special thanks to my sister and crit partner Jan Reynolds who read every word of this story umpteen times. Thanks also to Candice Speare and Rachel Hauck for great crits! And a great big thanks to my nephew Jeff and niece-in-law Lauren for letting me use your names. Y'all have something special. Praying many happy years ahead of you.

Chapter 1

S ure, Mrs. Whitfield. I'll be there in ten minutes."
Lauren Forrester flipped her cell phone closed
and slid it into her pocket. She turned her key
in the lock of the Pierce City Library door and headed
across the brightly lit parking lot to her car. Why was
solving other people's problems so much easier than
solving her own? The older woman, a regular at the
library, depended on Lauren to take her to get groceries on Friday nights. Lauren didn't mind. At least
she wasn't home moping. Or mopping, which was her
other choice these days. Her apartment had never been
cleaner.

Her best friend, Jeff, had been bugging her to tell
him what was wrong, but she couldn't put a label on
it. Restlessness? That wasn't really right. She had her
suspicions, but even in the dark of her own bedroom
when she poured out her heart to God, she wasn't ready
to face the truth yet.

Before she could delve deeper into her apparently

semi-warped psyche, she arrived at Mrs. Whitfield's little tin-roof house on the outskirts of town. Lauren quickly pulled out her tangerine-scented lotion and slathered it on her hands as she waited for the woman to come out. The lotion was her insurance against the elderly woman's hit-and-miss bath routine. Lauren could absently adjust her wire-rimmed glasses for a whiff of fresh tangerine if the odor was too bad.

A few minutes and several citrus inhalations later, Lauren dropped her passenger off in front of Town and Country. "Want me to come in with you?"

"No thank you, dear. When I get too old to buy my own groceries, they need to put me in a home. But that day's not here yet." Same answer every week.

Lauren smiled. "I'll be watching for you to come out."

She waited while the gray-haired woman shuffled through the automatic doors, then circled the lot to get a spot under a guard light so she could read her book. When she looked up from her story, the clock on the dash read nine o'clock. The library had stayed open until eight for a special Egyptian exhibit. Her friend and coworker, Becky, had a family to go home to, so Lauren had volunteered to work late.

The older woman should be done in a few minutes. And then what? Friday night and nothing to do except go home to her one-bedroom apartment over her parents' detached garage and clean the bathroom again. Lauren loved the small-town life, but she almost wished for the big city, a place where the sidewalks didn't roll up at nine.

The loud ring of her cell phone startled her out of her reverie. "Hello?"

"Hey, Laur. Meet me at the swings?"

"Jeff? What are you doing home this early on a Friday night?"

She'd known Jeffrey Warren so long she could almost hear the shrug.

"It didn't go so hot with Tina."

Big surprise. Why should Tina be any different than Jennifer or Mandy? Or any other girl in their singles group? "Give me half an hour."

"Half an hour? Since when does it take you more than five minutes to run down the stairs and across the field to the swings?"

She could feel a smug smile cross her lips. "For your information, I'm not home."

"Oh, that's right—the exhibit ran you late. You must be waiting for Mrs. W to get groceries."

The smile disappeared. How predictable could she get? "Yeah."

"You're too nice, Lauren."

"She needs me."

"Isn't there a service that would get her groceries for her?"

"We've been through this, Jeff. It's not the same thing. She feels independent this way."

He mumbled something she didn't catch. Sounded like "taking advantage," but she wasn't sure.

"I help her because I want to."

"I know. I hope none of your underdogs ever turns

on you. See you after a while."

"See ya." She disconnected and jumped out to help Mrs. Whitfield with her groceries.

Twenty minutes later, Lauren hurried across the moonlit backyard, running her fingers through her shoulder-length hair. At times like this, her exasperating natural curls came in handy. Not that Jeff would notice if she spiked her dark brown hair and dyed it green. They didn't worry about looks with each other. Considering the old Show-Me-State sweatshirt and ragged jeans she'd hurriedly thrown on, it was a good thing.

When she neared the border of her parents' property, she stopped. The moon hung high, silhouetting the old swing set. How many times had they met there over the years? No one really knew where the swing set had come from. Maybe it had been there when Jeff's grandparents had bought the small white house on two acres. Or it could have been his mother's and his uncle's when they were young. Either way, it was Jeff and Lauren's now. Had been since they were ten.

Jeff, his broad shoulders framed in the moonlight, gave her a sheepish grin and rubbed his dark curls. "Hey."

He'd certainly changed since the first day she saw him. At ten years old, his deep blue eyes had seemed to fill his thin face when he told her that his grandparents had just adopted him. Later that night, she'd overheard her parents saying that Jeff's mother had overdosed and died. Hiding there on the stairs, Lauren had determined then not to let anything else bad happen to her new friend if she could help it.

"Hey, yourself. What happened with Tina?"

"I can't seem to get the whole dating thing right."

Lauren sank into a swing, sliding her grip down the coolness of the chains. "Then she's not the girl for you."

Jeff folded his muscular frame into the plastic swing and began pushing it back and forth with his foot. "Maybe it's just me, but tonight she chattered the whole time about her bridesmaid's dress for her sister's wedding. I also know what her sister's dress looks like, and I don't even *know* her sister. It was worse than that time you dragged me to the mall to help pick out a birthday present for your mom." He looped his elbow around the chain and waved his hand in the air as if brandishing an imaginary scarf. "But do you think this orange will clash with her hair?" His falsetto rang through the night stillness in sharp contrast to his normal deep voice.

Lauren snorted. "Dragged you to the mall, my foot. You had a coupon for free curly fries. And for your information, Mama's hair is auburn and that scarf was red."

He held up his hand. "You're not going to tell me about your mama's new dress, are you?"

She laughed. "You knew Tina talked a lot before you asked her out. Face it. You like the challenge of making a girl like you, but after that it's over for you. Look at how you are about Krista. You can't stand it that she's engaged. But if she weren't, you'd find something wrong with her." Every time they had the "there's nobody in the singles group for me" conversation, he'd bring up

Krista as the example of someone who could have been the right one *if* she hadn't already been taken when she moved to Pierce City and joined their church singles group.

"Ouch. You know how to make a guy sound shallow, don't you?" He glanced over at her.

"Nah." She shook her head. "I know you're ready to settle down."

"But not with just anybody. It has to be the right girl."

The right girl. It didn't take a therapist to recognize that Jeff's strong desire to have a home and children was partly a result of living his first ten years with a self-absorbed drug addict who couldn't provide even his basic needs most of the time. "Let's see. Good with kids." She counted the words off on her fingers. "A sense of humor. Intelligent. Oh yeah, and don't forget blond, right? See? I know all your requirements—I should. I've heard them often enough." Did he know what *she* was looking for in a mate? For that matter, did she? Her heart seemed to have a mind of its own these days.

Back to the problem at hand. Time for a future-mate identity crisis later. "Jeff, there's someone out there for you. You just haven't found her yet." She couldn't think of one who could live up to his standards, but God must have someone special for a guy as great as Jeff. "Quit trying so hard. You've already broken the heart of every girl in Pierce City and all the neighboring towns. Pretty soon you'll have to go to Springfield or St. Louis to find someone."

"Can you see me with a city girl? I can imagine what would happen the first time I ordered frog legs."

"News flash. Even most small-town girls think frog legs are gross, Jeff." She grinned. Leave it to him to bring it down to food. "Besides, all you have to do is show your dimples, and she'll forget about supper."

His laughing denial barely registered as she thought about her own words. How true they were. Maybe if relationships with the opposite sex hadn't come so easy to the ruggedly handsome contractor, he wouldn't be so picky. Even as choosy as he was, though, eventually he'd find that one special girl. And where would that leave his faithful sidekick and best friend since fourth grade? Taking Mrs. Whitfield to get groceries every Friday night? Or accepting a pity invitation from Jeff and his new wife for dinner once a week? A pang shot through her heart as the scene played out in her mind's eye.

She could imagine Jeff, his arm draped affectionately around a gorgeous blond, a delicious secret sparkling in their eyes. "Say hello to Aunt Lauren," Jeff would say and pat his wife's little round tummy. Lauren would smile and congratulate them, then spend the rest of the night watching Jeff treat the mother-to-be as if she were a precious piece of fragile crystal.

Lauren pushed off hard with her tennis shoe and clutched the chains as the swing soared up into the darkness. The cool wind rushed past her face, whispering secrets in her ears. For a minute, she allowed herself a glimpse of a different future. When she came back down to earth, she looked over at her best friend gliding lazily in the swing beside her. After years of being satisfied with friendship, why had her heart betrayed her now?

∽∾∾⌒

Jeff Warren had planned at least to be engaged by now. His twenty-fifth birthday had just passed, his carpentry business was going well, and his personal building project was almost done. He'd worked on it every spare minute for the last four years. Since Lauren had been back in town, she'd helped him on Saturdays, and the little details were coming together.

He wasn't unhappy living in his grandparents' small frame house. It was empty anyway since Grandma and Grandpa retired to Florida, and they were glad to have him around to take care of things. But this place. He looked across the front yard at the sparkle of the rolling river. This place was different. This was his dream house.

His future home. And someday, soon hopefully, when he finally found the woman "God had in mind for him," as Lauren always put it, it would be their home. He hammered the last board of the porch railing in place, then leaned against it. A crisp breeze off the water tickled his face. But the tall chain link fence around the property ensured that a small child wouldn't wander too far. The world was a dangerous place for a kid with no protection.

He closed his eyes and listened. A cricket chirped a greeting to a friend across the grass, and the tree frogs forecast an evening shower. In the distance the garrumphing croak of a bullfrog made him smile. Wouldn't it be wonderful to go to sleep listening to that as a child? A far cry from the roaring bus engines and screaming neighbors, or worse, his own mother's voice screeching at her latest druggie boyfriend.

He'd finally found peace.

The national anthem jarred him from his reverie. He snatched his cell from his belt and looked at the caller ID. "Hi, Laur, what's up?"

"I thought you'd be here by now."

He paused. Be where? Suddenly he remembered. The singles group was meeting at the Taco Palace in Monett. He hit his forehead with the palm of his hand. He was supposed to pick Lauren up. When he'd finished his current job early, he'd only intended to spend a couple of hours working on his new house, but time had gotten away from him. "How about we meet there?"

Silence.

"Is that okay?"

"Oh. Okay. Sure."

"Listen, I'm running a little late and don't want you to have to wait."

"That's fine." She was using her bright smiley voice—like she did when she was hurt but trying not to show it. "I'll see you there."

What was her problem? "Lauren, wait—" He shook his head. Too late. She'd already broken the connection.

When he pulled into the Taco Palace parking lot, he looked at his watch. If Lauren had waited for him, she'd have been fifteen minutes late. Still, he felt a twinge of guilt. They'd made a pact to go to these things together because both of them were uncomfortable with the whole singles scene. Even though it was a church group, they felt less vulnerable together than alone.

Their friendship had been based on that foundation since they'd met. She'd helped him catch up in school, making up for time lost by being dragged from one seedy neighborhood to another, and in a small way, he'd returned the favor by protecting her from taunts of "brainiac" and "four eyes."

He spotted Lauren's bright red sweater immediately across the crowded restaurant. She always wore red when she was nervous. Said it gave her instant confidence. Guilt hit him again. Had she been wearing it before he'd stood her up?

Brad Lawton stood at the head of the table, and from his exaggerated hand motions, his story was a whopper. Everyone laughed.

Jeff walked up behind the medium-built blond man and clapped a hand on his shoulder. "Telling another fish story, Lawton?"

Brad grinned. "Had to do something to keep these women entertained. Thought you weren't going to make it." He and Jeff were two of the four men in the female-dominated group. Roger and Matt, the other two, were notoriously shy and barely responded when spoken to.

Choruses of "Hi, Jeff" came from around the table. He tried to catch Lauren's eyes to flash a silent apology, but she was talking to a couple of other girls.

"Hi." He started to take the empty seat next to her, but Brad slid into it before he did. The only other empty seat was between Tina and Krista, who was engaged to some guy in Indiana. He walked around and sat down. At least this would force Lauren to get over her mad spell. Seated straight across from him, she couldn't avoid his gaze all night.

"So, Jeff, Krista was just telling us that she and Ron broke off their engagement." Lauren smiled directly at him.

He floundered for words and looked at the gorgeous blond on his right. "Really?"

Lauren kicked him under the table as if to say, "Now's your chance. Don't blow it." Or knowing her, it could mean "Close your mouth. You look like a fish."

"Are you making it okay?" He looked at Krista, taken aback by her perfect beauty all over again.

She nodded. "I truly believe it's God's will. Things weren't working out with Ron, so He must have something better planned for both of us."

Her voice even sounded spiritual, innocent and childlike.

"Well, it's good that you found out now, I guess."

Krista smiled at him as if he'd said something brilliant. "Yes, I think so, too. But for a while I'm going to have to work to keep my mind off of it."

Jeff had some ideas about that. But asking someone out in a group setting just wasn't done. Maybe he could catch her afterward. He winked at Lauren across the table. She looked startled, then excused herself from the table. He hoped nothing was wrong with his best friend on this wonderful night. He'd have to tell her later that she'd hit the nail on the head with her prediction. The right girl had come along at just the right time.

Chapter 2

WANTED—CHILDREN'S LIBRARIAN:
The St. Louis Public Library system seeks an ener-
getic, upbeat individual who has experience working
with children. Picture yourself as part of our dream
team, where imagination, creativity, and knowledge
are rewarded. The only requirements are flexibility,
the ability to have fun, and an accredited MLIS.

When a girl unexpectedly falls in love with her best friend and he doesn't have a clue, distance is essential. Lauren double-checked her e-mail attachment, sent up a quick prayer, and hit SEND. The perfect job. Dealing with children, which she'd always loved. And most important, far away in the big city. Her résumé was on its way, and the rest, as her granny always said, was in the hands of the Lord.

She'd warned her parents and Granny of her intentions and asked them to pray, then tried to put the job application out of her mind. When the St. Louis

Library called and set up a phone interview a few days later, she was stunned. The head librarian set her at ease immediately and seemed impressed with Lauren's answers to her questions. She called back to offer Lauren the job without even having her come to St. Louis to interview in person, and Lauren felt like her whole world tilted on its axis. Could she really do it?

Becky would miss her, but Lauren knew the busy mom needed more hours. She could move up to full-time now. They'd easily find someone part-time to fill Becky's old job. Obviously, God even thought she should get out of town.

Lauren's hand trembled as she dialed Jeff's cell number.

"Jeff Warren here." She knew by his impersonal greeting that he'd been too busy to look at the caller ID.

"Hi. It's me." She suddenly felt shy, which was ridiculous. This was Jeff, the boy who'd shared every detail of his life with her for umpteen years.

"Lauren, what's up?" His deep voice covered her like a warm blanket, giving her strength and comfort.

"Want to meet tonight and get a bite to eat?"

"Sure, I'd love to. Any special reason?"

"I've got some news." Keeping her tone neutral was easy because she had such mixed feelings.

"How about we make it lunch instead of supper? I'm not sure I want to wait to hear something that important."

Lauren looked at the clock. Thirty minutes until lunch. "I can do that."

"Good. I'll pick you up at twelve and we'll run down to Thompson's for a burger."

"You don't have to—"

"See you then."

He hung up before she could tell him she'd meet him there. She wondered if he noticed that she'd been avoiding being alone with him for the last few weeks. Ever since that night at the Taco Palace when Krista had announced she'd broken her engagement, Lauren had steered clear of personal conversation with Jeff. She'd seen him and Krista out together once, but they hadn't seen her.

As she thought of how she'd gone home and watched every old sad movie she owned that night, she knew the truth. If she stayed here, she'd ruin what was left of her and Jeff's friendship with her crazy infatuation. If she moved, she'd quickly forget those feelings and they could stay friends. *St. Louis, here I come. Now I just have to explain it to Jeff without him figuring out the truth.*

Half an hour later, she climbed into his shiny black pickup and smiled. In his red flannel shirt with the rolled-up sleeves revealing the cuffs of a thermal undershirt, he looked like he'd stepped off the pages of a men's catalog. "Hey."

"Hey, yourself. What's the mysterious news you couldn't tell me over the phone?"

She'd always loved Jeff's propensity to go straight to the point, but today she'd hoped for some time to get herself together. "Not mysterious really. You know how

191

much I love working with children?"

He nodded but kept his eyes on the road.

"I've taken a children's librarian job in St. Louis."

He stomped on the brakes, and the truck squealed to a stop on the shoulder of the highway.

"Jeff! What are you doing?"

He looked at her. "What are *you* doing?"

A nervous giggle bubbled in her throat. "I'm moving to St. Louis."

"Why?"

How had she allowed herself to hope that question wouldn't come up? Her mouth suddenly felt so dry she couldn't speak. "It's a wonderful opportunity, Jeff."

His dark blue eyes seemed to be reading her most secret thoughts. She held his gaze, willing herself not to give anything away.

Finally, he looked back at the road. "I thought this was home to you."

She thought for a minute about the land she'd grown up on. Her grandparents had deeded twenty acres adjoining their farm to each of their four sons when they married. Lauren had grown up in the country, running and playing, skipping rocks, and flying kites with her cousins and then later with Jeff. "It is home. Always will be." A lump rose in her throat. "But trust me, Jeff. This move is what I need." She felt him looking at her again, and she forced herself to meet his eyes. "Okay?"

He stared at her, then grinned and pulled back onto the road. Was it her imagination, or did his smile look strained? "Okay. But I might as well buy stock in the oil companies. Think of how much gas I'll burn every time I need to talk to you in person."

"I'll be home for Christmas and a few days after. I made sure they'd give me a week off before I took the job. Besides, you won't need to talk to me as much since you're going out with Krista. How's that going, by the way?" She silently congratulated herself on both the smooth subject change and the casual tone.

"You'd know if you hadn't been so busy these last few weeks."

Ouch. So he had noticed she'd been avoiding him.

"I guess you had this secret in the works, so you didn't want to talk to me." He pulled into Thompson's packed parking lot and killed the engine. The hurt in his voice was as evident as it had been in ninth grade when she hadn't told him about her crush on Ricky Gray. When Jeff heard that Ricky was bragging he'd kissed Lauren, he'd been on his way to teach Ricky a lesson about lying when Lauren had intercepted him and admitted it was true. Of course, finding out Ricky was the type to kiss and tell had stopped that infatuation in its tracks. And Lauren had never really kept a secret from Jeff since then. Until now.

"I'm sorry. I was afraid you'd talk me out of it."

"I would have given it my best shot; I guarantee you that." He opened the door and looked over at her. "But if this is what you really want, I'll help you any way I can. It's the least I can do, as much as you've helped me."

She hated it when he acted like their friendship was one-sided because of where he'd come from. How many times had she told him that he'd given her as much as she'd given him? She opened her mouth to protest one more time, but before she could speak, he jumped out.

"Now, let's go get something to eat. Getting fired for being late back from lunch might make that big city library reconsider hiring you."

She climbed out of the truck and walked beside him to the door. Now that she faced the reality of being so far away from him, she almost wished the library *would* reconsider.

∽∾

"What should I do with this, Jeffie?"

Did Krista try to sound like a little girl, or had her voice just never matured? Jeff cringed at the irritation surging through him. Lauren was right. He must be bound and determined to find something wrong with any girl he was dating. *Not this time, Laur. If you weren't moving halfway across the state, you could watch and see.* He shifted the stereo box he was carrying so he could see Krista, who was holding a mixer out away from her as if it were a dead cat. "Um, my guess would be in the box of kitchen stuff." He forced a smile.

"Oh. I guess that makes sense." She disappeared back into the den, but not for long he was sure. Krista, along with the rest of the singles, had come over to help Lauren pack things and load the truck and

194

U-Haul trailer. But she was the only one who called him "Jeffie" and the only one who seemed to require his help with every item she picked up. He stomped out to place the stereo in the trailer. Sometimes he needed distance from his perfect girl.

The work went fast with everyone helping, and it wasn't long before he and Lauren stood in the doorway of her empty apartment and waved good-bye to the singles group. She'd said her good-byes to her family that morning, and her dad had taken her mom and her granny for a day trip to Branson. They'd all agreed it would be easier that way. Jeff had assured them that he would make sure Lauren got settled in her St. Louis apartment safely. He'd even loaded her car on a tow dolly behind the moving trailer so she could ride with him in his truck.

"Well, *Jeffie*," Lauren said with a wry grin, "are you ready to hit the road?"

He raised an eyebrow. Two could play the hated nickname game. "Sure am, Mutt. How about you?" Everyone in town had called them Mutt and Jeff until Lauren had hit her teenage years and had developed an aversion to being called Mutt. He dodged as she swatted at him. "Can't believe you're splitting up the team."

She spun around and walked through the tiny apartment. "It looks like we've got everything," she called back to him. "I'll be ready in a minute."

He heard the bathroom door close, and in a few minutes she came out, drying her face on a paper towel. "You okay?"

"Oh yeah, just grimy from all that packing. Thought I'd wash up." She wadded the paper towel into a ball with her clenched fist and brushed past him.

Right. Without a speck of makeup and her hair pulled up in a high ponytail, she looked about sixteen. And if he wasn't mistaken, she'd been crying. He was surprised by a sudden urge to keep her close and protect her. Instinctively he pulled up the mental boundary he kept between them.

Lauren had no idea, but in high school he'd come close to falling for her. His grandpa had realized it somehow. He'd taken Jeff aside for a man-to-man talk and explained the concept of "us" and "them." Sure, he'd said, the Forresters were good folk and friendly. But Jeff's grandpa would always be a hired hand to them. And Jeff would always be a drug addict's son and a hired hand's grandson.

Jeff argued that Lauren wasn't like that, but his grandpa had pointed out all the less fortunate people Lauren helped, even back then. Suddenly, Jeff knew that in spite of their undeniable bond, he would always be an ongoing "project" to her. And she would always be his best friend, but never more than that. Someday he'd find a woman who loved him for himself, not out of pity. He thought of Krista, blond and perfect. Who knew? Maybe he already had.

He looked across the truck cab at Lauren, so confident-looking in her bright red sweatshirt. "You scared?"

She flashed him a glance. "A little."

"Me, too."

She snorted. "Silly goose. You don't have to stay there and live. All you have to do is drive me there."

And leave you there. Even though her place in his heart was clearly defined, it was still going to be hard to make it without her. "Yeah."

She shot him a puzzled look.

"What? St. Louis is a big city. I might get us lost." He raised an eyebrow. "Truth is, Lauren, I hate to see you go."

"We'll still be friends. It'll just be different. We've grown up, and things are bound to change. One of us will end up getting married before too long. Nothing lasts forever, Jeff."

Wasn't she Miss Polly Platitude? He guided the truck and trailer through town and onto the interstate. If he didn't know better, he'd think his best friend was dumping him.

Chapter 3

D o you want to check out that book, Brian?"
Lauren asked.

"Yes, miss, if that's okay." The boy's jacket
was threadbare and his jeans stained, but his blue eyes
gleamed with subdued intelligence beneath his too-long
bangs. Lauren had been trying to gain his trust for the
past two months, but he still called her just "miss."

Lauren took the worn copy of *The Lion, the Witch,
and the Wardrobe* from his hand and stroked it lovingly.
"This is one of my favorites. Have you read it before?"

"No, ma'am."

"You'll have to let me know what you think."

"I will if I can." He pushed his dirty blond hair back
from his face.

Over the past couple of weeks, Brian had grown
more furtive and withdrawn, and for the hundredth
time Lauren wondered what burdens those small
shoulders were carrying. He showed up every day after
school, did his homework at a table in the corner, then

left right before closing time. On Saturdays, he stayed for hours. Did his parents care where he was? Did they allow him to wander the streets of the city without supervision?

"What do you mean?"

"I might have to drop it in the night box," he mumbled as she handed him the book back.

"Oh? Are you going somewhere for Christmas vacation?" It was still two weeks before the schools let out for the holidays. "Or are you moving?"

He looked up at her, as if measuring her trustworthiness. "I'm not sure." He clutched the book in his hand. "I've got to go."

Lauren looked out the window. Sheets of rain made it impossible to see the street outside. "Why don't you wait a few minutes until the rain lets up? Want me to call home for you?"

"No!" He shrugged his backpack onto the table and sank into a chair. "I'll wait. But you don't have to call."

Twenty minutes later when Lauren was about to leave, she noticed he was still sitting there staring at the rivers of water running down the window. "Brian, how far away do you live?"

He jumped at the sound of her voice. "Why?"

"I have a supersize umbrella," she said with a grin. "Big enough for both of us. I could walk you to your house." She'd been blessed to get an apartment less than a block from the library branch she worked at. Surely he didn't come from very much farther than that every day.

"No, thanks!" He grabbed his backpack and darted

out the door ahead of her, heedless of his gloves falling to the floor.

She snatched them up and popped her umbrella open. The cold rain took her breath away as she hurried outside. "Brian, wait! You're going to catch your death." She broke into a sprint. Whatever was going on with him, he had no business out in this weather.

She finally caught up with him as he slid open the side door of a battered white minivan. The rain had slacked up enough for her to see there were no seats, only blankets and pillows. Brian climbed in and spoke to the driver, a woman. As Lauren stood there on the wet sidewalk clutching his worn gloves, the van sputtered away from the curb and disappeared into traffic.

Why hadn't Brian wanted her to walk him to his vehicle? Were they living in the van? Lauren's heart squeezed at the possibilities. Then she scolded herself for being so silly. He probably thought he was too tough to be seen riding with his mom. Who knew with boys that age?

As she turned to walk the short distance to her apartment, her cell phone rang and she glanced at the caller ID. Jeff again. For that matter, who knew with boys of *any* age? She'd been ignoring most of Jeff's calls and e-mails. Probably not the most mature decision she'd ever made, but she missed him so badly that talking casually with him felt like pouring alcohol on an open wound.

Her two-bedroom apartment echoed with her footsteps as she padded from room to room, throwing together a grilled cheese sandwich and a salad, eating alone, then getting ready for bed. She picked up her cell. One missed call. Maybe she'd sleep better if she called him. Her finger poised over the keypad. She could find out how the house was coming along. How their friends were doing. How things were going with Krista. She gave the END button a vicious jab and tossed the phone on her nightstand. She could go to sleep fine without talking to him. Eventually.

The next morning Lauren wondered if she'd made the right decision. The dark circles under her eyes seemed determined to defeat her concealer. No matter how much she put on, they reappeared like magic. When Brian didn't show up in the juvenile section that afternoon, worry kept her awake again. A week later she was going through the motions, going to work, coming home. She missed Jeff more than she wanted to admit. And now she couldn't get Brian out of her mind. Why hadn't she beat on the van door when she'd seen the blankets and pillows and asked his mom if there was anything she could do to help? She wondered where he was spending his afternoons.

On Monday she had to run an errand to the reference section. There, huddled in a chair in the corner, devouring an encyclopedia article with his intelligent eyes, was Brian. He jumped when he saw her but quickly turned his attention back to the text.

"Fancy meeting you here," she drawled softly.

He looked at her as if she were speaking a foreign language, and she took that as an invitation to sit down.

Slowly. No sudden moves. "Everything okay?"

He stared at her, and for a minute she thought the dam might break and all the information he was holding back would flow forth with no restraint. But he just nodded.

She bent toward him and dropped her voice even lower. "Are you afraid I'll tell someone you live in the van?"

His eyelids opened wide. "We don't *live*"—he spat out the word, as if disgusted she could think such a thing— "in the van. We have a house." He stuck out his chin. "We own our own house."

Lauren felt heat rush to her cheeks. She'd done it again. Jumped to conclusions and embarrassed herself.

"We stay in the van some to get warm," he mumbled.

"You and your mom?"

He nodded.

"Because your house is cold?" Heating bills were high this time of year. But was gasoline cheaper?

He nodded again. "Our roof has big holes in it."

"Oh no."

"I gotta go."

"Wait, Brian." Her heart thudded. Would he run off again and never reappear this time? She prayed that God would keep that from happening as well as let her figure out the best way to help the boy and his mother. "I'm not going to tell anyone. I just want to help."

As if he read her mind, he said, "That's okay, miss. Mama says God will help us."

Lauren blinked back the tears that threatened to

overflow down her cheeks. Nothing made boys more uncomfortable than overemotional girls. Even grown-up girls. "She's right. But I have some ideas about how He might do that. Can I talk to your mom?"

"I'll ask her tonight, and if she says yes, I'll bring her with me tomorrow."

"Is she at work?"

He ducked his head and mumbled.

"I didn't hear you."

"She had to quit. It's too close to time for the baby to come."

Lauren's heart froze in her chest.

⁓

"Not coming home at all?" Jeff stared at Lauren's grandmother. "Did she say why?"

Granny shook her head. "Not really. Just that some things had come up and she wouldn't make it for Christmas."

Jeff cleared his throat, but it still felt like a golf ball was lodged there. "Did she say anything about me? I haven't been able to get in touch with her lately."

"As a matter of fact, she said to tell you Merry Christmas." The old woman patted his hand and pushed to her feet. "Oh, and she mentioned there might be someone special you wanted to invite for our Christmas Eve get-together." Her faded brown eyes twinkled. "You know any friend of yours is always welcome here, Jeff. You're part of our family."

"Thanks. That means a lot to me." He'd always been

203

at the Forresters' on Christmas Eve. But always with Lauren. He couldn't imagine coming without her.

As far as bringing someone, Krista was going home to Indiana for Christmas. With any luck, she'd work things out with her ex-fiancé. Jeff had been serving more as a counselor to her lately than anything else. She called him frequently for a man's take on what Ron was thinking. And that was fine with him. She was a nice girl, but her baby voice and constant worrying about her looks drove him over the edge.

Jeff clutched his coffee mug. He'd stopped by to check on Granny, but they both knew that he really wanted news of Lauren. And now he'd gotten it. Suddenly, the frustration of the past couple of months boiled up inside him. He clunked his mug down on the table and stood. "I'm going to St. Louis."

Granny looked up from where she was washing her own cup at the sink. "What about work?"

Odd that she hadn't asked him why he was going. "We finished up the Johnson job today, and I gave the guys their Christmas bonuses. I'd allowed a month off for the holidays until we start the next house. I had planned to work out at my place." He hugged the older woman and dropped a peck on her cheek. "But first I've got to make sure Lauren's okay."

Granny's smile wreathed her face in wrinkles. "That's my boy."

Jeff laughed aloud at the exuberance coursing through him since he decided to take action. "I'll see you Christmas Eve. And hopefully I won't be alone!"

Two hours later, he was St. Louis bound. He prayed the whole trip. Lauren was tenderhearted, but she was also stubborn. If she had some harebrained idea about proving her independence in the big city by cutting off communication with her best friend, there was no guarantee he could change her mind. But he was going to give it his best shot.

As he walked up the stairs to her apartment, his heart thudded in his chest like a teenager's on his first date. What would she say? Would she slam the door in his face?

He knocked and waited.

After a few minutes, he heard footsteps, then a muffled, "Who is it?"

"Lauren, it's Jeff."

The door cracked open, and a boy peeked around at him. "She's not home right now."

"Brian? Who's at the door?" Jeff heard a female voice ask.

"Just a minute." The boy who looked to be about nine or ten closed the door. Jeff heard the lock click.

He pounded on the door. Was someone holding Lauren hostage? What was going on?

"Jeff?"

He spun around. Lauren stood at the top of the stairs, two bags of groceries in her hands.

"Hey!" He stepped forward and took the plastic sacks. "Who are those people in your apartment?"

"What are you doing here?"

"Your granny said you weren't coming home for

Christmas, so I came to check on you."

"You drove all the way here?" Her voice was incredulous. "Why didn't you just ca—" Her face flamed. "Oh."

"Yeah," he said wryly, "I did think of that, but I seem to have some difficulty getting through."

"Jeff." Lauren slid her key into the lock. "I'm sorry. I've been really busy here."

"I see that. Are you sharing an apartment now with someone from work?"

"Not exactly. Their house has some damage to the roof. They were living in their van. . ."

Jeff shook his head, his heart pounding as the truth of what she was saying hit him. "Tell me you didn't really invite homeless people to live with you." He slammed his hand against his leg. "Have you lost your mind?" At least in Pierce City the people she insisted on helping were harmless. But in the city, con artists ate girls like Lauren for lunch.

"Could you keep your voice down?" Lauren nodded toward the door.

"Oh yeah. Wouldn't want to offend the people who are taking shameless advantage of you." Jeff couldn't stop the sarcasm. He felt his face growing hot. "You've pulled some good ones, Lauren. But this one takes the cake."

Tears sprung to her eyes, and he knew he'd gone too far. Still, the thought of people like his mother getting their claws into someone as innocent and trusting as Lauren made it impossible for him to be civil.

"I understand that you're upset, Jeff, but I think

you'd better go. Why don't you call me tomorrow?" She turned the knob and slipped into the apartment, closing the door firmly behind her. Jeff stared at the smooth white door. This wasn't how he'd envisioned their reunion.

Chapter 4

How dare he? Lauren shoved her hair out of her eyes and scrubbed at the tiny spot on the bathroom floor. He had no right to tell her what to do. She'd moved here to get away from him. She should have told him that. But then he'd have realized the truth. And that was the last thing she wanted.

Her cell phone hadn't stopped ringing since she'd closed the door on Jeff. She'd turned it on vibrate so it wouldn't disturb Connie. With the baby due in less than two weeks, Lauren's new friend wasn't getting much rest these days. She and Brian had gone to bed early. Lauren glared at the phone dancing across the bathroom counter. Did Jeff care about that? No, apparently not.

She paused mid-scrub and wiped away a tear with the back of her hand. *Lord, please help me to understand Jeff. And give me the courage to be his friend again. Even though I can't have the relationship I want to have with him, I don't want to lose him. Please.*

When she finished her prayer, she remembered

208

something her mother told her long ago. She'd been twelve and reeling from the sudden death of her beloved dog, Copper.

"Lauren," her mother had said, "you love God now and you believe in Jesus, but when you go through trials, that's when your faith becomes your own." Lauren remembered thinking that if growing faith had to hurt as badly as this, she'd be happy depending on what her mom and dad believed for the rest of her life.

But her mother had been right. The past couple of months had been empty in many respects, yet Lauren had grown closer to God. He'd kept her from giving up, from turning away from others in her despair. She was grateful.

She stood and rinsed out her scrub brush. Because of his mother's manipulative nature, Jeff had never been overly compassionate to those in need. But he'd never openly opposed Lauren's desire to help others. He'd even helped her sometimes. She knew from Granny's letters that he was taking Mrs. Whitfield to get groceries every week. Suddenly, an idea so outrageous that it had to work popped into her mind. Jeff's presence here wasn't an irritant. It was a blessing. An answered prayer, even.

The doorbell rang, and Lauren hurried to the door. She'd let him in and explain the situation to him with patience and understanding. Then she'd beg him to help. She automatically glanced through the peephole, and her hand froze on the knob. A pizza man stood in the hallway with a square cardboard box clutched in his hands.

"Can I help you?"

"Pizza delivery."

"I didn't—" Before she could finish, he interrupted.

"For Lauren Forrester courtesy of Jeff Warren. He says it's your favorite."

Pepperoni and anchovies? Oh, he knew how to break her down, didn't he? She groaned and opened the door. As the man handed her the pizza, she looked over his shoulder, half expecting Jeff to be lurking behind him, waiting to push his way in. But the hallway was empty. She didn't know if she was disappointed or relieved.

Pepperoni and anchovy pizza had been her favorite late-night snack when she was in college, but once she'd moved back to the country, she'd had to give it up. How many nights had she grumbled to Jeff that she'd love to have it again? Sneak. Trying to soften her up with food. Lucky for him she wanted to make up as much as he did.

She walked into the kitchen and plunked the steaming box down on the table. No need to let it go to waste. She grabbed a paper towel and flipped open the lid. A note in Jeff's handwriting was carefully taped inside the top flap of the box.

Dear Lauren,

I'm so sorry. It's none of my business what you do, but I want you to be safe. I promise not to discuss your guests if you will talk to me. Please.

Yours,

Jeff

She smiled. Leave it to him to cut to the heart of

the matter. She picked up her phone and punched in his number. He answered on the first ring.

"Hey," he said. "Meet me at the swings?"

"Huh?" She glanced out the window at the apartment complex playground below. Jeff, folded into a swing three sizes too small for him, lifted his hand in greeting.

"I'll be right down."

"Bring the pizza."

"I should have known you just wanted me for my food." As soon as she said it, she wished it back. The silly words sounded like banter between a couple in love.

She didn't wait for a reply. But just as she pushed END, she thought she heard him murmur, "Not hardly."

Her heart skipped a beat. What did he mean?

❦

Jeff pulled his denim jacket tightly around him and stared at the entrance to the brownstone apartment building. What was he going to say to her now that he'd coaxed her out? Before he could decide, she appeared at the door. He took the pizza box from her and set it on the picnic table. "Thanks for agreeing to see me. I'm sorry about awhile ago."

"Actually, I owe you an apology." Her voice trembled, and she looked about twelve. "For not taking your calls or being in touch. I—" She scuffed at the gravel with her toe.

"I know why you did that, Lauren." It had all become clear to him this afternoon when she'd stormed into her apartment.

She jerked her head up and stared at him, her eyes wide. "You do?"

He nodded. "Sure. I always thought I was looking out for you. But to you it must have seemed like I was treating you like a child. No wonder you were in such a hurry to move."

"No, Jeff. I didn't—it wasn't—" She grabbed the pizza box. "I can't think on an empty stomach. Let's discuss this later, okay?"

"Okay." He'd never understand women, but at least she didn't still seem to be mad at him. And he knew that was a good thing.

She sat at the picnic table and patted the seat beside her. "Actually, even though you promised not to in your very sweet note"—her eyes sparkled as she smiled up at him—"I want to talk about my houseguests."

"I'd recognize that 'Oh, Jeff. I've got a plan' look anywhere, so you go ahead." He shot her a wry grin. "I'll listen."

"Did you see Connie earlier? Or just Brian?"

"Just the boy."

"His name's Brian, and he reminds me so much of you when you were that age."

"His mama a druggie?"

She frowned. "No! Connie's a sweet Christian woman with tremendous faith."

"That's what she wants you to think, Lauren." Where had that come from? He'd been biting his lip, but the words had slipped out anyway. "Sorry. Forget I said that."

Lauren's tiny hand covered his, and the cool night

grew warmer. "I understand how you feel, Jeff. But she's just a woman like me, only she ended up in a bad situation."

He squeezed her hand. "I've got news for you. There aren't any other women like you." She cared so deeply about everything and everybody that it scared him. That quality kept him off guard, always made him afraid he would read too much into her affection for him.

"Good thing, huh? The world probably couldn't stand very many of me." She laughed. "Nice try at distracting me, but back to my story. Connie's husband is in prison. He *was* on drugs, and one day when he was visiting a friend's meth lab, the police showed up for a visit."

"Good for them," Jeff muttered around a big bite of pizza.

"Yes." Lauren leveled a steady gaze at him. "Good for them. And good for him, too. While he was incarcerated, he became a Christian. He was so excited about his new faith, that in one family visit, with some help from a prison ministry worker, he converted Connie and Brian, too."

Jeff stopped with his pizza slice halfway to his mouth. He'd always thought prison conversions were staged to look good at parole hearings, but if the man had taught his wife and son about Jesus, too. . . Of course, they could all be bluffing. "How long ago was that?"

"About seven months. He hadn't been in prison long when Connie found out she was pregnant."

"And they had nowhere to live?" Jeff hazarded a guess, unsure whether he was buying this story or not.

"They own a small house in a neighborhood downtown, but after he got on the drugs, the roof started leaking, and he didn't fix it."

"Typical."

"Part of the roof caved in last month. Doug's supposed to get out right away, but what about in the meantime? When I met Brian, they were staying in the van most of the time trying to keep warm. He spent the afternoons at the library for a change of pace. Connie had lost her waitress job because she couldn't stay on her feet. What was I supposed to do?" Love and compassion shone in her eyes.

What indeed? Lauren had no choice but to love people. It was who she was. And when she loved, she loved with her whole heart. "Just what you did, I guess." He cleared his throat. "You know, I remember what it was like when my mother was alive."

She waited.

"The crowd she ran with would use anything to get to people. They weren't above using their kids." He frowned at the memories flooding his mind. "Or even their pregnancies." He dropped the slice of pizza, forcing down the bite in his mouth that suddenly tasted like sawdust. "They—we would be Christians of any variety. One Sunday we'd hit the Baptist church for a handout. The next week it would be time to be Methodist. One year I went to five different vacation Bible schools." Shame pushed the words out of his mouth. "She made me wear the most raggedy clothes I had so people would feel sorry for us. There was nothing she and her friends wouldn't do for a fix. And that included getting religion."

Tears splashed down Lauren's face, and she put down her own pizza. "That must have been awful."

"It took a couple of years of living with Grandpa and Grandma—and hanging around you and your family—before I realized how unchanging true faith was."

"You sure know what it is now. Your whole life shows that."

If only she knew how far from the truth that was. How the bitterness rolled up in his throat like acid when he thought of his mother and his life in the city. "Why are you trying to butter me up?"

"I'm not!" she said with mock indignation. "But I do have a favor to ask."

Jeff would walk across hot coals for her, but he had a feeling this "favor" was going to be a doozy. "What's that?"

"Connie's roof. I have some money left from what Granny gave me when I graduated college. I'd like to use it to buy shingles and supplies."

"You want me to help you pick out the right things? Shouldn't you let the roofer handle that?"

She cleared her throat and tilted her head to one side, keeping her eyes fixed on his. "I only have enough money for the materials."

"Then who's going to—" Realization dawned on him before he could finish his question. He should have hightailed it out of town without looking back as soon as she said the word *favor*.

Chapter 5

Lauren stacked another book back onto the rolling cart and sighed. Only four days until Christmas Eve. Granny would have fresh greenery and sparkling lights throughout the house. Her cousins would be making their last-minute travel plans. Her parents would be plotting and planning Santa Claus surprises for the local kids.

She wondered if Mama was making her famous cheese logs this year. Or if Daddy had strung lights on the big red barn. She'd have to call and ask. One year, she and Jeff had spelled out "Santa, stop here!" with lights on the barn roof. People from all over the county had driven by to see it. Christmas was Lauren's favorite time of year, but this year she wouldn't be a part of the two-week-long celebration on Forrester Farms. How had she thought she could stand to miss it?

Only the thought of facing Jeff had kept her away, and now he was in the city with her. He'd leave day after tomorrow to go home, in time for Christmas Eve at

Granny's. But she would have to stay. There was no way she could leave Connie and Brian alone with the baby coming. And Connie definitely couldn't travel. Lauren blinked back hot tears.

A gray-haired man stopped beside her. "Excuse me, ma'am. Can you tell me where the books on vampires are?"

She directed him and turned back to the cart. She'd never seen him before. In Pierce City, she knew the library patrons by name. By the kind of books they preferred, even.

Take Thomas Maderro, for example. By day, he worked on the factory assembly line, but by night, he read cookbooks. Every variety he could find. Sometimes he'd bring in a plate of pastries for Lauren to try, other times, a nice casserole for Mrs. Whitfield. Whenever Lauren got a new cookbook in at the library, she always called to let him know. Did Becky do that for him now?

Mrs. Whitfield loved to pretend she was Miss Marple. She doted on mysteries. Lauren often noticed her watching the local residents with a suspicious eye, no doubt wondering who might have murder in his heart.

And little Samuel Evins. He read everything he could get his hands on and had since he was four. Brian reminded her of him, only Samuel had never missed a meal or gone to bed without a good-night kiss from his daddy.

She continued through the list of regulars in her mind, and by closing time she was so homesick she felt like she couldn't stay away another day. Funny thing, it wasn't even each individual person. It was the small-town life. The charming parts like the town square at Christmastime and the not-so-charming parts, like everyone knowing everyone else's business. She missed it all. Maybe she wasn't cut out to be a big-city girl.

She pushed open the double doors and stepped out into the frigid air. A bearded man with multiple face piercings bumped into her and kept walking without a word. On his bare right arm, a tattoo of a spider in a bikini belly-danced with the movement of his muscle. *Oh, Toto,* Lauren thought, *we're not in Kansas anymore.*

She ducked her head against the wind and concentrated on putting one foot in front of another. When her phone rang, she flipped it open with a grin. Jeff was right on schedule. "Hi, there."

"Lauren? Is that you?" In spite of the puzzled tone, Lauren recognized the voice of her old coworker Becky.

"Becky? What's wrong?" They were friendly but not close enough to call each other on a regular basis.

"Nothing's wrong. Something's right, actually. I'm pregnant."

"Congratulations! How wonderful." After Beth was born, Becky and Dan had wanted one more child, but Beth was ten now, and they'd just about given up. "I know you're excited."

"I sure am. But I'm going back to part-time. Before we advertised the full-time position, I wanted to be sure you were happy there."

"Oh." Was she happy here? It was a beautiful city, friendly people, pepperoni and anchovy pizza anytime, day or night. But it wasn't home. "Becky?" Lauren cleared her throat, but the lump stayed. "Can you give me a couple of days to think about it?"

"Sure! I'll hold the job until right after Christmas. Just let me know."

Lauren walked the rest of the way to the apartment in a daze. Why had she exiled herself like a criminal? Her only crime had been falling in love with the wrong man. Would it be so awful if she never married and went to eat with Jeff and his wife on Friday nights? Okay, that last part would be pretty awful. But staying single wouldn't be so bad. She might have to give up Jeff as a friend when he married, but at least she'd be doing it in the comfort of her own home, with her family nearby.

By the time she unlocked her door, she'd decided. She might not be able to get to Granny's for Christmas because of Connie and Brian, but after the baby was born and they were settled in, she was going to do more than visit. She was moving home.

⁕

By the next afternoon, Jeff knew without a doubt why he always tried to take a month off from mid-December to mid-January. This time of year, unless a man sported a red suit and a white beard while driving a sleigh pulled by reindeer, he definitely didn't belong up on a rooftop. A roaring fire would be more like it, along with a hot cup of coffee and a good book. Even an exasperating conversation with Lauren would beat trying to hold a shingle straight with frozen fingers.

He sat back on his legs and surveyed his work. He'd used over a bundle of shingles, and the job didn't look half bad if he did say so himself. Break time. He climbed carefully down the ladder and grabbed his coffee thermos. He might not be able to relax by the fire with a book, but he could drink coffee and call Lauren. She should be home from work now, and she'd been really worried about Connie the last time he talked to her. The doctors said it should be a few more days, but if there was one thing Lauren and Jeff knew from growing up on a farm, it was that babies came when they got good and ready.

He punched in Lauren's cell number and smiled. Now that he was in town, she'd gone back to accepting his calls. He still didn't know what that had been all about. But he was glad she was over it.

"Hello?"

"Hey, Laur. Everything okay?"

"Yes, unless you count Connie and Brian beating me at Monopoly."

"You're playing board games? I don't believe it! I'm stuck out here in the freezing cold, and you're all nice and cozy having the time of your life."

She chuckled and spoke softly. "Suck it up, you big baby. I'm not doing this for fun. I want to keep Connie's mind off these pains the doctor is calling false labor."

"You sound like you're not buying that assessment."

"I'm no expert, but it looks like the real thing to me, even if it is two weeks until her due date." He could hear the worry in her voice. "How bad is the roof?"

"Not as bad as it could be. I think I can have it done in a day and a half."

"That's wonderful, Jeff. Thank you so much," she whispered. They had planned to surprise Connie and Brian with the new roof.

"Hey, do you feel like having Chinese takeout for supper? I can pick some up after I stop by the hotel and shower."

"I know you're tired. Will you feel like it?"

"I can't think of anything I'd rather do." As Jeff said the words, he realized how true they were. Why was he in such a hurry to find his perfect girl? He could have a good time hanging out with Lauren and being single. Then when the right woman came along, he'd be ready, but it wouldn't be something he'd rushed into.

"Thanks, Jeff. I appreciate you so much. You're a lifesaver."

He dropped the phone back in his pocket. A throat cleared behind him. He spun around to face a tall, gangly stranger.

"Can I help you?"

The man ran his thumb across the bill of the grease-stained cap he held between his hands. Even though he didn't look to be over thirty, he appeared to have lived a lifetime already, and the solemn expression in his eyes reminded Jeff of someone. "Actually, I was hoping I could help you."

"I'm sorry, buddy," Jeff said and realized he really was sorry. He'd like to help someone out without

Lauren's prompting. "This is a volunteer job, so I can't afford to hire any help." Plus, his worker's comp probably wouldn't cover an indigent worker he hired in St. Louis—but no need to go into that.

"I don't need any money. Just want to help." The man's Adam's apple bobbed as he seemed to be weighing his words.

Jeff frowned. What kind of scam was this? He must be losing his mind. For a minute, he'd suckered right into the man's sincere-seeming demeanor and softly spoken words. "Thanks, but no thanks."

He walked away, hoping the con artist would take the hint, but the man hefted a pack of shingles onto his shoulder and started up the ladder.

"Hold it right there. I'm going to have to call the cops if you don't come down."

The man paused on the first step of the ladder. "The cops can't run me off."

Jeff stared in horror as the bum tossed the bundle of shingles to the ground with a thud and reached inside his right jacket pocket.

"And neither can you."

Chapter 6

Jeff jumped back and started to dive behind his truck.

"Whoa, man." The man held up a battered wallet. "Just showing you some ID. I live here."

"Says who?"

"Says the deed to the house and this identification." He stepped down and stuck out his hand. "I'm Doug Miller. I should have introduced myself, but when I saw you working here, I thought you must know Connie, and I was still figuring on surprising her."

"You're Connie's husband?" Jeff shook his hand as he suddenly realized who Doug looked like. He was a grown-up version of Brian. "I thought you were—" He stopped, unsure what to say.

"In prison? I was." Doug's soft smile took years off his age. "Up to a couple of days ago. Rick Watson down at Rick's Auto Shop teaches a Bible class at the prison, and when I got out, he took me on as a mechanic. I wanted to work a few days and get enough to start fixing the house up before I told Connie and Brian the good news." He shook his head. "It's hard not to rush to see her, though."

"I can imagine." Jeff found himself liking this man in spite of his history. Would his mom have been this nice if she'd ever gone straight? Who knew? "I'm a friend of Connie's friend, Lauren."

"Really? Lauren's an amazing person, the way she's taken Connie and Brian into her home. Most people wouldn't do a thing like that." Doug took off his cap again and clutched it.

"Lauren's one of a kind," Jeff agreed. "Have you talked to Connie lately?"

"We talk every Friday. I was hoping to be able to surprise her and Brian in person this Friday." He looked at the sunset and the darkening clouds. "Guess today's a bust. But tomorrow's my day off. I can help you all day." He chuckled. "I'm no roofer, so you'll have to tell me what to do."

Jeff clapped him on the back. "Get a good night's rest. With both of us working, we may get the roof done tomorrow."

An hour later, Jeff hurried into the brownstone, clutching a bag full of Chinese food. He hadn't known what Brian and Connie liked, so he'd gotten a variety. He decided not to mention Doug's return to Lauren. She deserved a nice surprise, too.

When she opened the door, concern lined her face. "Is Connie getting worse?"

"I don't know. Maybe not." She glanced over her

shoulder to where Brian and Connie sat at the kitchen table. "I can't be sure."

"Let's see if we can get her mind off it," he suggested. "They always say if you can distract them from the pain, it's not real labor."

"What do you know about real labor?" she teased.

"Not much, really." He raised his voice and smiled at Connie and Brian. "But I do know a lot about Monopoly. I was the Forrester Farms' champion."

They played until Connie finally stood. "I'm going to go to bed and try to get some rest." She ruffled Brian's hair. "You about ready to turn in, sport?"

"Sure. Good night, Miss Lauren. Night, Mr. Jeff." The boy hugged them both and bounded down the hall to the guest room, where Lauren had made up a cot for Brian.

"Thank you, both, for everything you've done," Connie said and followed her son.

"What did she mean? Did you tell her about the roof?" Jeff whispered when she was out of sight.

Lauren shook her head. "I think she meant caring for them in general. They've not had a lot of that in their lives."

"No, I don't guess they have. But I have a feeling things are going to take a turn for the better for them."

"Oh, really?" Lauren punched his shoulder. "Now you're telling the future? Is there anything you can't do?"

"Trust people. Apparently I have a real problem with that."

Her smile faded. "We're going to have to work on that."

He thought of his bargain with Doug Miller. "Believe me, I am." With a flick of his wrist, he tossed the empty food cartons in the trash. "Do you know it's only three days until Christmas Eve?"

She gave him an inquisitive look. "You read minds, too? I was just thinking about that."

"They're counting on me to bring you home, you know."

"Jeff, there's no way I can leave Connie and Brian all alone with the baby coming. Or even if it comes before then, they'll still need help."

Not if they have Doug to take care of them. "We'll wait and see what God has planned. How about that?"

She wiped off the table. "I guess. But don't get your hopes up about me going back with you. I'm not going to leave them to fend for themselves."

"Gotcha. How do you feel about leaving them alone for a few minutes right now and slipping out to look at Christmas lights with me?"

A huge smile wiped all the worry from her face. "Oh, Jeff, that sounds like something I can do."

When they exited the interstate at a suburb Lauren recommended, they could see the lights. Every house was trimmed with sparkling lights, and the lawns were decked out like the North Pole.

"Want to walk?" Jeff asked. He and Lauren shared a love of the outdoors.

"Sure."

He parked, and they ambled slowly down the street, taking in the intricate details of each display. "Even though they're all sort of alike, they're each one different," Lauren said softly. "Kind of like people."

Jeff pointed out a wobbly-legged reindeer with a bright red nose and hummed the first few bars of the familiar tune. Lauren grinned and broke into song. He joined in, and when they couldn't remember the reindeers' names, they made them up, until they were both laughing so hard they could hardly walk. "Sonnet? And Blondie?" He raised an eyebrow and looped his arm through hers. "Lauren Forrester, you just flunked Christmas 101."

"Right. You've got a lot of room to talk. Splasher and Stupid were definitely not pulling the sleigh."

"It's been a long time since we used to watch those TV Christmas specials when we were kids."

"For your information, I've never missed a year. I even watched them with Brian this year."

"I can't believe I didn't know that!" He knew she loved Christmas, but he had never dreamed she still watched the old TV specials.

"There's a lot about me you don't know." She punched him on the arm and took off to the truck at a dead run. By the time he caught up with her, she was in the passenger seat laughing.

❧

Lauren snuggled deeper into the patio chair with her down comforter tucked tightly under her chin and stared out at the city lights. The vastness of the city made her feel so small. A stereo played Christmas carols in the distance, reminding her of home. Loneliness welled up inside her. She was a friend to many, a good friend to a few, best friend to one; but when push came to shove, she was alone. Ever since Jeff had started his quest for the perfect girl, she'd felt their bond slipping through her fingers like buttered toffee.

She rested her head back against the frame of the chair and looked up at the dark sky. It wasn't like her to indulge in a pity party, but surely being away from home for the holidays gave her the right for a short poor-me session. Jeff would have a fit if he knew she stayed out on her patio at night. Someone might scale the building and grab her, he'd say. He was so protective. Sometimes she fooled herself into thinking that meant he cared about her as more than a friend; then she'd remember that her brothers were protective, too.

She'd almost let her guard down tonight when they were looking at the Christmas lights. As soon as she'd told him there was a lot about her he didn't know, she'd realized her mistake. Jeff would hound her until he figured out what she meant. So she'd hit him and run. Maybe it wasn't the most mature decision, but it was definitely the most expedient.

There had been a glint in his eye, though. And as she was running, it had flitted through her mind that if this were an old movie, she would let him catch her. When his arms were around her, he'd realize his deep love for her and kiss her passionately. If this were a movie, of course.

An unfamiliar sound pulled her from her cinematic fantasy. She clutched the comforter and hurried back into the apartment. Jeff's cell phone lay on the dining table playing a tune. Without even stopping to think, she snatched it up. "Hello?"

"Is Jeff there?" a female voice sobbed. For a split second, Lauren wondered if she'd fallen asleep on the balcony and was dreaming. This sudden drama seemed like a scene out of a movie.

"No, no, he's not. He left his phone—"

"This is Krista." Her words were barely recognizable.

"Krista, it's Lauren. Are you okay?"

"Oh. Hey, Lauren." She seemed to calm down some. "I'm sorry. I just need to talk to Jeffie. Would you ask him to call me?"

"I'll tell him tomorrow." Lauren realized Krista had broken the connection.

She sank down at the table, her heart pounding in her throat. How childish she'd been to think Jeff had come to St. Louis because deep down he loved her and didn't realize it. He'd probably just been restless, smarting from a fight with Krista, and decided to tool on over to see his buddy for a while. Too bad for him that he'd left his phone on her table or everything would be patched up by now. Krista obviously wanted to work things out. And Jeff? Krista was his perfect woman. What more could he ask for?

Lauren locked the patio door and unplugged her tabletop Christmas tree. Bah humbug. As she shuffled into her bedroom, her gaze fell on the picture by her bed—she and Jeff on the Ferris wheel at the county fair. They'd been seventeen and had the world at their feet in more ways than one. She picked up the picture and flung herself back across the mattress. How had she let her life get into such a mess?

A tap sounded on her open door. She looked up to see Connie standing in the doorway. "You asleep?"

"No." Lauren pushed to a sitting position on the edge of the bed, then looked down at the framed photo she still held in her hands and blushed. "Just thinking about what might have been." She motioned to the armchair across from her. "Come on in."

Connie waddled into the room, her arms resting on the top of her enormous abdomen. She looked at the picture as Lauren placed it back on the bedside table. "He's a great guy."

"Yep. The best friend a girl could ever have," Lauren said.

Connie lowered herself gingerly into the chair. "The connection between you two seems to go deeper than friends."

"Only on one side, I'm afraid." Lauren felt her grin tremble.

"Don't give up on him yet." Connie shook her head. "I thought Doug and I were through, but now that we're both Christians—I've never loved him more. And I know he feels the same way."

"Jeff doesn't see me like that. Never will. To him, I'll always be good old Lauren." She reached out to touch the picture one more time, then looked at her new friend. "But I'm going to stop obsessing over that and get on with my life. When Doug gets out and you and Brian"—she smiled at Connie's stomach—"and the baby are taken care of, I'm going to move home."

"Oh, Lauren, I'm so glad." Connie clapped her hands together softly. "The city is in my blood, and I love it here, but it's no good when you're only here because you're running away from something. You belong in the country. It's your home."

Lauren jumped up and hugged Connie. They embraced for a few seconds without speaking, then Connie took her hand. "I'll never forget what you've done for me, Lauren. God used you to take care of us. I'm so grateful that you were here."

"Even if I was running away?" She grinned.

"Proof positive that God can use anything for good."

"Touché."

Later, as she drifted off to sleep, she thought about Connie's words. God really had used Lauren's impulsive decision for good. And Jeff's presence had been for the best, too, since it had gotten Connie's roof fixed. And Lauren wasn't sure it was the handiwork of God, but she knew it was for the best that Jeff had left his phone there. If not for the phone call from Krista, Lauren might still be imagining what would have happened if she'd let him catch her.

Chapter 7

"Push me that bundle of shingles, will you?" Jeff glanced over his shoulder.

Doug slid the package across the roof. "You're pretty fast at this."

"Years of experience. I've been doing carpenter work since I was in high school."

"That's how I am with cars." Doug cleared his throat. "But I'm not bad with a hammer. There's no excuse for the shape the house is in."

"You were out of town," Jeff said, surprising himself by wanting to make the man feel better.

"Don't kid yourself. This disrepair didn't happen in eight months. It was the drugs. They took my life, and I let them."

"Like my mom. Except she could never see it. Right up until that final fatal overdose, she'd denied using drugs. Then it was too late."

"Overdose?" Doug asked quietly.

He nodded. "She was dead when I went in to tell

her I was leaving for school." He sat back on the roof, hammer hanging loose in his hand. "My grandparents took me in and raised me. Still, it always rankled me that my mom didn't care more about me than she did the drugs."

Doug scooted over beside him. "Ah, man, that's rough. Since I didn't know your mom, I can't say for her personally, but I can tell you that I loved Brian and Connie more than the drugs. But the drugs. . ." He picked up a roofing nail and flipped it around in his fingers. "They captured me. I was a slave to them. It was have them or die. Even after I got clean, I didn't have freedom. Not until Rick introduced me to Jesus."

"Mom knew about Jesus, but I don't think she really knew Him." Jeff thought back again to all the times they'd milked the local churches for charity. "There were times when she was sober that I thought she loved me, though. I wish she'd made different choices."

"That's a lot for a kid to handle. So that's why you're willing to help people like me get a second chance. I appreciate you fixing our roof more than you know."

Jeff felt his face grow hot at the undeserved praise. "We'd better get back to work if we're going to finish this today." He hammered one shingle on after another, but his heart was hammering, as well, as he thought about what Doug said. Why hadn't he tried to help others? Deep down, he'd believed people like Doug were getting what they deserved. How could he not have realized that if he wanted God's grace he had to share it with others?

He prayed as he hammered, and by midafternoon, he'd started the journey toward forgiving his mother. His heart was considerably lighter. "I think that about finishes it up here, Doug."

"It looks great. Thanks again, man." Doug gathered up an armload of tools and carried them down the ladder.

Jeff picked up what was left and followed him. As they packed the things in his truck, he smiled. "I have to go over to Lauren's and get my cell phone. You want to go with me and bring your family home?"

"I can't think of anything I'd like better. Seems like I've been waiting a lifetime for this moment. I think I'll change into a clean shirt, though." He paused with the front door half open and looked back at Jeff. "Want to see the inside? I've been working on it at night, trying to make everything like it used to be, only better."

"Let me close this up and I'll be right in."

Doug had just disappeared into the house when Lauren's little blue car pulled up to the curb. She and Brian got out and ran up the sidewalk.

"Jeff, Connie's in labor."

He looked behind her. "Is she with you?"

"She's at the hospital. They said it would be a while before anything happened, so we ran over to tell you." She held up his phone. "Since we couldn't call you."

"Thanks." He slid the phone into his pocket.

Brian had moved away from them and was staring up at his newly repaired roof, eyes shining.

"I wondered if you'd come stay with Brian at the

hospital," Lauren said softly. "I don't want to leave Connie alone."

Jeff grinned. Some days were made for surprises. "I will, but there's someone else who will want to come along, too."

"Really?" Lauren's brows knitted together. "To the hospital?"

The front door of the house opened, and Doug walked out, buttoning the top button on his shirt. He saw Brian and stopped, mouth open.

"Dad!" Brian threw himself at his father, and Doug picked him up and spun him around.

"In the flesh."

"I can't believe you're here!" The boy stood in the shelter of the man's arms. They showed no sign of separating.

Tears streamed down Lauren's face as she looked at them and then back to Jeff. "How did. . . ? Did you know?" She shook her head and laughed through the tears. "Are you behind this, Jeff Warren?"

"Not me, Laur. This is all God's doing." He blinked against the prickly moisture in his own eyes. "Let's go let Connie in on the surprise."

∾∾∾

"We named her Lauren," Connie said, her voice still a little weak.

Lauren stared through the blur of tears at the little bundle of pink in her arms. "I'm honored. It meant a lot to me to be here to welcome her into the world." She'd tried to excuse herself, but Doug and Connie had both insisted she stay in the birthing room with them. Jeff had kept Brian occupied in the waiting area.

"We couldn't have done it without you," Doug said from his perch on the edge of Connie's bed.

"We sure couldn't have," Connie echoed. "Does holding her make you want one of your own?"

Lauren looked down at her namesake again. How could she explain that she'd had an earth-shattering, plan-destroying revelation during the past few hours? She knew now, beyond a shadow of a doubt, that this was what she wanted. What Doug and Connie had, in spite of their difficulties. And yes, children, to love and nurture. She couldn't speak for the lump in her throat, so she just nodded and gently jostled the baby.

Connie and Doug continued to chat, but their voices faded to a muted roar in Lauren's ears as she put her finger in the baby's palm and watched her little fingers curl around it. How could she ever have considered staying single and childless? If God had planned that for her, she'd live with it, but how could she consciously choose it? She'd been crazy to think she could move home and be satisfied with her old job and Jeff's friendship. She'd never find someone else in the shadow of his presence.

"Lauren, are you okay?" Connie's voice jolted her from her thoughts.

Lauren nodded and walked over to the bed. "She's so beautiful."

"You won't get any argument out of us." Doug's thin face seemed to radiate light. He reached out his arms, and Lauren carefully placed the baby in them.

"I'm going to go let Brian come back in, okay?"

"You'll be back, right?" Connie asked.

Lauren forced a big smile. "You can't get rid of me that easy, girl. Aunt Lauren is here to stay."

They all laughed, but Lauren saw a twinge of concern in Connie's eyes.

She walked slowly out to the waiting area. "Brian, your folks thought you might want to come in and stay with them." She looked over his head at Jeff. "Want me to run you to get your truck?" They'd all been in such a hurry to get there that they'd piled into Lauren's car together. As much as she dreaded being alone with him, she knew he needed his truck.

"That would be great." He walked over and put his arm around her. "You worn out?"

She relaxed for a minute against him, then pushed herself upright. "A little, but nothing like Connie, of course."

"The baby's something else. Did they tell you her name?" He grinned at her as they walked through the parking garage.

"Yeah. I couldn't believe it."

"I wasn't really surprised," Jeff said as he slid into the passenger seat. "You made a huge difference in their lives."

"I didn't do anything special."

Lauren reached for the stick shift between the seats, but Jeff captured her hand in his. "Everything you do is special," he said softly. The cold interior of the car seemed to shrink and warm up as she felt his thumb caress her hand. His face was so close to hers, she could see his breath. "Home is not the same without you, Laur. Won't you at least go back with me for Christmas?"

He was right there, his eyes so blue, his mouth so chiseled and appealing. Lauren wondered if he could hear her heart pounding. If she leaned one inch toward him. . .

A loud ringing filled the small car. They both jumped, and he plucked his cell phone from his pocket. He glanced at the caller ID, then dropped it again without answering it.

Lauren put the car into gear and maneuvered out of the parking garage. "Was that Krista?" she asked, hoping her tone was casual.

"Yeah, but I'll get in touch with her later."

Lauren kept her eyes on the road. "She called last night after you left your phone at the house. I meant to tell you, but then Connie went into labor." She willed her eyes not to water. It had been an emotional twenty-four hours. "Krista sounded pretty upset."

"She's having a rough time."

Then why don't you hightail it home and make up with her? Put all three of us out of our misery? Lauren bit back the snippy questions, but in her heart she knew with certainty that she'd be spending Christmas in the city.

Chapter 8

W ant to go shopping?" Jeff asked, smiling when Lauren whipped her head around to give him an incredulous look.

"Shopping?" she repeated as if her hearing must be bad. "As in at the mall?"

"Yes." The way he figured it, here was a chance to kill two birds with one stone. Lauren was obviously feeling blue about something, and that precious little baby was going to need some clothes and nursery items. So the mall was the obvious cure for both problems. "I thought we might get baby Lauren a few things, then take them back to the house and set it up for when they bring her home tomorrow."

Her eyes sparkled, and she swung the car in a wide U-turn. "That sounds like a marvelous idea. I can't believe you thought of it."

He laughed. "Do you think I'm so dumb I don't know that was an insult?"

"I never said anything about you being dumb," she

said, concentrating hard on the road.

One objective down. She was cheering up already.

When they got to the mall, Lauren insisted they forgo the toy store for the clothes department. "She doesn't need a life-sized giraffe, Jeff. Her life will be enough of a zoo if you're ever around."

"It's not my fault you're always making a monkey out of me," he shot back. "But you're probably right. We should start with clothes. Then we'll hit the toys."

Jeff tucked his arm in Lauren's as they walked through the mall, but she jerked it away. "Got to keep my muscles in shape for carrying bags," she explained, flexing her arm.

Right. When did she get to where she couldn't stand for him to touch her? He didn't say anything, though. Assuming she went back home with him, they'd hash it out after Christmas.

Two hours later, they had enough baby clothes to last for a while. "What about nursery furniture?" Jeff asked.

"Connie has all of Brian's at the house. It might need to be cleaned up a little."

"Is that next on our to-do list?"

"Sounds good to me," she said, wandering over to a store window.

He followed her and stared up at the dress in the window. "That would look great on you."

"Not me, silly. Connie. I want to get them each a little something."

"Me, too. But not enough that they will feel obligated to get me something in return." He cleared his throat. "Actually, they've given me enough already."

She looked at his reflection. "What do you mean?"

"Talking to Doug made me face some truths about my mom. She was a flawed person, just like the rest of us, Lauren."

She stepped back against him, and he rested his head on the top of her head and lightly put his arms around her. Their reflection stared back at him in the shop window. To his amazement, they looked like—a couple. The idea shook him, and he barely heard her next words.

"I'm glad you got to know Doug and talk to him about things."

Jeff forced his thoughts away from how good it felt to hold her and back to their conversation. "Me, too. I've thought of Mom as a monster so long that I didn't realize how much that anger wore me down."

She turned, still in his arms, and for just a second leaned against him. He grinned. He'd always teased her about smelling like citrus fruit, but as the aroma of tangerines floated up to him, he realized how much he'd missed that scent. He pulled her closer and felt her stiffen. She pushed back, brown eyes wide, face pink. "I'm really happy for you, Jeff." She ducked out of his embrace and hurried into the store. He stared after her. What had gotten into her? For that matter, what had gotten into him?

∞≈

Lauren arranged the zoo animal mobile over the crib

and stood back. She and Jeff had compromised. He'd gotten his giraffe, but miniaturized.

She and Jeff had a blast gathering things for the baby and gifts for the rest of the Millers. They'd worked at the house last night, then met here this morning to do some last-minute things before going to the hospital to get Doug, Connie, Brian, and the baby. She'd invited Brian to stay all night at her house, but he'd wanted to be with his parents, and she didn't blame him.

She and Jeff had talked on the phone until late. It had been like old times. They'd talked about her missing Christmas Eve at Granny's and about him forgiving his mom. About everything. Except her feelings for him. And his feelings for Krista. They neither one mentioned her.

Lauren thought of all the awkward times yesterday when she'd pulled away from his touch. He probably thought she was crazy. Which in a way she was. Crazy about him.

She still saw the irony in the fact that she'd left home to get away from him and he'd followed her. Especially considering he did it based strictly on platonic feelings. What would it be like to have Jeff, in love with her, come charging into town to beg her to come home? She wouldn't last ten minutes.

"You ready?"

She looked up from where she was fussing with the crib dust ruffle. "When you are."

"That's an old stalling trick. Means you're not quite ready."

"Is that what it means?" She ran her hand over the

balloon wall hanging and edged toward the door. "Beat you to the car!" She threw the words back over her shoulder and took off for the living room.

"Oh no you don't." He caught her before she made it halfway down the hall and started to tickle her.

"We have to go," she choked out and slipped from his grasp, then hurried to the front door. She should have seen that coming. If he got out of town without her giving her feelings away, it would be barely short of a miracle. "Should we take my car so there will be room for everyone?" she asked, willing her voice not to tremble.

"Sure." His voice was subdued, and he hardly looked her way as they got into the vehicle.

The silence hung in the air between them as they drove to the hospital, but the Millers were so exuberant about going home that Lauren found it hard not to be excited with them.

The afternoon flew by as Jeff and Doug and Brian worked together to make everything perfect for an astonished Connie, who had assumed they were going to Lauren's apartment. After several trips to the nearby pharmacy and grocery store, the house was as well-stocked as Lauren had hoped. She put on a big pot of chili and threw some grilled cheese sandwiches together while Connie and the baby rested.

After supper, Jeff pushed to his feet. "I'm going to have to go."

Lauren raised an eyebrow. "Home?" She frowned when she heard her voice squeak.

Connie excused herself with the baby, and Doug

and Brian followed close behind.

Like rats deserting a ship, Lauren thought. *Just when I needed them most.* The last thing she wanted was to be alone with Jeff while she was trying to be strong.

"Yep. I checked out of the hotel this morning." He stood there in the kitchen and stared at her. "I'll wait for you to get your stuff together if you want to go. If you don't want to drive, I can bring you back whenever you're ready."

She shook her head and swallowed hard. "I appreciate it, Jeff, but I think I'm better off here this year."

"If I could make one iota of sense out of that, I sure would be happier," he said. "But I reckon it's your business." His blue eyes darkened.

She forced herself to remain seated between the wall and the table.

"You sure you won't reconsider?"

"I'm sure." She looked down at the faded plastic tablecloth and picked at an imaginary speck. Why didn't he just go? If she stood up to tell him bye, she'd run out to the truck as hard as her legs would carry her.

"Merry Christmas, Lauren."

She gave him a little wave. "Merry Christmas to you, too."

And then he was gone. And so was her heart.

When the door closed behind him, she put her head down on the table and let the tears fall.

Chapter 9

The snowflakes swirled at Jeff's truck windshield faster than the wipers could dispel them. If it were daylight, the snow would, no doubt, be beautiful, but as Jeff drove down the dark interstate, it surrounded him like an oppressive white blanket. Along with freezing temperatures and the starless night sky, the never-ending barrage of snowflakes fit perfectly with his mood.

Even though Lauren had repeatedly told him she wasn't coming home for Christmas, he'd never really envisioned himself making this return trip alone. In tandem maybe, paving the way in his truck as she followed close behind in her little blue car. He'd call her occasionally to make sure she was making it okay, and they'd stop at the halfway point and get a drink or a bite to eat.

But in the end, he'd left her behind. She hadn't even really given him a proper good-bye, although he wasn't sure anymore what would have constituted a proper good-bye from her. More than the wave of her hand he'd gotten, that much he knew.

He was grateful God was helping him work things out as far as his bitterness toward his mother. But Lauren. She unsettled him. Their friendship didn't fit anymore. It was like a pair of boots he'd loved but outgrown. It pinched his heart and made it uncomfortable.

He'd almost kissed her in the car yesterday. The realization shook him to the core. He would have if his phone hadn't rung. Assuming she'd have let him. She'd seemed agreeable to the idea, but maybe that was his imagination. Ever since that moment, things had been out of sync between them. She was avoiding him. He'd tried to play around and even started to tickle her while they were over at Connie and Doug's house getting things ready for them to bring the baby home, but she'd slipped from his grasp without a giggle.

As he remembered how she'd been in his embrace one moment and gone the next, he gripped the steering wheel and fixed his eyes on the snowy highway. Familiar scenery greeted him now, but he felt like he was getting farther and farther from home.

∽

"Lauren? Are you going to stand there and watch the snow fall all night?" Connie called.

Lauren turned away from the window. "Did you see how the flakes are coming down sideways? The wind, I guess." She walked over to the worn orange and brown plaid couch where Connie cradled the baby in her arms and sat down beside her. "I'm just glad we're going to have a white Christmas."

"Hard to believe tomorrow's Christmas Eve, isn't it?" Doug asked from his seat on the rug next to Brian. They'd dragged out an old Lego set and were trying to outdo each other with their elaborate creations.

"Yeah." Lauren sighed. It would be the first Christmas Eve morning she'd ever missed eating breakfast at Granny's and hanging ornaments on the tree with her cousins.

"You seem thrilled about it." Connie shifted the baby to her shoulder and patted her gently on the back. "Tell me again why you're not going home."

"Connie, I'm afraid to. This thing with Jeff. It's gotten too big for me to keep it a secret. And I really don't want to spend the holidays making an idiot out of myself over someone who views me as a good buddy." She grimaced and fiddled with the baby's little crocheted bootie. "Plus, I've got to make a clean break if I'm ever going to meet someone else."

Connie motioned toward Brian and Doug, who were absorbed in building their Lego structures, then waved a hand at the rest of the modest house. "Who are you hoping to meet here, girl?"

"It's too soon to be thinking about that, really," Lauren said, fully aware of how ridiculous she sounded.

Connie raised an eyebrow at her. "Do you ever really listen to yourself?"

"What do you mean by that?"

"You are the oddest mixture, Lauren Forrester. You forced Brian to bring me to the library that day to talk to you and then insisted we move into your apartment. I'd never met anyone so straightforward. Yet you won't tell this man—this man that you've known since forever—that you're in love with him and take a chance that he might feel the same way."

"What about Krista?"

"What about her? From what you've told me, you don't know that he has any feelings for her at all, only that she called him crying." She motioned toward the muted TV with her free hand. "If I called the star of that TV show crying, would that mean he was in love with me?"

Lauren ran a finger down the soft skin on the baby's neck. "Your mama should be a lawyer, little Lauren."

"That's what I tell her all the time," Doug said.

Connie's face turned red. "I'm looking into getting a grant for college. We'll see after baby Lauren gets a little older." She turned back to Lauren. "If I can consider going to law school, you can surely march yourself down to your granny's and tell Jeff how you really feel. Give him a chance to tell you he feels the same."

"You never give up, do you?"

"Not if I think there's any hope of success."

Lauren pushed to her feet. "Anybody want a cup of hot chocolate?"

"Sounds wonderful," Connie said. "You're not going to poison me because I'm telling you like it is, are you?"

Lauren laughed. "I don't think I have the nerve to do what you're saying. Risk a lifetime of friendship on a chance of love."

"Are you happy being just friends?"

"No."

"Then I don't see where the risk is."

Lauren ambled into the small kitchen and fixed four cups of hot chocolate. She craved the comfort of chocolate. And if she were honest, anything to get her mind off of tomorrow and off the fact that Jeff was gone.

As she was setting the cups onto a wicker tray, her cell phone jangled. She snatched it up. Had Jeff decided to stay in town? To ask her one more time to go home with him? "Hello?"

"Lauren? It's Krista."

Lauren's heart thudded against her ribs. "Hi, Krista. How are you?"

"I'm okay." The girl laughed softly. "I got your phone number from Jeff. I hope you don't mind."

"Oh. That's fine."

"I felt bad about being so upset on the phone the other night. I just wanted to say I'm sorry—and to tell you my good news."

"What good news?" Lauren's legs suddenly felt like jelly, and she sank onto a bar stool.

"I'm engaged."

"Oh." Tears filled Lauren's eyes, but she forced herself to speak. "Congratulations."

"It's mostly because of Jeff."

Of course it is, Lauren thought, head spinning. She clutched the phone like a lifeline, even though she wanted to throw it down and stomp on it. "Really?"

"Yes, he helped me to understand how Ron was feeling."

"Ron?" Lauren felt like someone had switched channels in the middle of a show. She shook her head to clear it.

"We had a big spat the other night," Krista continued as if Lauren hadn't spoken. "That's why I called Jeff, to get his take on it. But it's all worked out now. Ron was going to give me my ring back for a Christmas present, but he couldn't wait. So tonight he asked me to marry him."

"Krista, I'm so happy for you." Lauren meant every word, but she still wasn't sure exactly how this had all happened. "Are you going to Indiana right away?"

The girl laughed. "I'm in Indiana! Didn't Jeff tell you? He advised me not to stay away from Ron another minute, so I took all my vacation time two weeks before Christmas and came home."

"Oh, that's good." Lauren tried not to growl, but why hadn't Jeff told her that? At least that miscomprehension wouldn't have stood between her and telling him the truth.

"Everyone should be home at Christmas. When are you leaving for Pierce City?"

"I'm heading out first thing in the morning."

She heard a cough and looked up to see a beaming Connie standing in the doorway giving her the thumbs-up sign. "Good night, Krista. Congratulations again. Thank you for calling." When she pushed END, Connie started laughing.

"Krista's engaged, huh?"

"Yep." Lauren sat at the table, still trying to take in the news.

"And not to Jeff?"

"No."

"So is it possible, Miss Forrester," Connie said in her best lawyer voice, "that if you were mistaken about that detail, you could also be wrong about Mr. Warren's feelings or alleged lack of feelings for you?"

"I don't know," Lauren said, smiling. "But tomorrow I intend to find out."

Chapter 10

At 1:00 a.m. Jeff gave up on sleep, got dressed, and peered out his living room window. The snow had stopped, so he padded out to the old swing set. He kicked the snow off the swing and sank down to lay his confusion down at the feet of the One who could make sense of it. As he finished praying, a figure tromped toward him from Lauren's parents' yard. The man drew closer, and he recognized Lauren's dad, a big overcoat thrown over a white T-shirt and black sweatpants tucked into his snow boots.

"Jeff? You okay?" Concern filled Mr. Forrester's voice.

"Yes, sir. I'm all right. Just couldn't sleep."

"Me, either. I was getting a drink and saw you out the window. Thought I'd come out and keep you company. Hope you don't mind." The older man perched in the other swing and almost lost his balance. He chuckled. "Truth is, I miss my little girl."

Jeff took a deep breath. "Truth is, that's my problem, too, sir."

"You two have been close for a long time." Mr. Forrester gave Jeff a sideways glance. "It's bound to be hard not to be together at Christmas."

Jeff had to stand up if he was going to say what he had to say. He pushed out of the swing and walked over in front of the man. "There's more to it than that. At least there is on my part. I don't know how she feels because I haven't told her yet, but I'm in love with her." He felt like all the breath had been pushed out of his lungs. The long ago conversation with his grandfather about "us" and "them" played over and over in his mind. He rushed on. "I'd like to ask your permission—"

The swing set shook as Mr. Forrester jumped to his feet. "You don't know how proud I am to hear that!" He grabbed Jeff's hand and shook it. "I thought you were never gonna wake up, boy."

"I—I—I. . ." Jeff wanted to tell him that Lauren probably didn't love him back, so there was really nothing to shake his hand about, but Mr. Forrester pulled him into a hug.

"I guess you know we've always loved you like a son."

A lump the size of the Ozarks filled Jeff's throat. "I love you and Mrs. Forrester, too. You've all been really good to me over the years."

"So when's the wedding?"

"I'm going to drive to St. Louis in the morning, but I can't guarantee anything." What a difference a few minutes could make. He'd been certain that Lauren's dad wouldn't think he was good enough for his daughter. "I might go back right now."

"Take some advice from an old man," Mr. Forrester said. "No woman wants to be proposed to while she's still got morning breath and no makeup. Get a good night's rest and give her time to miss you. You show up around noon tomorrow, and she'll be tickled to death to see you."

Jeff remembered how casual Lauren had been when they'd said good-bye. He was probably setting himself up for heartbreak, but what would his life be like if he didn't try? He shook Mr. Forrester's hand one more time and forced himself to go to bed. When sleep came, he dreamed he was on one knee proposing to Lauren. She had the baby's little zoo mobile in her hand, and she was shaking the monkey in his face and laughing. Finally, he fell into a sound sleep and didn't wake until morning. The snow had started falling again.

He prayed as he dressed in his least-faded jeans and blue and green flannel shirt. Just before he walked out the door, Granny Forrester called.

"Jeff?"

"Good morning, Granny." He'd been surprised by Mr. Forrester's proclamation of love last night, but he'd never doubted that Granny loved him like he was one of her own grandkids. "What's going on?"

"That's what I want to know. You got in from St. Louis last night?"

"Yes, ma'am, but I'm heading back there this morning."

"Whatever for?"

"This is just between you and me, so if you talk

to her on the phone before I get there, you can't say anything—"

"I won't say a word. What's the big secret?"

"I'm in love with Lauren and I want to—"

"Whoo-eeee!"

He held the phone away from his ear. *Like mother, like son,* he thought, remembering Mr. Forrester's premature celebration. "Now, wait a minute, Granny."

"Stop by here before you go, Jeff."

"I'm running late—"

"I won't hold you up. See you in a few minutes."

"Yes, ma'am."

Five minutes later, he stood on the snow-covered porch of the big, old, white house and rang the doorbell. No one answered, so he pushed the button again. Finally, he heard running on the steps and the door flew open.

His heart flip-flopped. Staring back at him, her gorgeous brown eyes wide with surprise, was Lauren.

∾∾

"Jeff? What are you doing here?" Lauren cringed as she realized how that sounded. She'd spent the whole trip from St. Louis this morning gathering her nerve, but she'd also promised herself a leisurely breakfast and a confidence-building girl talk with her cousins before she confronted Jeff about her feelings. Yet here he stood, on the doorstep, as breathtakingly handsome as she'd ever seen him.

"Granny called and asked me to come by. I was on

my way to—what are *you* doing here?"

"Why don't you come in and I'll explain?" She stepped back for him to enter, then closed the door behind him. Forget the confidence building; it looked like it was now or never.

When they were settled on the sofa, Jeff touched the fresh greenery that laced between Granny's snow globe collection on the coffee table in front of them. "Granny didn't cut back on her decorating this year, I see."

Lauren shook her head. "If anything, I think she added a few things." Her mouth felt as dry as the inside of the Santa birdhouse gourd that sat on the table across from her. "I'm actually glad you're here."

"You are?" Jeff reached over and took her hand gently in his.

She resisted the urge to pull away. She was done running.

"I'm glad you're here, too." He kept his gaze on her thumb as he caressed her hand absently with his thumb. "Saved me a trip back to the city."

"Why were you going back to the city?"

He looked up at her then, and she saw stark fear in his eyes, but unless she was crazy, there was something else behind the fear. Suddenly she knew. He loved her. "Lauren, I need to tell you something. And if you don't feel the same way, I hope we can still be friends."

"I thought I was the one who talked too much. If you don't hurry up, I'm going to have to tell you first."

She looked down at their hands, completely intertwined now. Their hearts had always known the truth; it was just taking their brains a little while to catch up.

"Tell me what first?" He stared at her. "Lauren? Are you saying you love me?"

"Of course I do. Why do you think I ran halfway across the state to get away from you?"

"I tried to get you not to go." He grinned, and a glint of mischief sparkled in his eye. "Anyway, I guess you know it's your fault I never did find my perfect girl, you know."

"It was not. I even memorized your list." She jerked her hand from his and began to count off the qualities on her fingers. "Good with kids. Blond—"

"See? That explains it. It was always brunette. I just hated for you to know that you were pretty much my idea of the perfect girl."

"Pretty much? What do you mean pretty much?" Lauren couldn't believe how free she felt. Her best friend was back, only better than ever, because he— "Wait a minute. You still haven't told me you loved me."

"You know what your Granny always says."

"Never go out in the cold with your hair wet?" Lauren gave him a cheeky grin, but her heart thudded against her ribs.

"No, silly. Actions speak louder than words." He leaned toward her and whispered, "I love you," then lowered his mouth to hers. For a while no words were needed.

CHRISTINE LYNXWILER

Christine thanks God daily for the joyous life she shares with her husband and two daughters. They work, play, and worship together in a small town nestled in the gorgeous Ozark Mountains. She loves to write and has had several novels and novellas published with Barbour Publishing.

Joy comes from many corners, and at this point in her life, Christine's list of blessings include a wonderful husband and two amazing daughters, a large family (including in-laws) who love God and each other, a close group of writer friends, a loving congregation of believers at Ward Street Church of Christ, and readers like you who encourage and support her dream of being a writer. Please visit her Web site at www.christinelynxwiler.com and sign the guestbook to let her know you stopped by!

Dreaming of a White Christmas

by Kathleen Miller

Dedication

To Brittany Bodden, Kristy Bodden, Sally Miller,
Meagan Holman, Lauren Adams, Megan Adams,
Alison Goss, and Sarah Goss, my precious nieces. . .
may the Lord always lead you and guide you.

*And the angel said unto them, Fear not: for, behold,
I bring you good tidings of great joy, which shall be to
all people. For unto you is born this day in the city of
David a Saviour, which is Christ the Lord. And this
shall be a sign unto you; Ye shall find the babe wrapped
in swaddling clothes, lying in a manger. And suddenly
there was with the angel a multitude of the heavenly host
praising God, and saying, Glory to God in the highest
and on earth peace, good will toward men.*
LUKE 2:10–14

Chapter 1

Cade's Point, California—Thanksgiving Eve

I t's the day before Thanksgiving and I'm sitting in a store window up to my eyeballs in work."

Ducking beneath the swag of brilliant green tinsel, Casey Forrester surveyed her progress as she suppressed a yawn. It must be near to midnight. She'd know the exact time if she hadn't lost her watch somewhere in the simulated red snow.

Casey leaned against the paper-covered glass of Callahan & Callahan's easternmost window. *Honey, you're a long way from the Ozarks, but this is a whole lot better than a double helping of Granny's turkey and Aunt Lou's pumpkin pie.*

All right. So it wasn't really better, but if she repeated the thought enough it might push away some of her homesickness. After all, she was doing exactly what she'd always wanted to do: design store windows.

And how bad could it be to have all your dreams come true in a place where palm trees and beaches were the standard scenery? After all, Cade's Point had the benefit of being situated comfortably between Los Angeles and Malibu on the Pacific Coast Highway. While their neighbors to the north and south paid city prices for their oversized homes, the post–World War II beach shacks and bungalows bordering Riverside and Cade's Beach Boulevard could be had for a steal.

Someday she would make one of those lovely cottages hers. Until then, she'd settle for two rooms and a bath in a converted attic across from the beach. If she stood on the toilet and craned her neck, she could see Cade's Beach and the glorious Pacific beyond.

"Sun, sand, and a view of the beach from my bathroom window. What could be more perfect?" She stumbled over a cable, then righted herself by reaching for the first of three blue tin trees. "All right, I admit it, Lord. I don't want to be here tonight. I'm tired." Casey punctuated the statement with a yawn.

Obviously the Lord wanted her here or Mrs. Montero, the store's manager and Elias Callahan's daughter, would never have entrusted Casey with the job of creating the Christmas displays for Callahan & Callahan Fine Clothiers, the most fashionable store on the entire West Coast. Considering this time last year she was planning what to wear to the Christmas formal at Ole Miss, Casey considered herself extremely blessed. Mrs. Montero told her she'd beat out a long line of much more experienced competitors to win the position.

Casey's first assignment: create a drop-dead amazing set of store windows to celebrate Callahan & Callahan's newly remodeled Cade's Point store. The offices where the big brass worked were just two floors up, so Casey had spent the past few months designing windows that would be seen by most of America come Thanksgiving Day under the watchful eyes of everyone from the janitor to the CEO himself, Elias Callahan. At least they *tried* to watch. Mrs. Montero had upped the pressure by electing not to preview Casey's designs and decreeing that anyone caught looking over Casey's shoulder would be summarily dismissed.

Given all the hype, gratefulness at being given her big chance had soon turned to sheer terror at the prospect of messing up. When the three windows of Callahan & Callahan opened on Thanksgiving morning, the whole world would be looking at Casey's work for the first time.

Well, anyone who watched local TV or cable news, anyway.

Fear overtook her, and Casey had to sit. She sank down beside a pile of gifts wrapped in rainbow colors and topped by bows of silver and gold, and rested her head on her knees.

What if the world wasn't ready for her designs? What if she had created a huge flop?

What will I wear?

Mrs. Montero told her preview photos of the windows were considered a hot commodity on the Internet. Yesterday, Mr. Riley, a security guard, caught a guy from the *National Questioner* posing as a deliveryman so he could peek at the design.

Brenda from accounting and Liz, the new hire in cosmetics, told her at lunch they'd been approached by e-mail from several journalists offering payment for pictures of the famous Callahan & Callahan windows. Neither accepted, not that they had any more access to the designs and the actual windows than anyone off the street.

Casey felt her pocket where the keys rested against a partially wrapped peppermint and a note reminding her to grab milk on the way home. As of this afternoon, she held the only key to the three locked windows. Even Mrs. Montero couldn't get in, although in theory she could order Casey to hand over a key anytime she felt the need to peek.

Slowly she rose, then reached down to fluff up the faux snow where her rear had made an impression. One final check of the display Casey called Neon Noel and she tiptoed to the exit hidden behind the brilliant orange bag of toys. The door clicked behind her and she fitted the key into the lock, then rested her forehead on the steel door.

"Lord, what have I done?"

"You've created a right interesting set of windows, I'm sure."

Casey jumped, her breath caught just shy of her throat. Resplendent in his Christmas-green coveralls stood Mr. Riley, a man whose age defied calculation. Rumor was, he'd been hired by the original Callahans, although Mr. Riley refused to confirm or deny this.

"I'm sorry, little lady. I ought not to have spoken without first letting you know I was here." He cocked his head to the side, then pointed to a spot just north of her eyebrows. "Did you mean to have that red fuzz in your hair?"

Swiping at her forehead, she watched a sizable chunk of cherry-colored faux snow land between her sock feet. Casey quickly picked it up and stuffed it into her pocket alongside the mint and note.

"Thanks," she said, as she pushed on the door one more time to be certain it had closed tight. One more window to check and she could call it a night. Or a morning, if it was as late as it seemed.

"If you'll excuse me."

She ducked past Mr. Riley to head to the south end of the building. This side faced the ocean, thus lending itself nicely to a beach theme she'd come to call Sandy Claus.

"You done for the night, Miss Forrester?" he called as she rounded the corner at foundations.

"Not yet," she said, "but you don't have to stay on my account."

It was a well-known fact that Mr. Riley's job was a token one. The real security for Callahan & Callahan's flagship store was an alarm system handled by a firm out of Los Angeles whose prototype was in use at the governor's mansion in Sacramento.

Casey didn't know he'd caught up with her until he banged his flashlight against the escalator. She jumped.

"You're a skittish thing, aren't you?"

She gulped to slow her racing heart. "Well, sir, I guess I'm just not used to watching a big-time security man like yourself on the job. I sure do appreciate the work you do here, Mr. Riley."

The old man hitched up his coveralls with one hand and gripped his flashlight with the other. "You ain't from around here, are you?"

Well who was? With few exceptions, the folks she'd met since she arrived in town last July were all from somewhere else. The California native seemed as rare as the California condor.

"No, sir," Casey said. "Pierce City, Missouri, by way of Ole Miss."

He gave her an appraising look. "Thought as much."

Okay. "Yes, well, if you'll excuse me." She unlocked the door to the beach scene and stepped inside.

"You going to be in here long?" he called.

"Fifteen minutes at the most." She stuck her head out to see him standing where she'd left him. "Were you in a hurry?"

"I don't suppose," he said. "I'll go make my rounds one more time before I leave. Ought to take about fifteen minutes, twenty at the most."

She stepped into the window and reached for an errant elf whose swim trunks had been put on backward. "That should give me plenty of time." A moment later, Casey left the display and locked the door, satisfied that all was well at the North Pole Pier.

One more window, her favorite, awaited her final

inspection. She called it Dreaming of a White Christmas, and it was a near-perfect reproduction of Granny Forrester's front parlor back in Pierce City. Complete with a towering, bedecked spruce and gifts wrapped and tagged with the names of her cousins, it boasted a well-worn King James Bible open to the story of the Nativity and a cane rocker just like Granny's. Wooden ornaments sat waiting in a basket on the hearth, a reminder of the Forrester family tradition.

Casey stepped inside and hit the switch, bathing the window-turned-room in a homey combination of warm lamplight and cozy orange firelight from the faux fireplace in the corner. She walked toward the fireplace, marveling that the flames were no more real than the cherry-colored snow in the Neon Noel window.

It seemed as though, if she were only a few feet closer, she could warm her hands by the fire and fill her empty stomach with the freshly melted ingredients for s'mores that waited on the hearth. And the stockings? Exact replicas of the ones she and her cousins hung every year on Christmas Eve.

Closing her eyes, she wondered what Granny Forrester was doing right this minute. Probably sleeping, she decided, for the matriarch of the Forrester family rose before dawn and, in her own words, went to bed with the sun.

Definitely not California hours. Even now Casey could hear the sounds of traffic dashing past on the boulevard.

She shrugged the tiredness from her shoulders, then

reached for the crocheted granny-square afghan currently draped on the arm of the plaid sofa. Cuddling the soft material against her cheek, she turned to peruse the details of the room.

Doilies on sofa arms. Check.

Braided rug on floor. Check.

Framed photographs of family. On this she had been forced to compromise. While they weren't actual family members, they would fool just about anyone except her family.

Casey lowered herself into the rocker and arranged the afghan over her legs. Two days until her big debut. She reached for the Bible, a happy find in the back of a dusty shop in the valley, and sighed. Words from the second chapter of Luke rose unbidden in her mind: *"And the angel said unto them, Fear not: for, behold, I bring you good tidings of great joy, which shall be to all people. For unto you is born this day in the city of David a Saviour, which is Christ the Lord."*

She settled deeper into the cushions of the cane rocker and pulled the afghan to her chin, closing the Bible. The firelight beckoned, so she turned her attention there as she suppressed a yawn.

"And this shall be a sign unto you; ye shall find the babe wrapped in swaddling clothes, lying in a manger. And suddenly there was with the angel a multitude of the heavenly host praising God, and saying, Glory to God in the highest and on earth peace, good will toward. . ."

A moment later, Casey jerked as something hit the floor with a thud. The Bible. She reached over to set the heavy volume back in its place on the chair-side table, then rose and stretched before heading toward the door.

Stepping out of the window, she walked into total darkness. "What. . . ?"

She reached behind her to open the door, then flipped the switch inside. Light streamed through the opening and lit the space around her.

"Mr. Riley?" When he failed to answer, she called again. "Must not be able to hear me."

Casey took a few steps out of the rectangle of light, then froze. She'd never get anywhere like this.

Ducking back into the window, she grabbed the battery-operated floor lamp and headed for her office in the back of the store. Once there, she snagged her purse and empty lunch bag and made her way to the employee exit. It was locked tight.

"Mr. Riley?"

Still no answer.

Gripping the floor lamp, Casey retraced her route, then turned toward the doors on the east side. They, too, were locked, as were the ones on the south and north sides. Until she found Mr. Riley, she was good and truly locked in, the only alternative being to trip the alarm by opening an emergency door.

In her exhaustion, Casey briefly considered doing just that. Then she took that scenario one step further. Not only would she rouse the security guard and the Cade's Point Police Department, but Mrs. Montero and Mr. Callahan would also be summoned.

Then there was the matter of the press. If anyone

saw the windows before the big opening, decades of tradition would be ruined.

Better to ferret out Mr. Riley. Perhaps the elderly fellow had fallen asleep somewhere in the store. Lamp in hand, she set off in search of the security guard who held the key to her exit—literally. Unfortunately, after a half hour of searching and much banging on doors, walls, and other structures, she failed to raise the security guard.

Panic edged into the corners of her mind and threatened to creep further. Casey shook her head and reached into her purse for her cell phone. If she couldn't get out, she could at least call out.

Casey opened the flip phone and punched the green button. Nothing happened.

She tried again. And again. Dead. What a time to realize she hadn't charged her phone.

"Great." Casey closed the phone and dropped it into her purse. "Now what?"

Using a store line sounded like a great plan, until she realized she had no idea who to call. Back in Pierce City there were any number of folks who would get out of bed to come and rescue her from a locked department store or see her through whatever emergency had befallen her.

But here in the city she knew no one that well. She did have a lunch table companionship established with Brenda from accounting, and Liz from cosmetics had offered a free makeover anytime she desired. Still, a live body across the lunch table and a pal who could hide your dark circles did not equate to a good friend you could call at midnight.

Or whatever time it was.

If I get out of here with a job, I am going to make sure Brenda and Liz know I'm that kind of friend. If . . .

Casey leaned against the locked door and closed her eyes. Now what?

Granny Forrester's parlor beckoned, and she headed back toward the Dreaming of a White Christmas window to settle into the cane rocker. Best-case scenario: Mr. Riley would return to let her out or someone arriving early to work would take pity on her.

Worst case? "Well, I just won't entertain those negative thoughts. The Lord will get me out of this mess. He always does."

She'd nearly fallen asleep when she thought better of it. Staying awake was her only hope for keeping this minor emergency from turning into a major fiasco.

Casey rose and rubbed her eyes. She'd make a pot of coffee up in the break room, then get something to read from the books-and-gifts department. Before she knew it, dawn would break.

Or, better yet, Mr. Riley would come out of hiding and release her.

The coffee made, she carried her mug and the most gripping mystery novel she could find into her office. Settling into her soft leather chair, Casey placed the book in front of her on the desk, then took a sip of strong black coffee.

"This should keep me up."

Half an hour later, she lifted her head off the desk to realize she'd soaked the edges of the novel with the remains of the overturned coffee mug. Casey straightened the mess as best she could and fought to knock the cobwebs from her brain. What to do? She certainly couldn't be caught sleeping at her desk. That would be more embarrassing than sleeping in the window and much more of a public spectacle.

Sleeping in the window. Of course.

She opened her desk drawer and picked up her notepad, then scribbled two notes, one each to her two companions. After placing the notes on their desks, she headed for the Cade's Point Boulevard window where Granny Forrester's parlor waited.

Back in Pierce City, she and her cousins had spent many nights sleeping by the fire. They'd called it camping out. Tonight Casey would be camping out alone, at least until someone came to rescue her.

Chapter 2

Ben Callahan was a mess and he knew it. That last call, a four-car accident out in Hidden View, had done him in. Between the bumpy ride up the canyon's fire road and the combative patient they'd transported to Valley General, he'd ended up feeling like he ought to be the ambulance's next occupant instead of the EMT.

If he weren't so tired, he'd probably have the strength to count the number of runs the ambulance crew had gone on tonight. It numbered in double digits; this he knew for sure. The last time he'd spent a night like this, he'd been on the other side of the world in a combat zone.

But then, some nights it seemed as though he'd never left the patch-'em-up-and-ship-'em-out mentality of the military. There certainly seemed to be parallels here in civilian life.

Slamming his locker, Ben sank onto the hard wooden bench and rested his elbows on his knees. Soon as he gathered the strength, he'd change into his street clothes and head home.

Home. Well, that brought a chuckle. The studio apartment he shared with an empty fridge and a dead plant could hardly be called a home. He let his chin drop and cradled his head in his hands.

"Callahan?"

Ben lifted his head and slid the shift supervisor a sideways glance. "Yeah?"

The captain wore his uniform like a Brooks Brothers suit and never failed to comb his hair back with something slick and sweet smelling before he came on duty. Tonight he'd added a gold chain to his ensemble. Ben figured he either had a crush on the cleaning lady or himself; he wasn't sure which.

He pointed in Ben's direction. "Brody called in sick. I'm going to need you to stick around until I can find someone to take his shift."

"Aw, Cap. Come on." He rose to address his boss. "I'm beat. Send Fisher or Cappalini."

"Fisher's already left and Cappalini's wife went into labor three hours ago." The captain shrugged. "That leaves you to ride along with Abrego. If it's any consolation, Vinson will probably jump at the chance for overtime. He's got those two kids in college now, and he's forever pestering me. Anyway, I left two messages."

Ben sank onto the bench. Even if he'd managed to gather the strength to protest, what would he say? All he could do was pray there would be no more calls before Vinson arrived.

Before he could fashion an official prayer, the radio crackled to life and another emergency call came in. He hit the rig running, then waited while Jerry Abrego slipped behind the wheel.

When Jerry called out the address, Ben froze. "Say that again." Of all the places to be called to, his exhaustion level aside, this one was the worst.

Jerry repeated the address.

Callahan & Callahan. Last time he left there, he swore to his father he'd never return. Four years, three months, and five days later, here he was, rolling toward it with lights flashing and sirens screaming. So much for getting in and out without his father seeing him.

Ben checked his watch. "It's a quarter to two in the morning. Are you sure this isn't a crank call? That's a department store."

Jerry shrugged and threw the vehicle into gear. "All I know is we got a call there's a dead woman inside the Cade's Point Boulevard window."

As the unit rolled toward its destination, Ben felt his heart begin to pound. *Get it together, Callahan. You've got a job to do.*

"You all right, Callahan?"

He cast a sideways glance at Jerry. "Yeah. Just tired, I guess."

"I heard you all blew out the old record last shift."

"Probably."

Ben scraped his fingers through his hair and focused on the road ahead. Two more turns and the building would come into view. He gripped the door handle and paced his breathing as they headed left on Riverside, then sped through the light at Wayland to turn onto Cade's Point Boulevard.

A police cruiser sat waiting, lights flashing. Jerry cut the siren and pulled up beside the officer.

"Over there." He pointed to the sole illuminated window, then gestured toward a man seated in the back of the cruiser. "That guy found her. Photographer. Seems as though he thought to get the scoop on these windows. Didn't expect to find a body when he looked inside that little tear in the paper."

"Male or female?" Jerry asked.

"Female," came the response.

While Jerry radioed the captain, Ben jumped out and grabbed his equipment before trotting toward the window. *Forget where you are, Callahan. This has nothing to do with Elias Callahan.*

"Anyone call the store manager?" he tossed over his shoulder.

"Not yet," the officer said. "Figured I'd wait until we knew what we had on our hands first."

"Probably could wait until morning at this point." The last person he needed to see tonight was his sister.

Ben shrugged off the last of his ire and leaned against the window at the spot the officer directed. Sure enough, a fair-haired woman lay prone beside what looked like a roaring fire. While he watched, her fingers twitched and she reached to rub her eyes.

"She's not dead!" he called as he tapped on the window. "I think she's sleeping!"

"Sleeping?" Jerry jogged up beside him. "Are you kidding?"

"Best I can tell through that little tear in the brown paper." Ben pointed to the spot. "Look for yourself, Jerry."

He did, then shook his head. "Don't that beat all?"

While Jerry went over to speak to the officer, Ben continued his efforts to awaken Sleeping Beauty. A moment later, the officer left with the newsman still seated in the back of the cruiser.

"Any luck?" Jerry asked.

"Not yet. What's the story with the guy in the cop car?"

Jerry shrugged. "I just got him for trespassing. Seems as though he was on the roof trying to shoot pictures through a skylight."

"Yeah, that'll get you in trouble every time."

"Especially at two in the morning." Jerry peered in at the woman. "How about I do the paperwork while you beat on the window some more?"

"I've got an idea." Ben nodded toward the unit. "How about you hit the siren a couple of times? I think that ought to do it."

When Jerry complied, the woman on the floor sat bolt upright. Ben tapped on the glass.

"Ma'am? City of Cade's Point EMT here! You need to come on out!"

She seemed bewildered and a bit lost. When he repeated his command, she rose and stood in the center of the window. Once more he tapped on the glass. This time she followed the sound.

A single eye peered back at him through the tear in the paper. It was blue—the color of a summer sky over the Pacific.

Ben took a step back, then tapped once more on the glass. "Come on out now! It's time to go home!"

She pulled the paper back at the corner and shook her head. Her lips moved but he couldn't quite make out what she said. Repeating his demand had the same effect.

He walked over to the trash can and yanked out a fast-food bag, tossing the contents back into the container. COME OUT OF THERE, he wrote on the bag, then walked back to the window to show it to the woman.

To his surprise, she lifted the corner of the paper to look out, then shook her head and disappeared. A moment later, she returned with a piece of what looked like a sales receipt. I CAN'T. THE DOOR IS LOCKED was written on the back of the receipt.

OPEN IT. YOU ARE THE ONE INSIDE.

The woman made a face as she wrote, then lifted the receipt into view. I CAN'T. I DON'T HAVE A KEY AND THE ALARM WILL GO OFF.

He responded with a quick, IT'S OKAY. THE POLICE ARE ALREADY HERE.

She shook her head. I WILL LOSE MY JOB IF MY BOSS FINDS OUT.

He gave this last claim a bit of thought. Alexis had the reputation of being a tough cookie, but would she fire someone for falling asleep on the job? Probably. She once gave away a puppy because it refused to come when she called. Then there was the episode with the peace-loving Chinese fighting fish.

Ben sighed then wrote, WHO ELSE HAS A KEY?

The woman turned the receipt over and scribbled, MR. RILEY.

Mr. Riley. Hal Riley. Ben smiled.

As a kid, he'd followed Hal all over Callahan & Callahan, and the old fellow never once complained or failed to answer any of his questions. The man must be well past retirement age by now.

GIVE ME A MINUTE AND I WILL GET YOU OUT.

Before she showed him what she wrote, she pointed to the glass. DO NOT BREAK THIS WINDOW.

Suppressing a chuckle, he gave her the thumbs-up sign.

She nodded and crumpled the receipt, then tossed it behind her. As he walked back to the rig, he couldn't help but wonder why he was going to so much trouble for a total stranger.

It didn't take him long to find Hal Riley's number; it was the same one he'd had for six decades. He answered as if he were sitting by the phone and said he'd be up at the store in under fifteen minutes.

Hal made it in ten, and despite the fact that he kept stopping to hug Ben, he found the proper key and fitted it into the side door nearest the window where Sleeping Beauty had been held prisoner.

"Thanks, Hal," Ben said once the door swung open.

The ancient security guard replied, "Anything for you, Bennie."

"No one's called me that in years."

"Well, now, I guess I should have called you Corporal Bennie." Mr. Riley looked him up and down. "Only it don't look like you're still on Uncle Sam's payroll."

"No, sir. I've been with the City of Cade's Point almost a year now."

"Well, how about that? Wonder why your daddy didn't mention that you were back in town."

Ignoring the question, Ben stepped inside. The familiar scent of designer suits, expensive perfume, and big money stopped him in his tracks. If Hal noticed Ben's discomfort, he had the kindness not to comment. Rather, the old man weaved his way through the darkened aisles with the expertise of a man who'd been clocking in at Callahan & Callahan since Eisenhower sat in the White House.

Ben, on the other hand, stumbled and picked his way through the maze, unable to match Hal's pace. He did fine, even at his slower pace, until he slammed his knee against the umbrella display.

"Want me to hit the lights, Bennie?" Hal called.

"No, don't do that. I'm fine." He wasn't, but somehow it seemed appropriate to be entering Callahan & Callahan in the dead of night under cover of darkness.

"Oh, there you are!" he heard a voice call. "You all just don't know how glad I am to see you."

Definitely not from around here, Ben decided from the way she drew out her words. Beautiful, he realized when he turned the corner and caught sight of her.

The woman came his way, right hand outstretched. Before he realized what happened, she was shaking his hand. Those eyes, much prettier when viewed without the glass between them, peered up at him with what looked like a mixture of gratitude and exhaustion.

"Casey. Casey Forrester. I don't know what I would have done without you, Officer."

"I'm not an officer." He withdrew his hand. "I just work for the city."

She studied his face for a second, then her attention fell to his lapel. "Callahan." Her gaze met his, the exhaustion turned to amusement. "Same as the store. What are the odds?"

Here we go. How he hated having to explain away his connection to the Callahan fortune—or rather his lack of it.

"Yeah, what are the odds?" He caught Mr. Riley staring and gave the old man a wave. "Appreciate the help, Hal."

"Anytime," he said. "You take care."

Ben responded, then turned and headed for the door. Between his forced return to the store and the sleepy-eyed blond, he'd just made a memory he'd be hard pressed to forget. The sooner he got out of here, the better.

Chapter 3

"H ey, hold on a minute, Officer Callahan!"
Casey picked up her pace to try and catch the long-legged fellow who'd just saved her budding career from ruin. Unfortunately, the man seemed more intent on getting out of the department store than in obliging her by slowing down.

"Wait," she called, "these are *not* my running heels!"

As soon as his broad shoulders cleared the front door, he whirled around to stare at her. She grabbed the door to keep from slamming into him.

"I told you I'm *not* an officer."

And you're not very nice right now, either. She upped her smile in the hopes his grim look might soften. It didn't. *All right. Plan B.*

"Sorry. The uniform confuses me. Back home, only cops and security guards wear that. But then the closest hospital's a 'fur piece,' as my granny always says."

Casey waited for the medic to smile. He didn't.
Plan C.

"Look, I just want you to know I'm really grateful to you for being my Prince Charming and rescuing me from the tower tonight. If anyone found out I was sleeping on the job, I'd probably be headed back to the Ozarks for Christmas."

Again she waited for some sort of smile, maybe even a glint of amusement in those ocean blue eyes. Again, nothing.

"Honestly, you saved me from a huge mess. Can't I repay you in some way? Maybe take you out for dough-nuts and coffee?"

"It's not necessary, really. That's my job, ma'am," he finally said without enthusiasm. "I'm no Prince Charming, but if you appreciate the service, call the city manager."

"I'll do that." She gave him a playful nudge. "Shall I mention you by name?"

The paramedic raked his hands through his surfer-style hair and sighed. "That won't be necessary. Just tell him it was Prince Charming."

"Oh, I'll do that, but I'll still make good on that coffee and doughnuts. Just name the place."

Casey waited for the grin that would indicate he was teasing. It never came.

Without a Plan D, she shrugged and walked past the Callahan fellow. *Odd that a man who makes his living helping people would be so crabby.*

Stifling a yawn, Casey settled behind the wheel of her VW Bug and stabbed the key into the ignition. Maybe the Cade's Point paramedic was tired, too.

The car protested rather than started, a usual occurrence lately. Casey pulled out the key, counted to five, and replaced the key in the ignition.

Out of the corner of her eye, she saw the EMT approaching. Rolling down the window, she waved at the Callahan fellow. "It does this all the time," she said when he reached her window.

For the first time, she saw something besides aggravation on the man's face. He actually looked concerned. "You sure?"

Casey offered a genuine smile. "Positive."

She turned the key and prayed as the engine cranked to life on the third try. Someday she'd have to replace the only car she'd ever owned. In the meantime, she gave thanks that she had no car note to pay.

"All right then." He glanced over his shoulder, then back at her. "Hey; you're welcome." The paramedic stuck his hand through the open window. "Ben Callahan."

Casey smiled and shook his hand. "Nice to meet you, Ben Callahan. I'm Casey Forrester."

"So you said." His gaze swept across her face. "Get some sleep, okay?"

What beautiful blue eyes. *Focus, Casey.* "I'm headed home."

His badge glinted silver under the streetlight as he took a step backward. "Would you like us to follow you to be sure you're all right?"

"No, I'm fine. Thank you, though."

He stayed a moment longer, then gave her a nod and turned to sprint toward the waiting vehicle. Before she could shift the Bug into drive, the paramedics had pulled onto Cade's Point Boulevard.

Casey slowed for the stoplight at Riverside and Cade's Point Boulevard. Up ahead she could see the vehicle signal to turn left, then disappear down Grant Drive.

"Well, that was an interesting night, Lord." As she crossed Grant Drive, she looked to her left and saw the ambulance off in the distance. "And an interesting man, too."

∞

Exhaustion rolled over Ben like the waves at Cade's Beach, each one dragging him further toward the oblivion of sleep. Maybe he'd bunk upstairs tonight instead of going home. When he got this tired, any bed would do. Besides, he had too much to think about and not nearly enough functioning brain cells to do the thinking.

Stepping back into the world he swore he had left for good was enough to do any man in. Combine that with meeting a woman who'd literally taken his breath away, and he was a goner.

Ben closed his eyes. *Lord, what are You up to? I thought we had a deal.*

"Well, that was different."

He opened his eyes and glanced over at Jerry, then let out a long breath. "Yeah. Different."

"Who woulda thought our dead girl in the store window would turn out to be sleeping?" Jerry shook his head. "It takes all kinds. She was a cute thing, though."

"Yeah. Cute." Ben closed his eyes. When he opened them, Jerry had begun his turn into the station. A quick glance at the parking lot told him his replacement had not yet arrived.

"Hey, I'll do the paperwork on this one, then I'm heading home." Jerry cut the engine and released his seat belt. "You go get some shut-eye. If the boss wants someone to roll out again tonight, he's gonna have to do it himself."

As tempting as that sounded, Ben wouldn't leave his post. Even if it hadn't officially been his shift any longer for several hours.

"I'm fine." He gestured toward the stairs. "Look, I'm going to find an empty bunk. Tell the boss if he needs me, call me, okay?'

"Yeah, whatever." Jerry pointed to the closed door of the supervisor's office. "I still say he can handle this himself. What is it with you? Don't you understand this is just a job?"

Despite his exhaustion, Ben smiled. "You really want me to answer that?"

Jerry nodded. "Sure."

"It's like this. If you knew someone really important— someone like the city manager or maybe the mayor, with the power to decide your future—was watching you work, wouldn't you do the best job you could for him?"

He palmed the keys and leaned against the front bumper. "Sure, who wouldn't?"

"Exactly. That's how it works with me and God. Even when no one else is watching, He is." Noting

Jerry's surprised expression, Ben shrugged. "I don't want to sound like I'm preaching or anything, but you asked."

"Anybody else said something like that to me and I'd be tempted to call it preaching. You?" He slapped Ben on the back. "You're the real deal. I'm glad you've got something to believe in."

You could, too, he wanted to say. Instead he smiled and parted company with a handshake and a quick, "Anytime you want to know more, I'm here."

As he lay in his bunk a short while later, Ben's thoughts drifted between what to say to Jerry next time he asked about the Lord and whether he should call to check up on Sleeping Beauty. The issue with Jerry was much more important than a slight infatuation with a blond Kate Hudson look-alike, and yet Ben knew that when the time came, the Lord would give him the right words to speak to the searching paramedic.

The blond? That was another story altogether.

Then there was the issue of his father. Ben rolled over and punched the skimpy pillow. Thanksgiving mornings in the past, he'd headed for the house in the canyon to be poked and prodded by maiden aunts who thought him too thin and teased by uncles who resented his firm stance on bachelorhood. Then came the big blow up with his father at the store.

Callahan males were a pigheaded bunch and Elias Callahan was the most pigheaded of them all. Ben's sisters would say Ben had inherited a good measure of that family trait, as well, but what did they know? He drifted off to sleep, wondering if even his mother, rest her soul, could have negotiated a truce in this ongoing war between father and son.

Probably not, as Ben refused to apologize for choosing to serve his country in the Marine Corps over serving his father's business interests at Callahan & Callahan.

Ben awoke from a dreamless sleep to the smell of something cooking. Lunch, he discovered a few minutes later when he slipped into his boots and headed downstairs. Passing on the turkey and dressing, he situated a slice of pumpkin pie on a paper plate and anchored it with a cover of foil. It sat beside him on the seat of his truck until the light at Mountainview and Riverside when a Channel 43 news truck ran the light and nearly broadsided him.

He pulled to the curb to scrape the pie off his floor mat with an out-of-date map of Los Angeles, then climbed from the truck and deposited the mess in a trash receptacle. So much for his Thanksgiving feast. Glancing up Riverside, he noticed what looked like a traffic jam at the next light.

"The big unveiling," he muttered as he jogged back to the truck and climbed inside. "Big deal."

At one time it *had* been a big deal. Being the sole male heir, Ben had done the honors at the annual post-parade Thanksgiving morning unveiling ever since he was out of diapers. Photos of Elias Callahan's future business partner went out on the wire services along with images of the store windows that never failed to draw a crowd. Afterward, at the traditional meal in the company dining room, he'd been given first chance at the turkey leg.

Ah, the perks of inheriting the keys to the kingdom.

Somewhere along the way, he'd lost interest and still he honored the tradition. Until four years ago.

Ben let out a long breath and shook his head. Easing onto Mountainview, he accelerated. Three blocks away a soft bed awaited, while up on Riverside a painful memory of what used to be was being filmed for the evening news.

The choice was simple. Why then, did he slip his cap on and hang a U-turn to head back toward Riverside?

Chapter 4

C asey, you do the honors." Elias Callahan leaned close. "And don't be nervous."

Don't be nervous? That was like saying don't breathe or don't blink. Oh, anyone could manage it for a moment or two, but any consideration of accomplishing it long-term was out of the question.

Casey glanced over at the store owner and he gave her what looked like an encouraging nod. As she raised her hand to press the giant candy-cane-colored button, cameras began to flash. She lost track of where the button had been placed. It took her two tries to make contact with the device, but when she managed, the music started and the curtains opened.

Through the spots dancing before her eyes, Casey watched the crowd's astonished faces turn to smiles. Then the applause broke out.

She'd chosen to stand near her favorite window, the scene from Granny's house. Whether the other two windows were a hit or a flop was uncertain. But she knew from watching the crowd on the other side of the glass that this one had met with appreciation. Granny would be pleased.

Elias Callahan grasped her elbow and guided her away from the throng. "Miss Forrester, perhaps you would do the honors of posing in the window nearest the door."

Neon Noel. Not her favorite.

"Oh, I don't know, Father." Mrs. Montero gestured toward the replica of the Forrester family parlor. "I think I like this one."

A moment later, Casey stood in front of Granny's fireplace. A half dozen journalists awaited her upstairs, each having been selected to write about the new window dresser at Callahan & Callahan.

It was all too much, really, this attention. Coupled with her lack of sleep, the excitement made her woozy and she swayed. Catching herself on the mantel, she stared past the crowd on the other side of the window to the vehicles passing on Riverside.

A truck slowed and edged to the curb, its occupant's face hidden beneath a cap. He leaned against the steering wheel before turning to look her way.

Elias Callahan cleared his throat. "Miss Forrester, shall we?"

When she glanced in his direction, she saw he wore an odd expression. He, too, was staring at the man in the truck.

The look on the older man's face concerned her. "Someone you know, sir?"

Mr. Callahan turned his back on the window and headed for the exit. "Not anymore," he said, as he disappeared into the store.

The interviews lasted until midafternoon, then the group headed for Thanksgiving dinner in the employee dining room, an event that had begun years ago when the late Mrs. Callahan balked at serving Thanksgiving dinner after spending the morning at the unveiling. She'd elected to bring the feast to the store and a tradition was born.

By the time Casey left the store, she was sleepy, stuffed, and floating on air. Gary, the store's Web guy, had a stack of articles on the store printed out for her while Mrs. Montero advised her to go home and tape the news broadcasts. The clincher was when Granny Forrester called Casey's cell phone to say she'd been contacted by a wire service for her opinion on the room that was supposed to be a replica of hers.

"How do they find these things out, Granny?" she asked as she snapped her seat belt and threw the Bug's gearshift into reverse.

"I don't know, honey, but don't worry. I told them it was the prettiest store window I'd ever seen. Well, actually. . ."

"What? Don't you like it? I tried hard to make it look just like your parlor."

"Oh, I like it fine enough, honey. I just don't understand why you'd want my plain-old house featured in a fancy store window. Now that beach room? That was a pretty one. Oh, and the window with the red snow?

Well, I just loved it, even if I never would have dreamed up that color combination."

"I'm glad you liked it, Granny."

"I did, that's for sure. So did your mama and daddy. They'll be calling you next. I told them they had to wait until I had my turn since it was my house you used." She chuckled, then grew silent. "Casey, honey, I wonder if it's too soon to ask what day you'll be here next month."

"What day?"

"For Christmas. You *are* coming home for Christmas, aren't you?" She paused. "Why, the Forrester Christmas tradition wouldn't be the same without you here to be a part of it. All your cousins will be here. You've never missed a year, you know. None of you have."

Casey shifted into drive and headed the Bug across the parking lot. "Yes, of course I'm coming home. I wouldn't miss it. I just haven't had a moment to think about exactly what day."

"I understand. Just as long as you're here in time to have our special Christmas get-together with your cousins."

"I'll be there. I promise. I'll let you know the minute I make the plane reservations."

Signaling to turn onto Riverside, her phone beeped. A number she didn't recognize scrolled across the screen. Rather than cut short her call with Granny Forrester, she waited until she reached home to check her messages.

"Casey, this is Elias Callahan. I want to congratulate you on a job well done. I've been at this all my life and I've never seen a more enthusiastic reception to our store windows than I saw today."

She gulped and plopped onto the threadbare sofa. Elias Callahan was pleased with her work.

"I've left instructions with your supervisor that you're to be given a week's paid vacation starting Monday morning. When you return from your well-earned sabbatical, we'll talk about a raise, eh?"

A week off *and* a raise. She gulped again. She'd only take it if it didn't affect her planned vacation over the Christmas holidays. Nothing could keep her from Pierce City at Christmas.

"Oh, and don't make plans for Christmas Eve. I'm hosting a dinner in your honor. The invitations went out this morning. How's that for a Thanksgiving surprise, Miss Forrester?"

❧

Ben stabbed at the last piece of pumpkin pie, then washed it down with milk straight from the carton. The football game ended and a commercial for a delivery company came on as he rose to head for the kitchen to toss his paper plate and fast-food wrappers into the trash.

While he tried to convince himself that somewhere in the Bible it said that a turkey sandwich eaten alone was preferable to a feast shared with a contentious parent, the nightly news theme song floated toward him. Without dishes to rattle or anything to clean, Ben followed the sound of the talking heads into the living area.

There, in living color, was the smiling face of Sleeping Beauty. The camera panned back a bit to show her standing in the window that resembled someone's living room—the window where he'd first seen her.

The window where he'd spied on her from a distance this morning. Now *that* had been a dumb move. Not only had he seen Sleeping Beauty, but he'd laid eyes on his father for the first time since he left the military.

Ben pushed the newspapers out of the way and perched on the edge of the coffee table. Snagging the remote from beneath yesterday's sports section, he hit the VOLUME button.

"The inspiration for that window came from my grandmother's home in Pierce City, Missouri," she said. "Every year my cousins and I get together for our traditional celebration before Christmas Day. Inevitably, it is snowing or has snowed, so that's a part of what I think of as Christmas. I call this window Dreaming of a White Christmas."

A reporter questioned her further but Ben heard none of it. Instead, he stared at the window designer's name, then reached for a pen and jotted it down in the margin of the comics' page.

Not that he intended to look her up. The last thing he needed was any connection to Callahan & Callahan. Still, she *had* seemed nice and she *did* offer to thank him. That rarely happened in his line of work. Most folks weren't too worried about who was saving them, just that they were being saved. Some actually complained.

Maybe he'd let her buy him a cup of coffee.

A commercial came on and Ben hit the MUTE button as his phone rang. He groaned as he rose and padded toward the sound.

"Who would be calling me on Thanksgiving? Surely I'm not being summoned to work on my day off. Not again."

The phone rang a second time. He picked up without checking the caller ID.

"Look, I'm not coming in to work today, Cap. You're going to have to find someone else."

A click was followed in quick succession by the sound of a dial tone. Ben hung up and pressed the caller ID.

"Callahan & Callahan Fine Clothiers?" Ben took a step backward. "Who would be calling from there on Thanksgiving night? Casey Forrester, maybe?"

He smiled and punched the code for the call-return feature. As the phone rang, he ran over what he would say in his mind.

Unfortunately, he needn't have bothered. No one answered.

❧

It was Friday morning, and Casey's shoe-box-sized apartment smelled like a florist's shop. Between the dozen red roses her mama and daddy sent her, the huge arrangement of blossoms from her boss, and the fragrant fruit basket from Mr. Callahan, she could barely breathe.

Slipping into her running shoes, Casey tucked her key into her pocket and headed outside for fresh air. Her walk to the beach turned into a run as soon as her shoes hit the sand.

What a glorious day. The sun rode above a light wisp of clouds and added just enough warmth to the morning to keep the stiff breeze from being chilly.

Casey vaulted over a clump of smelly seaweed, then picked up her pace. Mama told her this morning that back home in Pierce City, the streets were covered in a light dusting of fresh snow. It was hard to imagine that back home there were snowmen in the yards and fires in fireplaces while here in her new home there were people enjoying the beach and surfing.

She ran past Java Hut and headed toward the pier. A half-dozen fishermen sat in silence, their lines bobbing in the surf. Toward the horizon, she noted more sailboats than usual. Must be the holiday weekend, she decided, as she completed her lap on the pier and returned to the beach.

A half hour later, she landed on a stool at Java Hut's beachfront counter. The combination of Christmas music on the sound system and the beach on the other side of the counter made her smile. Only in California.

Someone had left the lifestyle section of today's *Times* on the counter, and she slid it over while she waited for her coffee.

"Sleeping Beauty?"

Casey turned to see a familiar face coming toward her on the sand. The EMT, her rescuer from two nights ago, only today in place of his uniform and medical bag he wore a wetsuit and carried a surfboard.

"Well, if it isn't Prince Charming. Hi, Ben."

He looked surprised. "You remembered my name."

"It's a gift. I remember everyone's name. Just don't ask me for directions." She stuck out her hand and shook his just as she heard her name being called. "Oh, my latte is ready. Can you stay a bit?"

Ben took a step backward and stuck the end of his surfboard in the sand. "Well, I don't know, I—"

Again, her name was called. "Hold that thought," she said as she jumped up to retrieve her latte. When she returned, Ben had leaned the board against the side of the building and come around to take a seat beside her.

Drops of water glistened in his short hair and dropped to his shoulders as he shook his head. The slightest hint of a sunburn touched high cheekbones and faded into the stubble along his jaw.

And then there were those eyes. Green? No, blue but with a band of deep gold around their centers.

What am I thinking?

Casey set the latte on the counter. "I'm sorry, Ben. I told you I would buy you a cup of coffee next time I saw you. And here you are. What would you like? Vanilla latte, maybe?" She pushed the steaming cup toward the EMT. "Here, you can have mine. I'll get another."

He eyed the coffee, then scooted it back in front of her. "Thanks, but I like my coffee a little less fancy."

"Without the vanilla?"

His smile was amazing. "Without anything but coffee in it."

298

She jumped to her feet. "One black coffee coming right up."

Before she could reach the counter, he caught up with her. "Let me."

Casey stood her ground. "No way, buddy. I promised you coffee and doughnuts, and that's what you're getting." She glanced over her shoulder at the gentleman behind at the cash register. "A black coffee and two doughnuts for the officer."

"I'm not—"

"An officer." Casey grinned. "I know. I'm just teasing."

"And I'll pass on the doughnuts." He turned his attention back to Casey as he followed her to their seats, coffee in hand. "Thank you for the coffee. You didn't have to do that, you know."

She settled on her stool and watched the EMT find his spot beside her. "And you didn't have to save my bacon the other night. I really appreciated how you handled things. I was afraid I might have lost my job over what happened. I want you to know I've never fallen asleep on the job."

"I believe you." Ben lifted the coffee to his lips and blew on the steaming liquid before making eye contact with her. "So, what do you do when you're not sleeping in store windows? I mean, working at the store." He set the cup down and upped his smile. "See, I can tease, too."

Now that was an interesting statement. Casey gave her attention to the latte in her hands rather than meet his gaze. "Honestly, I haven't had much time to do anything else other than work since I've been in California. Well, I like to run. Does that count?"

"Sure."

"What about you, Ben?" She leaned on her elbow. "What do you like to do when you're not saving damsels in distress?"

Ben glanced at his wetsuit.

"Besides surf," she added.

"Knit."

She nearly choked on her latte. "Really?"

He chuckled. "No. There's nothing better than surfing. You should try it."

"I wouldn't know. The closest thing I've done to surfing is to try to sled down Jenson's Hill standing up." Casey giggled. "Trust me. That wasn't pretty."

Chapter 5

Why don't you let me teach you to surf, Casey? You're in shape. I'm sure you'd be great at it."

Ben tried not to groan as he went back to his coffee. There wasn't a thing about what he'd just said that hadn't come out sounding stupid. *You're in shape?* What kind of thing was that to say to a woman he barely knew?

Casey didn't seem to notice his embarrassment. "Honestly, I'd rather watch. I find it fascinating that someone can get on a board and ride a wave all the way to the beach without getting hurt."

"Oh, I don't know about that." Ben jerked up his sleeve and pointed to the pale crescent-shaped scar on the inside of his left wrist. "See that? Hawaii, five years ago." He turned his hand over and flexed his forearm, revealing the reminder of a run-in with a piece of coral. "Bali."

Casey grasped his right wrist and touched the back of his hand, tracing the network of scars that ran from wrist to elbow. "What happened here?"

Ben jerked his arm back and yanked on the wetsuit. "Afghanistan, three years ago."

"There's no beach in Afghanistan," she said with a slightly confused look.

"Exactly." *But there's a buddy of mine who never made it home.*

He shook off the thought and searched his mind for a change of subject. Thankfully the sound system did it for him.

"Oh, I love this song." She smiled and her face took on a faraway look. "It reminds me of home and snow and my family."

"Tell me about home, Casey."

For the next few minutes, his companion waxed poetic about life in the Missouri Ozarks, about a close-knit family that included three cousins who were like sisters to her. Ben listened and tried to imagine what that sort of life was like.

Sisters, he understood. He had four of them. But a family that let nothing come between them? Who were so close that their property literally adjoined one another? *That* he didn't quite have a handle on.

Too soon she finished her monologue and turned her baby blues his direction. "That's enough about me. Tell me about your family, Ben."

He swiveled on his stool and leaned his elbow on the counter. "Oh, you don't want to hear about that. It'd bore you, and it's such a beautiful day. How about we get out of here?"

She hesitated before nodding, then followed him around the counter and out onto the sand. Her Ole Miss sweatshirt and running shorts complemented her slender frame and fresh-scrubbed good looks, making her appear more like a teenager than a grown woman. She certainly was a fresh face among the usual California blonds he tended to date.

Not that he had dated anyone in a long time.

Ben reached for his board and hitched it up under his arm. "So, what would you like to do now? Looks like you've been running. I don't guess you'd be interested in a walk."

Casey placed her hand on his arm. "You know what I'd really like to do?"

"What?"

"Watch you surf." He must have looked as surprised as he felt because she quickly added, "Only if you want to, I mean."

"Yeah, sure, of course I want to." Ben paused to search her face for genuine interest. "Are you sure? I mean, I'll be the one having all the fun."

"I assure you," she said with a giggle, "watching will be much more fun for me than putting on a wetsuit and making a fool of myself."

"I don't know, Casey." He swept his gaze in her direction, then shamed himself for doing so. She was just so pretty, all the more so because she seemed to have no idea of her beauty. "I think you'd look much better in a wetsuit than I do."

"We'll never know, will we?" She tapped his arm,

then pointed to the shack where beach chairs were rented. "I'll grab a chair and you go do whatever it is that surfers do."

"Um, Casey, we surf." Ben waved at the familiar face behind the counter at Jim's Surf Shack. "Hey there, Jim. A chair and a towel for the lady, please."

"A towel?"

"The wind gets cold down by the water, Casey."

Jim came around to give him a bear hug, then grabbed a chair and towel. When Casey reached into her pocket, he waved her money away.

"It's on the house, little lady. Your boyfriend here saved my life. It's the least I can do."

"Cardiac arrest," Ben said by way of explanation as they crossed the sand to the water's edge. "And I didn't save his life. The doctors did that. I just kept his ticker going until he could get into surgery."

Casey accepted the towel and watched while he set the chair a few feet back from the water's edge. "Do you always do that?"

Ben looked up sharply. "Do what?"

"Refuse gratitude. Sometimes that's all a person has to give."

He opened his mouth but found he had no answer.

"Never mind." Casey settled into the chair and crossed her legs, then draped the towel over them. "Go ahead. Wow me."

"Wow me?" He grinned despite himself. "Is that a command, Sleeping Beauty?"

"It most certainly is, Prince Charming." She affected

304

a bored pose. "To the waves with ye before I'm forced to nap."

Ben reached down to snap the safety line around his ankle, then straightened to see Casey's questioning look. "In case the board and I get separated."

A few minutes later, with the board beneath him and the rolling Pacific all around, he thought of her question about gratitude. Did he really do as she said?

True, he hated to be complimented, but with good reason. He'd fought the monster of pride most of his adult life. Born the nearest thing to a crown prince in a royal family that valued the male bloodline hadn't exactly equipped him for the life of humility the Lord called His people to.

Ben turned the board and waited for a good wave, searching the coastline until he found Casey Forrester. As if she sensed his gaze on her, she stood.

His ride wasn't particularly impressive, but Casey seemed to think it was. She laughed and clapped, then ducked away from the water he shook off as he approached.

"Again!" she called.

"You sound like my nephew."

"Oh, come on." She pointed to the water. "That was a little wave. I want to see you ride a big one."

"You do?" He gave her a sideways look. "What if I'm not that good?"

Casey dropped her towel onto the chair and planted her fists on her hips. "You're kidding, right?"

Ben's eyes narrowed. "I might be."

She swatted his shoulder. "Stop being so modest, Ben. Just once more, please?"

He knew she was right about his abilities. What he didn't know was how she'd figured him for an expert surfer.

This time it was a beauty, one of those perfect waves with just enough potential to warn the average surfer away. As always, the moment his feet hit the board everything went into slow motion.

Balance.

Speed.

Instinct.

Ben filled his lungs with salt air while adrenaline pumped a rhythm through his veins. He ducked under the curling water and rode the wave out until he could see daylight and Casey Forrester again.

As he floated to shore, he saw her. She feigned boredom, then giggled.

"Did I wow you?" he shouted.

"Oh, I suppose it was all right," she answered in a teasing tone. "*Wow* is such a strong word."

"All right. Watch this!"

Ben began to clown around, doing the handstand he'd perfected during his freshman year at UCLA. Casey rose and pointed to a spot behind him.

At least that's how it looked from upside down.

He flipped back to a standing position and opened his mouth to speak. That's when the wall of water hit him.

Chapter 6

Casey threw down the towel and raced for the spot where Ben went down. She barely felt the frigid water as it pounded against her legs and fought her progress.

One after another, the waves slammed her, but thankfully none were as large as the one that took Ben down. When the water reached a depth where she could no longer run, she dove in and began to swim.

Forcing her eyes open against the sting of the salt water, Casey kicked off her sneakers. Years of competitive swimming had not prepared her for this dip in the icy Pacific, and yet she couldn't turn back.

Ben was out there somewhere.

Something large and black caught her attention and she prayed it wasn't a shark. Casey bobbed up to catch her breath and saw Ben's board floating in the distance. Unless the line snapped, Ben should be attached to the board.

Casey ducked back under the water and swam

toward the black object. Another surfer reached Ben before she could and yanked him out of the water.

She surfaced in time to see the surfer drape an unconscious Ben facedown over his board. Blood trickled from a spot just above his right eyebrow and disappeared into a dark pool in the ocean. His lips moved as if trying to speak, but no sound emerged.

"You, there!" the surfer called. "Can you help me? We need to get him out of here before the sharks get a whiff of all this blood!"

Following the young man's directions, she climbed onto Ben's board and waited until he positioned his board beside her. With Ben's head and shoulders on one board and his legs on the other, they paddled at a maddeningly slow pace toward shore. Trying to speed up their progress only brought a warning.

Any faster, he asserted, and Ben would slip from the board.

Any slower, she retorted, and the tide would haul them back out in the opposite direction. By the time they reached shallow water, Casey felt like screaming.

The surfer eased Ben onto the sand, then stood back to address the knot of people gathered there. "Anyone know CPR?"

Casey turned Ben onto his back and put her training as a lifeguard at the YWCA into use. She'd repeated the process twice before she realized her patient was staring up at her.

"Hey there, Ben." She forced a tone of calm into her voice.

"Don't stop, Sleeping Beauty," he whispered. "You were just beginning to wow me."

The next hour was the most humiliating of Ben's life. Thankfully it was Jerry Abrego who was on call. Any other EMT and he'd never hear the end of it.

Ben looked around and determined he was in the back of the rig, his back flat on the gurney. "You rolling alone, Jerry?" he managed.

"Yeah; they're still shorthanded. Funny thing is, the cap tried to get you on your cell. Now sit still and let me do my magic."

He grunted as Jerry began his work. "Where— is—she?"

Jerry nodded toward the front of the vehicle, then bandaged him up in silence.

"She—okay?"

Ben had no memory of how he got from the water to the beach, but he had no problem remembering awakening to find Casey leaning over him.

When Jerry finished, he gestured toward the glass separating the treatment area from the cab. "Your girlfriend?"

"Nah." Ben eased into a sitting position. "Just someone I—" He paused to let a wave of dizziness pass, then continued, "Met recently."

"You think I don't recognize her, buddy?" Jerry chuckled. "She's the dead woman from your daddy's store."

He shook off the dizziness and shrugged his shoulders to ease the tightness between them. The fog cleared and he could think again. His first thought was of the woman who'd rescued him.

"Yeah, about Casey. . ." Ben leveled Jerry a serious look and exhaled. "I'd appreciate it if you didn't mention anything to her about my connection to the store."

"You think she doesn't know?"

"Nah. She thinks the name's a coincidence. I didn't see any reason to correct her."

Jerry shrugged. "Suit yourself, buddy, but don't you think she's gonna figure it out eventually?"

Ben slid off the gurney and waited for his sense of balance to catch up. When the rig's back door came into focus, he psyched himself up and headed toward it.

"Ben, hey, where're you going?"

"I need to see how she is. You *did* check her out before you worked on me, didn't you?" Ben's feet hit the sand as he held tight to the door and then the bumper. The world tilted once, then righted. He heard Jerry follow a step behind.

"Yeah, I gave her a couple of blankets and turned on the heater in the cab. Told her to knock on the glass if she needed anything. Hey! Go slow, Ben!" Jerry called. "Come back here. You know the drill. You blacked out. I gotta take you in to check for trauma."

"Forget it, Jerry. I'm fine. The only trauma I've suffered is to my ego. I need to see Casey. I'm such an idiot. This is all my fault." He made his way around the rig to yank on the passenger door. "Casey? Are you okay?" She nodded but he didn't buy it. "Hey, Jerry, how about we take her in to get checked out?"

"No." Casey sat bolt upright. "I'm fine, really. I'm more worried about you. Are you okay?" She touched the bandage, and tears welled in her eyes. "I'm so sorry. This is all my fault."

"I insist you see a doctor, Casey. You have no idea what damage hypothermia can do."

"Are you kidding me? I'm from Missouri where it actually gets *cold* in November." She fixed him with a stubborn glare. "I insist *you* see a doctor, Ben. You've had a head injury."

Jerry stood back, hands on his hips, and chuckled. "Yep. You're two of a kind, all right." He turned to look in Ben's direction. "You sure she's not your girlfriend?"

"Yes," they said in unison.

"All right then, kids," Jerry said, "how about I take you two home?"

While Jerry loaded Ben's board, Casey shifted over to allow Ben a spot up front. Her lips held a slight tinge of blue but otherwise she seemed to be unharmed.

"Hey, Casey, I was an idiot clowning around like that." He smoothed a strand of wet hair off her forehead while he checked her face for bruises. Under cursory examination, he decided she had suffered nothing worse than a swim in cold water without a wetsuit.

Truthfully, Ben was glad to have an excuse to sit, although he'd never let on to Jerry or Casey. When Jerry rolled the rig to a stop in front of Casey's apartment in the attic of a converted beach shack, he realized he only

lived two blocks away from her.

"I'll walk it from here, Jerry," he said as he opened the door and climbed out.

"No you won't," Casey and Jerry said in unison.

Ben grinned. "She your girlfriend, Jerry?"

"Very funny," Casey said.

"Nice place you got here, Casey," Ben said.

"I'd hoped for a cottage on the beach with white roses and a balcony overlooking the water, but then I saw this."

"She's a regular comedian, Ben," Jerry said. "I say she's a keeper."

"On that note, I'll be saying good-bye and thank you to both of you."

Sliding over to the door, Casey let the blanket fall from her shoulders before climbing out. She'd walked halfway to the front steps before she turned abruptly. Ben stopped short to keep from slamming into her.

Casey took a step backward and studied her nails. "It's been an interesting day, Ben."

He touched the bandage, then turned the gesture into a salute. "I'm glad I could wow you, Sleeping Beauty."

"Oh, you did better than that, Ben." She lifted her bare foot to pointedly study her toes. "You knocked my socks off. My shoes, too."

"Yeah, about that. If you tell me what size you wear I'll replace them." Her lip began to tremble, giving evidence that the fair maiden was not yet over her distress, and he jumped into action by reaching for her elbow. "Let me help you."

"Are you kidding?" She stepped away from his grasp and took two steps up the stairs before she turned to chuckle. "I don't want to have to give you mouth-to-mouth again."

"Oh, I don't know about that, Casey. That was the best part of the whole day." Ben leaned on the stair rail and offered her the broadest grin he could manage under the circumstances. "In fact," he said slowly, "Miss Forrester, I can honestly say that you wowed me."

Chapter 7

Casey's vacation wasn't starting off as the relaxing week she'd hoped. Rather, she spent the beginning of it wrapped in one of Mama's quilts with a box of tissues at her side. She'd missed church in favor of treating her fever and aches with chicken soup and hot tea.

By Monday afternoon, she'd exhausted her supply of tissues and moved on to paper towels. Her Jane Austen videos were groaning from overuse, and she had made short work of the pile of books she'd set aside to read in her spare time.

She'd made excellent progress in her sketches for the spring windows, even though the job had not yet been assigned to her. Still, memories of her day with Ben Callahan intruded. He popped up in the books, the videos, and even the few TV shows she watched.

Every time a handsome man attempted to sweep a woman off her feet, Casey thought of Ben and his silly handstand. When a chaste kiss or the proper words of adoration turned the heroine to mush, she remembered Ben's parting words: "You wowed me." Even now they made her smile.

Then her cell phone rang.

She'd been careful to avoid calling Mama this weekend, choosing to e-mail instead. There was no need in causing her mother worry, and worry she would if Mama knew Casey was ill.

Casey leaned over the edge of her chair and fished for the phone beneath the magazines she'd collected on a brief foray to the corner grocery this morning. While she collected the phone, she also snagged another tissue.

"Casey, it's Ben."

"Ben?" She dropped her tissue into the overflowing trash can and sat up straight. "How did you get my number?"

A long pause.

"Ben?"

"You sound like you're sick."

Casey reached for another tissue and dabbed at her nose. "It's nothing," she said.

Another pause. "Oh, man. I'm really sorry, Casey."

"I'm the one who should be sorry. My cold will be gone in a few days but you'll bear the scar of our day at the beach forever."

"Oh, I don't know. I worked half a shift last night, so when I got off I went to the early service at church. My sister was there and caught me with my bandage. Next thing I knew, she had me at the pharmacy buying stuff to get rid of the scar." He chuckled. "And here *I'm* supposed to be the medical professional."

"Yes, well, trust a woman to know about skin care." A thought occurred. "Say, do you go to church around here?" When he told her the name, she shook her head. "I can't believe it. That's where I go. You said you go to the late service?"

"When I'm not working a weekend shift, I do. You must be one of those who likes to get up early."

Casey shifted positions and burrowed into her nest of covers. "Now you know my secret. I'm a country girl at heart. Up with the chickens and sound asleep before the evening news. I figure that's why I'm not much of a sports fan. I never can stay awake to see who wins."

He laughed, then his voice returned to its serious tone. "Casey, I was wondering—that is, if you're not doing anything—well, of course, you're not because you're sick but. . ."

Casey gathered the quilt under her chin and tried not to smile. Was Prince Charming nervous about something? Could he be about to ask her out on—

"A date isn't out of the question, is it? I mean, if you're not feeling up to it, I'll understand."

It was her turn to be nervous. "When?"

"When? Well, I have four sisters, so I know I can't call you today and ask you out for tonight. How about tomorrow night? Seven?"

"You have *four* sisters?"

"Yes. Now answer the question."

"Tomorrow at seven." Casey pretended to think about it a moment. "I suppose I could do that," she said in the most casual tone she could manage.

Hanging up, she threw back her covers and jumped from the chair to do a happy dance. A moment later, the room began to spin and she fell back into her quilt.

"Slow, girl," she said as she reached for another tissue. "You've got twenty-four hours to make suffering from a cold look good."

∽∾

Ben dropped the phone onto the seat of his truck and threw the vehicle into reverse. If he'd been home, he would have whooped for joy. Instead, he settled for a ridiculously broad smile and a trip to the florist.

"Callas and a white ribbon for Alex Montero," he said. "Just put 'Thanks for the number, sis. I'm seeing her tomorrow. Love, Ben' on the card."

Ben wrote his sister's home address on the card, then fished in his pocket for his cell phone so he could provide her number. Too late, he remembered he had left the phone in his truck.

"Is a number necessary? I don't remember Alex's home phone number and it's unlisted." He shrugged. "The convenience of cell phones. Sorry."

"What about an office number?" the florist asked.

"That I remember." After he gave the main number to Callahan & Callahan, he reached for a card from the counter. "I'll write this one myself." When he was done, he sealed the card inside the envelope and reached for the shopping bag at his feet. "I know this is nuts, but can you work these into an arrangement?"

"Sure. But this one won't go out until tomorrow."

∞

Between the prayer and the chicken soup, Casey's cold had been reduced to the occasional annoying sneeze. She tucked a tissue into her purse and stuffed another in the pocket of her khakis, just in case.

Slipping her favorite blue sweater over her head, she reached for the brush and gave her hair a quick styling. When the doorbell rang, she dropped the brush and glanced over at the clock on her nightstand. Ben was early by half an hour.

She snagged the brush and tossed it onto her bed, then took a deep breath and let it out slowly. Heart racing, she walked to the door.

"This is silly." Casey reached for the handle and gave it a tug. "It's just a date. No big deal." The door swung open and Casey put on a smile despite her nerves.

Instead of finding Ben on her porch, there stood a young man wearing a T-shirt with FLOWER POWER emblazoned on it. "Miss Forrester?"

"Yes."

"Sorry this took so long. I thought I'd never find this place. I didn't even know this apartment was here." The man gave her a receipt to sign, then thrust an oversized bouquet of white roses in her direction. "Have a nice day, ma'am," he said over his shoulder as he raced down the stairs toward a green van.

Casey set the arrangement on her kitchen table and reached for the card. That's when she saw the shoes:

a tiny pair of white sneakers with pink laces attached to the soft pink bow. She removed the card from its envelope.

Since I knocked your shoes off, I thought it only right to replace them. I hope you're feeling better. Forgive me?

Ben

Smiling, Casey replaced the card in its envelope and set it beside the vase. She touched the toe of one of the shoes. "What an interesting man."

By the time Ben arrived, Casey had changed clothes two more times. When she answered the door, she'd donned a pair of black jeans and the green sweater her parents gave her for Christmas last year. This time she peered through the peephole first.

No great surprise. Ben looked fabulous. He'd traded his wetsuit for a pair of jeans and a navy sweater. The bandage over his eye had been replaced by a small strip of white tape, and the slight sunburn from Friday had faded to a burnished bronze.

"Hi," she said as she opened the door.

"Hi," he repeated.

"The flowers—they're beautiful. Just one problem."

Ben's grin sank. "What's wrong?"

Casey leaned against the door and pretended to study her nails. "Well, Ben, it's the shoes." She met his gaze. "They're too small."

Chapter 8

Dinner was shrimp and crab, under the stars on the patio of a beachfront hole-in-the-wall in an enclave a few miles down the road. A lone guitarist played Spanish tunes while the Pacific kept rhythm. The ever-present wind died down to a gentle breeze by the time the coffee arrived.

Throughout dinner, the conversation had been about impersonal things like the mild temperatures last week, the headlines in the local paper, and the success of the fund-raising campaign at church. Casey had barely noticed any of these things, but listening to Ben talk made her smile.

Actually, everything about Ben made her smile. It also made her wonder what the Lord was up to.

Rather than dwell on the odd sensation that she'd never had a more wonderful evening, she leaned back in her chair and watched the waves break against the shore. "This is a lovely place, Ben." She turned her attention to her companion. "Thank you for bringing me here."

"My pleasure, Casey."

Casey took a sip of coffee and watched Ben order two pieces of the house special, Wow Cake, from the dessert cart. With a flourish, the dessert chef sliced two overlarge pieces of the flower-covered Italian cream cake and set them on the table.

"I guarantee this will be the best dessert you've ever had." Ben reached for his dessert fork. "My mother used to make this cake and, much as I loved her, she never made it this good."

Loved?

Several questions begged to be asked, chief among them what the current status was with his mother. Granny Forrester always said if a man didn't care about his mama, then run for the hills because he won't love you right, either.

She placed a small bite—just a nibble, actually—of cake onto her fork. When Ben made a face, she scooped up a bit more and added a touch of frosting before popping it into her mouth.

All she could say was, "Wow."

Ben nodded. "Hence the name."

Despite her good intentions, Casey ate the whole thing. After a refill of her coffee, she was ready to broach the topic of Ben Callahan's family life. What she couldn't quite figure was how to do it without sounding nosy.

She decided to start with his childhood. "So, Ben, did you grow up here in Cade's Point?"

He nodded. "Yep."

So much for getting the man to talk about his past. Now what?

"Ben, is that you? What happened to your eye?" a man asked.

A man in a dark suit and a well-dressed woman with upswept black hair and tiny, wire-rimmed glasses approached the table. Ben rose to embrace her, then shook hands with her companion. "Delia. Bob. Good to see you." He touched the tape over his wound. "Surfing accident."

"Looks like a nasty laceration, Ben," the man named Bob said. "I can take a look at that in the office tomorrow if you'd like."

"I'm fine, Bob. Honestly. Nothing to worry about. Say, where are my manners? Let me introduce you to my friend, Casey." He smiled in Casey's direction. "Casey Forrester, I would like you to meet my sister Delia Jenson and her husband, Dr. Bob Jenson. Delia's the eldest, so she's a bit bossy."

"And Ben's the baby of the family, so he assumes we all think he's adorable even when he's behaving badly."

Casey searched the older woman's face and noted eyes that matched Ben's, as well as a broad smile and twin dimples that marked her unmistakably as his sibling. Delia and Casey exchanged pleasantries while Bob spoke to Ben about the latest buzz at the hospital. Casey got the impression Ben did not see these folks on a regular basis.

Another warning bell went off.

The doctor studied her intently. "Casey Forrester.

Why does that name seem so familiar? Are you in medicine?"

"Oh no," she said with a giggle. "I'm the new window dresser at Callahan & Callahan."

Bob and Delia whipped their attention toward Ben. "Isn't that interesting?" Delia said.

"Interesting indeed," Bob echoed.

"Tell me, Casey. How did you come to work at my fath—" Delia shook her head. "I mean at Callahan & Callahan?"

"Oh, that's quite a story. I graduated from Ole Miss in the spring with the goal of someday working at Callahan & Callahan, but in my mind it would be way in the future."

"Why that particular store?" Dr. Jenson asked.

"Promise you won't laugh?" When he agreed, she continued. "Ever since I was a little girl, I've dreamed of living in one of the store windows at Callahan & Callahan. They were just so beautiful."

Delia chuckled. "I assume you altered your goal a bit as you matured."

"Oh yes. Once I realized that what I loved about those windows was the creativity and the ability to transform a small space into a place where everything is good and happy, then I knew I was hooked."

"Hooked?" asked Dr. Jenson.

She felt the heat rise in her cheeks. "This is silly, really."

"Oh no, I'm interested," Ben said as the other two nodded.

"Well, I mean, it's not like I am a doctor or an EMT or a. . ." She turned to Delia.

"CEO of an international marketing firm."

Casey nodded. "Yes, or the CEO of an international marketing firm. I'm just a girl from the Ozarks."

"Casey, God can use anyone," Delia said, as she entwined her fingers with Ben's. "Absolutely anyone. Sometimes the less you know about His plan and purpose, the easier it is for Him to have His way."

"Yes, well, anyway," she said, "I believe the Lord put everybody on this earth for a different reason. Me, well, somewhere along the way I figured out He intended me to be someone He would use to add a little happiness to the world. Well, as much happiness as a store window can give, that is."

"I think a store window can bring an incredible amount of happiness. What do you say, Ben?" asked Delia.

Ben's gaze met Casey's and his smile broadened. "Yes, I'd say those windows have made a number of people happy. Just looking at them makes me smile."

"So you've seen them, little brother. Interesting." Delia fixed her attention on Ben. "So, Ben, we missed you at Thanksgiving. Were you working?"

The statement seemed harmless enough to Casey, but Ben's countenance darkened. "Yeah, you know how it is. The guy without the family draws all the holiday overtime."

Ben's sister placed her hand on his. "You have a family, Ben. Whether you choose to be a part of it is

DREAMING OF A WHITE CHRISTMAS —

up to you. Don't ever forget that."

All the air seemed to go out of Ben as he looked down at his sister's hand. "It was good seeing you tonight, guys. We were just leaving or we'd invite you to coffee."

Delia went up on tiptoe to give Ben a kiss on the cheek, then Bob shook Ben's hand. When Delia stepped toward Casey, she paused. "Wait a minute. You didn't finish your story, Casey." At Casey's confused look, Delia explained. "You were going to tell us how you ended up at Callahan & Callahan."

"Oh, that. Well, all I can say is that it was a God thing. There's no other explanation. I was in my last semester at Ole Miss when I got the idea to send a résumé to Callahan & Callahan. It was a silly thing to do, because they weren't even interviewing on our campus but still, I felt God telling me to give it a shot. After all, it *was* my dream job."

She shrugged. "So I put a few of my sketches from design class in an envelope along with my résumé. I was about to write a cover letter when I realized I didn't know who to address it to. I called the main number for the store, not realizing I'd called an hour before the store opened. Would you believe the person who answered the phone was Mrs. Montero, the store manager?"

The trio didn't seem surprised by this. In fact, something akin to a knowing look passed between Ben's sister and her husband. Ben, however, looked positively pale.

"Mrs. Montero and I had a great conversation. Did

you know she went to Ole Miss? Anyway, by the time I got off the phone I had an interview. Two weeks later, I had a job offer. I've been with the store since July. I don't know how to explain it except to say that God made it all possible because He's got some purpose in all of it. What that purpose is, I can't imagine."

Delia and Ben wore matching looks of stunned silence. Dr. Jenson took the lead and grasped Casey's hand. "I, for one, will pray that His purpose will become clear to you, Casey. And if I may say so, I may have an idea what that purpose is."

Ben's sister stepped forward and offered a smile. "Honey, I think this is between Casey and the Lord. I wouldn't advise you to spoil the surprise."

"Surprise?" She caught Ben's startled expression. "What's wrong, Ben?"

"Wrong?" He reached for his glass of water and downed half of the contents, then gave his brother-in-law the oddest look. "Oh, I don't know. Like my sister said, it's probably best that *the Lord* reveal things."

Bob seemed to think about the statement a moment before nodding in agreement. "Casey, it has been a delight meeting you. You have *no idea* how much I've enjoyed it."

Casey had the oddest sensation she was the only one in the group who was missing a piece of information. "My pleasure, Dr. Jenson," she said.

Delia stepped forward to embrace Casey, then held her at arm's length. "Take care of my brother. He's a pain but he's the only brother I have."

"Cool it, Dee," Ben said. "This is just our first date, okay?"

Ben's sister ignored her brother and broadened her smile. "As my husband said, it has been delightful. I will pray that the Lord reveals His purpose in your coming to Cade's Point very soon. In fact, Bob and I are having our annual Christmas get-together in a few weeks. I would love it if you'd come. May I send you an invitation?"

"Oh, thank you," she managed.

Delia nodded. "I'll call you for an address. Are you listed?"

"Actually, all I have is a cell phone. I'm never home so I figured I didn't need two phone numbers."

"Well, what if I just sent your invitation to you at the store? That's probably the easiest way to handle things."

"Dee," Ben said, "could I have a word with you?" He didn't look happy.

"Well, of course, little brother. I would love to stay and chat but Bob and I were just leaving, weren't we, honey? Bob's got an early tee time tomorrow."

"Yeah, right." Ben wrapped Delia in a hug that lifted her into the air. When he set her feet back on the ground, he touched the tip of her nose. "Keep this where it belongs, dear sister, or I'll have to tell Pop the story of how Mom's favorite Faberge egg got cracked."

"Benjamin, you know that ugly egg got broken when you tried to throw my doll up the chimney, you little brat." She winked. "Besides, to tell Pop, you'd have to speak to him. So, in this instance, I would welcome being tattled on."

Chapter 9

Pant legs rolled up and shoes in hand, Casey and Ben crossed the sand to walk toward the water's edge. With the waves breaking at low tide, the wet sand shimmered under the full moon.

They walked a few moments until Casey broke the silence. "What really happened back there, Ben?"

"Oh, you know, it's that brother and sister stuff."

He'd offered to take her for a stroll, as much to clear his head as to enjoy her company. Then there was the matter of the surprise he'd planned. The encounter with Delia and Bob had left him wondering if he ought to forget the plans he'd made for the end of the evening.

Casey looked up at him with eyes that shone in the moonlight. His vague response had clearly not been sufficient.

"There was a weird vibe going on between you and the Jensons."

What were the odds that Delia and Bob would be

dining at the Surfside Inn tonight? Worse, how had he managed to extricate himself and Casey from the encounter without his date knowing his secret?

Ben sighed. Eventually, he'd have to tell her.

A thought stopped him in his tracks. What if Delia went to Pop? By morning, Casey might be out of a job.

After all, if he were persona non grata at the store, anyone associated with him would most likely suffer the same status. What a shame. He was really beginning to like Casey Forrester. Telling her good-bye would not be easy.

He should do it now and avoid dragging out the inevitable. Yes, he'd speak his piece, tell her things between them were never meant to be, then go on about his business.

It was the only way to save Casey's job.

Once more, he looked down at Casey. Moonlight turned her face to a luminous pale, which served to accentuate her clean-scrubbed beauty.

Then she smiled.

Ben's heart sunk as his knees went weak. Oh, man, was he in trouble! All he could think about was how he could make this walk last forever. He'd tell her *afterward*.

Lord, is that okay? Just one evening—then I'll break it off.

Casey tugged on his hand and urged him to continue walking. When he caught up with her, he noticed she looked pensive. "Look, everything's fine, Casey. Don't let whatever's concerning you ruin a perfectly good evening, okay?"

For a moment he thought she might pursue the subject of Delia and the weird vibe. She surprised him when she took the conversation in an entirely different direction.

"Have you ever gone night fishing, Ben?"

Now this was a multifaceted woman. He guided her around a clump of seaweed, then steered her toward the rocks jutting out at the water's edge a few yards away.

"Night fishing? Yes, actually I have. Pop used to take me to the Cade's Point pier all the time. Why do you ask?"

She shrugged. "My daddy used to take me night fishing, too, and I wondered something."

"What's that?"

"Well, you know that look the fish has when it breaks the surface? The one where he realizes he's out of the water and in for trouble?"

Ben chuckled. "Yeah, but I'm not sure where you're going with this, Casey."

They stopped at the edge of the small gulf between the rocks and the shore. Unwilling to commit to spending more time here, Ben prayed that the Lord would either lead him home or urge him to climb up to where a spectacular view of His light show would soon be had.

Casey touched Ben's sleeve and looked past him to the pounding surf. "Here's where I'm going with this, Ben: Back there at the restaurant before your sister showed up, you were doing just fine. I mean, we were having a good time, weren't we?"

He nodded.

"Then, here comes Delia and Bob, and pretty soon you were snagged up in something that made you look just like one of those fish. I just haven't figured out what that something was."

Ben closed his eyes and took a deep breath. He released it slowly with the intention of telling Casey everything. Instead, a soft whisper crossed his heart and he found other words.

"Casey, I can't explain this—I mean, it's crazy to say this, seeing as how we barely know one another, but I. . ."

She waited expectantly yet silently while he struggled to put together a meaningful sentence.

"What I'm saying is, there is so much you don't know about me, and yet I feel like I'm not able to tell you. I want to, believe me." He raked his hand through his hair, then touched the spot over his eye. "Every time I look in the mirror I'll think of you."

"Past tense." She looked down to study her hands. "Well, Ben, maybe it's time we head home. It's been a wonderful evening."

Out of the corner of his eye, Ben saw a streak of light followed in quick succession by two more. "Actually, if you'll bear with me, I did have one more thing planned."

Even as she nodded, she looked doubtful.

"How are your climbing skills?" He pointed to Outlook Rock, the centermost and tallest of the three formations. "Because we can either watch from down here or up there. Down here's not bad, but if you don't mind the hike, the view from up there is spectacular."

Casey smiled. "You forget. I was raised in the

country. I was climbing trees while you were still playing dolls."

"Playing dolls?" He feigned indignation. "So, that's how it's going to be, is it? Let's see how you like California rock climbing."

Casey leaned against the smaller rock and dusted the sand off her feet, then donned her socks and sneakers. "Now I see why you told me to wear these shoes. I wondered when I saw the restaurant if I'd misunderstood."

"Follow me, little lady. You're about to see the show of your life. By the way, this is called Outlook Rock. We had the name before the software guy thought of it."

She giggled at his bad joke, then forged ahead. "One thing we don't have in Missouri is a coastline. I don't think I'll ever get tired of the smell of salt air and the feel of sand under my feet."

She'd just spoken his heart—odd how a girl from a landlocked state could feel the same as a man who'd been raised with swim fins and a wetsuit.

"Come on then," Ben said. "We don't want to be late for the opening act."

They traversed the maze of low-lying rocks, then reached Outlook Rock. "I'll go first and you stay right behind me. The trail's not steep, but there are a few spots that are a little tricky."

Five minutes later, they stood atop Outlook Rock. The view was spectacular in the daylight, with a panorama that included the mountains on one side and the sparkling Pacific on the other. On a clear day, you could see all the way to Catalina Island.

Ben pointed to a bag he'd stashed under a natural crevice this afternoon. He unzipped the duffel and pulled out a plaid stadium blanket. As he arranged the blanket, he smiled up at Casey. "Our box seats, milady." He pointed to a spot on the blanket. "You can lie there and I'll be over here. No funny business, I promise."

She didn't seem convinced. "Maybe this wasn't such a good idea."

"Remember, Sleeping Beauty, we are here to see the show. I'll put the duffel bag between us."

"Well, I suppose it will be all right." Casey took her spot on the blanket, leaning back to rest her hands beneath her head.

Ben settled beside her and leaned up on his elbows. "Even my sister will tell you I am a perfect gentleman."

Casey turned to look his direction. "So, what's the name of this show?"

"Just watch, Casey," he said. "It has no name—at least none that I know of."

As he spoke the words, another streak dashed from the heavens. Her smile warmed his heart. Until now, he'd watch a meteor shower over anything else. Now all he wanted to do was watch Casey Forrester.

Oh yeah, he had it bad. *Lord, what are You up to?*

"Did you see that?" Casey pointed straight up. "It looks like God's throwing stars."

Ben chuckled and leaned back to see the meteors streak overhead. Occasionally, he succumbed to the temptation to turn his attention to the woman at his side.

Watching her watch the Lord's handiwork was the best show of all.

∞

Casey said good-bye to Ben at the bottom of the stairs with a hug and a handshake, then nearly floated up to her door. What a wonderful evening. Sure, there were a few questions lingering in her mind about Ben, but her thoughts spun past them to remember more pleasant things. She'd seen starry nights and her share of falling stars back in Pierce City, but nothing as beautiful as tonight's spectacular display.

Ben had been the perfect gentleman, keeping to his promise to place the duffel bag between them. She'd stolen a few covert glances and even caught him looking her direction a few times. Still, he'd only offered a quick smile before turning his attention skyward.

Just as she closed the door, her cell phone rang. It was Ben.

"Did you lock the door?"

"Yes, I locked the door." She peeked out the curtains to see Ben still sitting in his truck by the curb. Letting the fabric slide back into place, Casey leaned against the wall and smiled. "Why?"

"Just checking."

In the background she heard the *ding* of the ignition and the sound of the truck's engine roaring to life. "Well, thank you for checking."

"You're welcome. Casey?"

Casey took another look out the window. "Yes?"

"I have to go. I'm useless trying to drive and talk on the phone."

"At least you know that about yourself. Most don't."

Ben chuckled. "I don't want to hang up."

She watched the headlights come on. "You have to. I don't want you to risk getting a ticket."

"I suppose not." He paused. "May I call tomorrow?"

It was Casey's turn to laugh as she glanced up at the clock. "Ben, it *is* tomorrow."

"So it is. Well, then, how about I call you later today?"

Chapter 10

Ben waited a respectable nine hours before phoning Casey. He caught her on her way out the door for a run, and, at Casey's insistence, he talked to her until she stopped for coffee at Java Hut. The topic: *It's a Wonderful Life* versus *Miracle on 34th Street*, the Natalie Wood version.

If he hadn't been on duty, Ben might have met her at the counter and took his turn paying. Instead, he settled for taking the rig out to gas it up and driving past to see if she was still there.

When he found himself circling the block to be sure he hadn't missed her, Ben realized he might be falling for the window dresser from Missouri. Funny how he didn't mind.

The rest of the week passed in a flurry of phone calls to and from Casey, all sandwiched in between runs in the ambulance. His day off was Friday, and they planned their second official date: a compromise from Ben's original idea of a surfing lesson, which Casey nixed. Instead,

Ben borrowed Jerry's sailboat and conned Alexis's cook into preparing an impressive picnic lunch.

God blessed them with a beautiful day for a sail, and He added a fine wind for good measure. Casey learned quickly and soon took her turn at navigating the channel. Only the threat of missing lunch could coax her away from the wheel.

"Did you make all this?" Casey reached for a handful of grapes and added them to her plate of roasted chicken and Greek salad. "It's wonderful."

Ben carried his plate beside her. "It would be easy to take credit for this, but my sister's cook did the honors. Does it count that I thought of it?"

Her smile was glorious. "Yes, it counts. Now, tell me about these sisters of yours. You have four of them?"

The mention of his family usually froze his blood, but somehow he found he wanted to tell Casey about his sisters.

"Yes. Delia, whom you've met, is the oldest and by far the bossiest. Alex comes next. She's the smart one. Then there's Alex's twin Andrea, who is five minutes younger and a world different. Alex calls her the domestic diva because Andi's goal in life is to make the perfect pot roast and never have a pillow unfluffed. She's the most like Mom. Finally, there's Jill. She's a nurse. Last I heard she was working out of a hut in Sudan providing medical care to war victims. Her husband is a missionary."

"What an interesting family. You must be proud of your sisters."

Ben nodded. "Yeah, the girls really are a quartet of unique women."

Casey set her plate aside and leaned against the cushions. "Do your parents have any grandchildren?"

"Seven." He popped a grape in his mouth, then swallowed. "Delia's got two, Alex one, and Andi had four at last count."

"What about Jill?"

Ben shrugged. "She says it's too dangerous to bring babies into the world where she and Kent live. I suppose it's all in God's hands, but I would like to see her with children of her own." He glanced at Casey and caught her staring. "What?"

"You like kids, don't you?"

"Yeah, they're great. Why?"

She turned to look in the direction of the wind, eyes closed, and her hair blew away from her face. "No reason," she finally said. "I'm just trying to figure out who you are."

"I'm just me."

Casey opened her eyes and regarded him with an odd look. "Just you? No deep, dark secrets?"

Uh-oh. I don't like the tone of that.

"W—w—what do you mean?"

She sat up straighter. "I mean, it surprises me that a man who knows so much about his sisters doesn't sit down with them on Thanksgiving."

He tried not to scowl. "I told you before. I had to work."

"Yes, you did, but I happen to know you got off

early enough to stop in front of Callahan & Callahan and watch the windows being unveiled." Casey ran her hands through her hair and tilted her chin to meet the early afternoon sun. "But what you didn't tell me is why you don't talk about your parents."

Time to change the subject. But how?

He rose to yank at the rope holding the anchor. To his surprise, Casey came up behind him and put her hand atop his.

"I'm sorry, Ben," she said softly. "I don't mean to pry. You don't have to say another word if you don't want to."

Ben turned slowly. Casey stood close. Too close.

He sank onto the cushions and buried his head in his hand. *What now, Lord? Do I tell her?*

From somewhere deep inside, he felt the words well up. "My mother went home to Jesus when I was very young. I haven't spoken to my father since I enlisted." At her confused look, he continued. "Pop wanted me to go into the family business. I felt medicine calling me but knew I would never be able to afford med school with my father set against it. I settled for enlisting in the Marines. It seemed like a good way to get the training I wanted and get out of town at the same time. When I told him the news, he told me he no longer had a son."

Ben watched Casey take it all in, seemingly digesting the news fairly well.

"So, let me understand this. Your father was grooming you to take over his business but you became a Marine instead?"

"That's right."

"And because you chose the military, he broke off contact."

Ben shrugged. "That's about the size of it, except the breaking off contact thing was mutual."

He knew he'd answered all Casey's questions about his family when the topic turned away from the personal nature of his rift and toward the finer points of tacking against the wind. Glad for the interruption, he tutored Casey in the more difficult aspects of sailing until the sun began to sink toward the horizon. Too soon, he drove up to her house.

"I had a wonderful time," Casey said. "Thank you."

Ben smiled. "My pleasure."

Casey gestured toward the house. "I should go."

He released his seat belt and turned off the truck. "Let me walk you to the door this time." A statement, not a question.

When they reached the top of the stairs, Casey fished her keys from her purse. She seemed reluctant to unlock the door.

"Something wrong, Sleeping Beauty?"

She looked up at him with a concerned expression. "How old is your father?"

Ben did a quick calculation. "I'd say he's past eighty by now."

"I see." She touched her lips with her fingers, then sighed. "So, how long are you going to let this continue? I mean, neither of you seem to be walking where God wants in the relationship, don't you think?"

Her question offended him. Then, it challenged him. Finally, it concerned him.

"I hadn't thought about it that way. Keeping this silence hasn't honored God, has it?"

Casey shook her head. "So what are you going to do about it?"

"Do?" Ben moved closer. "Well, Pop's not here right now."

"No, he's not." Casey smiled.

"And I have to work tonight, so going out to see him now is out of the question. So, what I thought I would do is. . ."—he leaned toward her—"is kiss you."

And he did.

❦

Casey awoke on Saturday to a text message on her phone. MEET ME AT JAVA HUT ASAP. TEXT ME WITH TIME. B.

She slipped into her clothes and sent him a response. TEN MINUTES? C.

In no time, she received her answer. MAKE IT FIVE. I AM ALREADY THERE. B.

When she arrived, she found Ben at the cash register purchasing a vanilla latte. "Good morning, Sleeping Beauty."

She accepted the coffee. "It is now," she said as she took a tiny sip.

He wore his uniform and a tired expression. "I wanted to thank you for yesterday," he said.

Casey felt herself blush. The kiss had been even

more spectacular than the day. In fact, she had been reliving it this morning when he'd called.

"What do you mean?"

Ben raked his hands through his hair. "If I weren't so tired I'd go talk to Pop right now. See, you were right. I'm not honoring God with my behavior."

"Did I say that?" She took another sip of her latte. "It sounds kind of harsh now that I am hearing you say it."

"It was the truth, Casey." He paused and seemed to be studying the counter. "There's something else I need to tell you, and I don't think you're going to like it. See, my father is—"

His radio squawked to life. Once again, he was being summoned for overtime work. Jerry was running late and the captain needed a man to cover his shift until the EMT could arrive. He'd only be there an hour, no more, the captain promised.

Ben took Casey's hand and lifted it to touch his lips. "We need to finish this conversation. Can I come over tonight?"

Casey frowned. "I'm sorry, Ben. I made dinner plans with two ladies from work. I realized when I got stuck in the store that I needed to cultivate my friendships here." She paused to offer him a grin. "Just in case I need to call someone in the middle of the night and ask for help."

"Tomorrow after church then?"

"Sure. Now, come on. I'll walk you out." Casey rose and tossed her empty latte container into the trash bin.

He stopped in his tracks and shook his head. "I promised the guys in my men's group I'd have lunch with them. We're trying to decide on a Bible study. I'm on the evening shift, so I will have to go straight from my lunch to work."

"We'll figure something out, Ben," she said as they stopped beside the ambulance.

Ben looked to the right and then to the left before embracing Casey. He held her for a moment, then brushed her cheek with his lips. She looked up into his eyes and grinned.

"What a nice way to start the day."

"No, *this* is a nice way to start the day." He kissed her quickly. "Casey, I don't know what's happening between us. Do you?"

Yes, I know, Ben Callahan. It's crazy but I'm in love. Are you?

Chapter 11

T hanks for covering my rear, Ben." Jerry slipped behind the wheel of the rig and buckled his seat belt. They had a call, a nonemergency, and thankfully it came in just as his buddy arrived.

"I wanted to tell you why I was late."

"Yeah, okay," Ben said, "but you don't have to."

Jerry smiled. "See, I was all set to walk out the door when my kid comes in and starts asking me all these questions about God and stuff. Well, since you and I have been talking, I had some of the answers. The rest, we looked up."

Ben clapped his hand onto Jerry's shoulder and grinned. "That's great, Jerry."

"Yeah, and while we were looking up stuff, I found that bookmark you gave me. The one that talks about how to ask Jesus into your heart." He paused and looked away, swiping at his eyes. "Well, um—the kid, he gets ahold of that bookmark and he says, 'Dad, you and me, we need to do this. We need to get right with

Jesus.'" Jerry turned back toward Ben. "My boy's fourteen and he's got more sense than me. But now, thanks
to you, we both got Jesus."

∽

Casey found waking for work on Monday morning
harder than she remembered. One week of languishing in
bed and watching movies or talking to Ben on the phone
had made her sadly inept at the work routine. To top it
off, her in-box was overflowing with a week's worth of
work. She would have to stay late to clear it out.

Ben called just as she sat down at her desk.

"Casey, we really need to get together tonight. It's
important."

Casey cast a glance at the in-box pile that threatened to turn into an avalanche. "I can't see you tonight.
I have to work. What about tomorrow?"

She heard him sigh. "No, I have to work."

The sound of Mrs. Montero's voice warned her of
her boss's presence in the hall. "I have to go. I'll call
you at lunch." She clicked off the phone and stashed it
in her desk drawer just as Mrs. Montero rounded the
corner with another woman in tow.

"Welcome back, Casey. Meet my twin sister, Andi."
She smiled. "Andi, this is Casey Forrester, the genius
behind the Christmas windows."

"It's a pleasure, Casey." Andi reached across Casey's
desk to shake her hand. "Alex has told me so much
about you. Delia, too."

Mrs. Montero looked confused. "Delia?"

"I'll tell you all about it over coffee. It was nice meeting you, Casey. I hope to see you again soon."

Casey sat back in her chair and tried to make sense of what she'd just heard. Alex, Andi, and Delia. Where had she heard those names in conjunction with one another?

"Ben."

She rose on shaking legs and headed for the break room to fortify her brain with the store's signature French roast. Before she could pour her coffee, Mrs. Montero's secretary came in carrying an enormous arrangement of flowers.

"Those are lovely, Susan. Are they yours?"

"No, Mrs. Montero's brother sent them. The florist made a mistake and delivered them here instead of her home last week. Guess this was the only number they had for her. Anyway, aren't they pretty?"

The phone rang across the hall at Susan's desk. "Do you mind watching this until the water fills to the top?"

Casey eyed the card as she took hold of the slowly filling clear-glass vase that Susan had put under the tap. "I'll keep an eye on it," she said as Susan scurried away.

The envelope had been discarded, leaving only the card on the plastic holder. Casey parted the foliage in order to read the inscription.

Thanks for the number, sis. I'm seeing her tomorrow.

Love,
Ben

"Thanks for the number? I'm seeing her tomorrow?" Casey's eyes narrowed. "And he let me believe the Callahan name was just a coincidence."

"Yes, I did, and I'm sorry."

"Ben! What are you doing at my office?" Casey dropped the arrangement and it crashed into the sink. She looked at the mess, then back at Ben. It was all she could do to keep from crying.

"I came to see you." He shook his head. "Actually, I came to see my father first, then you."

Elias Callahan stepped off the elevator. "There you are. Oh, good, Casey, you're here, too. This is perfect."

Casey stared at Ben. "He's your father."

"Yes." Ben crossed the distance between them. "I wanted to tell you." He paused to capture her hand with his. "No, that's not true. I didn't want to tell you at all. Then you talked to me about God's will and I knew I had to." He gestured toward his father with his free hand. "I also knew I owed this man an apology."

Elias came to stand at Ben's side. It was obvious the man had been crying. "Casey, I owe you a huge debt of gratitude. You brought my son back to me. More important, what you said to him, he repeated to me. Those words brought me back to my son."

"There's more, Casey." Ben released her fingers to take her into an embrace. "I don't mind saying this in front of Pop. I love you. I can't explain it, and I know we haven't known one another a long time, but my prayers have told me that this has to be something God approves of."

Casey stood quiet a long time, struggling to find the words to respond.

"It's a lot to take in, Casey, but I know we were meant to be. Will you give us a chance?"

She tried to nod but couldn't. Finally she managed to speak. "I love you, too, Ben."

While Elias beamed his approval, Ben went down on one knee. "Casey Forrester, you are the world to me. Will you be my wife, Sleeping Beauty?"

This time Casey found her ability to nod. She also said, "Yes, Prince Charming, I will."

"This calls for a celebration. I know!" Elias clapped his hands. "We will turn Casey's Christmas Eve party into an engagement party for the two of you."

Casey's heart sank. "About that party. I've been trying to figure out how to tell you this, sir, but I can't be there Christmas Eve. I have plans to go home to Missouri. Granny Forrester and the family are expecting me."

Ben exchanged glances with his father. "What if I accompany you to Missouri, Casey? I want to speak to your father before I make our engagement official." He turned to Elias. "You understand, don't you, Pop?"

"Understand a man in love? Of course I do. What if we hold off on the party until Valentine's Day? We can plan the party to coincide with Casey's Valentine's Day windows."

"I got the Valentine's Day windows?" Casey jumped into Ben's arms and kissed him soundly. When he set her on her feet again, she realized she now stood in her bare feet.

"You did it again, Prince Charming," she said as she looked up into the eyes of the man she loved.

"What did I do, Sleeping Beauty?"

"You knocked my socks off. Well, my shoes, anyway."

KATHLEEN MILLER

A publicist for Glass Road Public Relations, Kathleen is a tenth-generation Texan and mother of three grown sons and a teenage daughter. She is a graduate of Texas A&M University and an award-winning novelist of Christian fiction whose first published work jumped onto the Christian Booksellers Association best-seller list in its first month of release. Kathleen is a former treasurer for the American Christian Fiction Writers and is a member of Inspirational Writers Alive, Romance Writers of America, Words for the Journey Christian Writers Guild, Fellowship of Christian Writers, and The Writers Guild. In addition, she speaks on the craft of writing to schools and writing groups and teaches an online creative writing course through Lamar University in Beaumont, Texas.

A Letter to Our Readers

Dear Readers:

In order that we might better contribute to your reading enjoyment, we would appreciate your taking a few minutes to respond to the following questions. When completed, please return to the following: Fiction Editor, Barbour Publishing, Inc., P.O. Box 719, Uhrichsville, OH 44683.

1. Did you enjoy reading *Ozark Family Christmas*?
   ❏ Very much—I would like to see more books like this.
   ❏ Moderately—I would have enjoyed it more if _____
   _____
   _____

2. What influenced your decision to purchase this book?
   (Check those that apply.)
   ❏ Cover   ❏ Back cover copy   ❏ Title   ❏ Price
   ❏ Friends   ❏ Publicity   ❏ Other

3. Which story was your favorite?
   ❏ *Making Memories*   ❏ *Home for the Holidays*
   ❏ *A Christmas Wish*   ❏ *Dreaming of a White Christmas*

4. Please check your age range:
   ❏ Under 18   ❏ 18–24   ❏ 25–34
   ❏ 35–45   ❏ 46–55   ❏ Over 55

5. How many hours per week do you read? _____

Name _____

Occupation _____

Address _____

City_____ State _____ Zip _____

E-mail_____